NO STONE UNTURNED

M. S. PEKE

FROST FREE MEDIA

This is dedicated to my wife, Susan, and my children, Liz and Katie.
They're all the inspiration I'll ever need.

1

Winnie Hackleshack beamed as she pointed her phone up and toward her, taking a selfie next to the Yellowstone National Park entrance sign. After making sure she got herself and the sign, Winnie posted it to Facebook with the caption "I'm finally here!"

As Winnie walked away, a family of five moved in front of the sign, and Winnie offered to take their picture.

"Say cheese." Winnie snapped a couple of photos. She looked at the camera's screen to make sure they came out. "These look great. Have fun!"

Handing their camera back, she waved goodbye and stopped for a moment to admire the view, but when she saw the line of people pulled over, waiting to take their picture with the sign, Winnie jumped back into her motor home and continued on.

"This place is beautiful." Winnie paid her entrance fee to the woman attendant. She was at the east entrance station, having come in through Cooke City, Montana, all the way from Madison, Wisconsin. "There's nothing like this where I'm from."

"Wait until you get inside." The attendant handed her a map of the area and an activities pamphlet. "There's no other place like this. How long are you staying?"

"Eight days. Is that enough time?"

"You won't be able to see everything, not by any means, but you'll get through the highlights of the park. You have to see Old Faithful, but there are many other spectacular water thermals scattered throughout. Boiling mud and steaming, simmering pools are all over the park. This time of year, Lamar Valley is bustling with buffalo, so you'll want to check that out. There are lots of hikes, too, and plenty of activities to keep you occupied." The attendant looked over at Winnie's copilot. "Just be careful with your friend and follow the rules—they're in place for everyone's safety. And the bears are quite active now."

Winnie smiled and thanked her, pulling forward to a turnout to check the map. Soon, she was back on the road with the window down to take in the fresh late spring air. With an average elevation of 8,000 feet, summer came late to Yellowstone, and the temperatures were still mild in June. It felt good to be out, and the excitement of being somewhere new brought with it a surge of energy. An energy she hadn't felt in a long time. Twenty minutes later, Winnie saw the sign she was looking for.

The Winnebago sputtered as it turned into Yellowstone's Pebble Creek Campground. The thirty-four-foot motor home had each side emblazoned with a caricature of a smiling woman in a yellow sundress with short, curly red hair and freckles. Next to her was the phrase "Winnie's Winnie." The entire motor home was painted in a color called electric blue. Electric was a good name for it because it stood out. Wow, did it stand out. None of the other motor homes looked anything like it, and she drew a few stares as she pulled in. Winnie was getting used to the attention the RV got. She smiled and waved at the gawkers as she drove past. The custom-painted RV was a marketing tool that people didn't forget. Her website address was on every side with the tagline "Creative, Professional Writing...Explore New Possibilities."

Pebble Creek Campground had twenty-seven campsites. The campground operated on a first-come, first-served basis. Winnie timed her entrance to make sure she got a spot. Even at 10:00 A.M., two other campers pulled into the campground ahead of her, and Winnie was worried there might not be any sites available. At least not the size she needed.

Each site was a simple gravel pad nestled between shrubs to provide privacy. A picnic table and grill completed the amenities. Some campgrounds provided hookups, connecting the motor home with electricity, water, Wi-Fi, and even cable television. Pebble Creek wasn't one of those campgrounds. There were no hookups for power or water, so each camper had to use whatever provisions they brought with them. Winnie shook her head as she drove past a few hardy campers using tents. *Maybe twenty, no thirty years ago.* She continued on.

The outer loop of the campground went next to the outhouse. Winnie shuddered at the thought, grateful her RV had a regular bathroom. The RV wasn't as nice as living in a house, but it was far more comfortable than sleeping in a tent or stumbling to a cold outhouse in the middle of the night. Not to mention what creatures might lurk about after dark. Some people called RV camping "glamping," but Winnie thought of it as a practical way to explore the country and still be comfortable. Besides, she needed a place to work on her assignments.

"I'll take this one," Winnie called out as she spotted one of the last sites available. She pulled into space eighteen, which had just enough room for her RV and the car she was towing. Dust flew up as she came to a stop along the gravel, and Winnie breathed a sigh of relief that the four-day drive from Wisconsin was over. The trip was Winnie's first big excursion, her first real trip outside of test runs and weekend trips near Madison.

Looking over at her companion, Winnie smiled. "We're here, Patches! It's almost time for that walk I promised you."

Responding with an enthusiastic bark, Patches wagged his tail as he hopped off the passenger seat and went to the door. With a nice black spot around his right eye, the name Patches was a perfect fit. A Rat Terrier/Jack Russell mix, he was her confidant for over a year now, and the two seemed meant for one another. A rescue dog, he had lived a hard life. He was found wandering along the side of a road and taken to the shelter. A bath and an exam revealed he was badly bruised and malnourished. No one at the shelter knew what Patches had been through, but his fearful reaction to people made them think he had been abused. Patches cowered in his cage when someone came near, and the volunteers at the shelter told Winnie they didn't think anyone would adopt him. But Patches's personality changed when he saw Winnie come to his cage with a big smile and a dog treat. He must have sensed Winnie was his guardian, and he took tentative steps toward her. It didn't take long before the two were playing together. And they'd been together since.

"Nice rig," a man walking by said as he noticed Winnie's license plates. His bright red T-shirt, emblazoned with the words "Git R Done," strained against the seams in an unsuccessful attempt to keep everything in. A mangy head of hair flopped out of a baseball cap turned backward, and a belt buckle the size of Texas with a skull and crossbones on it completed the ensemble. Winnie tried not to roll her eyes, nodding and offering a quick smile before looking away.

"You come all the way from Wisconsin in that thing? By yourself?"

Why do I attract these people? Whatever it is, I need the antidote. "Sure did." Winnie offered a half-turn before moving back toward her RV. Winnie breathed a sigh of relief when she looked back and saw the man had moved on. She shook her head and chuckled. It always amazed her how some people seemed to be so curious about her driving a motor home by herself. Like somehow this was a man's domain, and a woman had no place doing it. And it wasn't just men that questioned her. Even her mom tried to talk her out of it.

"Traipsing across the country in that thing is dangerous, especially for a woman by herself," her mother, Sabrina Hackleshack, warned Winnie before she left.

But Winnie wouldn't have any of it. "I'll be fine, Mother. I need a change of scenery. Especially after what happened."

"But you need to support yourself. You quit a perfectly good job as a reporter to do this. How can you make a living when you're in the woods?"

"Mother," Winnie heaved a big sigh. "My clients don't care where I am as long as I make my deadlines. We've been over this before, and I really don't want to rehash it. I'm going."

Winnie seldom used the mother card, preferring to keep it mom. But she knew her mom understood what it meant. Thankfully, her mom let it go, with only occasional attempts to convince Winnie to stay.

After spending the day getting settled and playing with Patches, Winnie was ready for a night out. Her RV automatically kept the temperature comfortable for Patches, and, after saying good night, Winnie unhitched her car from the motor home's tow bar and set off for a thirty-minute drive to Roosevelt Lodge. Her car was a Mini Cooper, painted the same shade of blue as her motor home. It sported the same smiling woman caricature but had "Winnie's Mini" on the sides and back.

The sky was still bright, with small puffy white clouds dotting here and there. Even though the sun was high, the early June evening weather was chilly and a little breezy, and Winnie was glad she put on a jacket before she left.

Winnie turned right onto US Route 212, which traversed the northern part of Yellowstone along Lamar Valley, a beautiful plain surrounded by mountain peaks. She'd read about cars stopping along the highway, with people staring at grizzlies, black bears, elk, or other animals roaming the large plain. This early in the season it was still quiet, with only the occasional car. Looking out into the valley, Winnie spotted the distinctive furry face and hump of four buffalo grazing in the distance.

"My first buffalo." She pulled over to take pictures. After a few minutes, and several photos, her growling stomach turned her attention back to dinner and Roosevelt Lodge. Waving goodbye to the buffalo, she pulled back onto the road, heading west.

Winnie was excited about eating at the lodge. She read up on its history and was eager to experience it for herself. The lodge was built in 1920 and named after Theodore Roosevelt, even though he never camped there. No longer a lodge, it was converted into a nice restaurant, and being the only restaurant for miles, it was often packed. Surrounding the lodge were over one hundred rustic cabins, each miniature log homes. Some of them offered a bathroom, but the "Roughrider Cabins" had no electricity or running water. A wood fireplace was their only amenity. The thought of trying to stumble out of a log cabin in the middle of the night seemed worse than the tent option. *A bit too rustic for me.*

Winnie smiled. She felt calm and peaceful and happy, all rolled into one. It took almost a year to get over what's-his-name, but she finally did. This trip—the first of many, she hoped—was her way of celebrating. A rebirth, of sorts, even if she were in her mid-forties. Sliding in a CD, she started to sing as she drove along. Her favorites were Christmas songs, and Winnie belted out an almost unrecognizable version of "It's beginning to look a lot like Christmas."

Turning off the highway, she pulled into the Roosevelt Lodge parking lot. Constructed like a log cabin, its architecture included two huge stone fireplaces and a large porch filled with rocking chairs. Winnie was looking forward to sitting on the front porch, idly rocking while she waited for a table, then enjoying a good meal inside.

The parking lot was crowded, and Winnie had to circle around to look for an open spot. On the second pass, she noticed a couple walking to their car and followed them, putting her blinker on to let the car behind her know she was waiting for the space. The couple smiled as they pulled out, and Winnie waved as she took their spot, parking next to a park ranger's car.

Winnie got out and watched a group of about twenty riders along a trail near the restaurant. She had never been on a horse and wondered if she'd have the nerve to try it. But doing new things was a part of the trip, so she decided to check about rides after dinner.

As she turned toward the lodge, she nearly collided with a park ranger, who looked up, staring at Winnie before storming off without saying a word. Winnie noticed his name tag said "Taggart" as he passed her.

Winnie watched the ranger, who seemed oblivious to everything around him. His pants were dirty and worn in spots, and his untucked shirt had wrinkles throughout, with deep sweat stains under his arms. Not the model of a park ranger you see in pictures.

The ranger backed up in a hurry, and the car shook as he sped off, throwing rocks and creating a cloud of dust in his wake.

Winnie shook her head. *I could have stayed in Madison and dealt with drivers like that.*

She looked in the direction the ranger came from, trying to figure out what had him so angry. That was when she noticed a young woman sitting on a log, wiping tears from her eyes.

2

Winnie looked over at the young woman and wondered what to do. If this was some sort of lover's spat, she'd rather not get involved, but Winnie didn't think the woman's sobbing had anything to do with romance. And she got a good look at Taggart before he stormed away.

I know that look. I've seen it a thousand times in my ex.

Deciding she had to do something, Winnie walked over. The woman sat curled up in a ball by the side of the parking lot, her blonde hair covering her face. As she got closer, Winnie could hear quiet sobs.

"Hey, what's wrong?" Winnie asked softly.

The woman looked up, startled. "It is nothing, thanks." She wiped her eyes and tried to smile, but it was a halfhearted attempt.

Winnie sat down next to her. For a while, neither one said anything.

Finally, the woman looked over at Winnie. "Do you work here? I have not seen you around before."

Her accent was unfamiliar, but Winnie thought it sounded

Eastern European. "No, I just arrived this morning." Winnie was happy the woman was at least talking. "I came here for dinner. Yellowstone is so beautiful. I can't believe I waited this long to come."

The woman nodded. "It is beautiful. We have nothing like this at home."

"I'm Winnie," Winnie smiled as she extended her hand. "Where are you from?"

The woman looked at Winnie's hand for a moment then reached out to shake it. "I am Anita. And I am from Ukraine, working here for the summer."

They sat in silence for a while longer until Winnie spoke up. "You want to talk about it now?"

"The ranger you saw, it was nothing. He tried to get me to go out with him, and when I refused, he got mad. Since then, he has been coming around threatening me, telling me he will have me deported or put in jail. He is just a bully. I deal with them all the time back in my village."

"Well, he won't get away with that here. I'll report him."

Winnie reached for her phone, but Anita took her hand. "Please stop. It will just make things worse."

"We can't let him continue to harass you, Anita. I'm sure we can file a complaint and get him to stop."

Winnie was used to being harassed and bullied. She spent over twenty years enduring criticisms and putdowns, until she'd finally had enough and filed for divorce. Winnie was done being pushed around, and she wouldn't stand for anyone else to be, either.

"Please," Anita pleaded. "I can handle him. He is not that bad, really."

Winnie looked over at Anita. She wasn't hurt physically, and she seemed to be a strong, sensible woman.

"Okay." Reaching into her purse, Winnie pulled out a card

and handed it to Anita. "Here's my phone number in case you need anything."

Anita looked at the card. "Winnie Hackleshack, Explorer," she read out loud. "What is explorer?"

Winnie laughed. "It means I'm unemployed. And I'm free to do whatever I want."

Even though Winnie worked as a freelance writer, she considered herself first and foremost a traveler, and she wanted her business cards to reflect that.

Anita sighed. "I wish I was explorer."

Winnie stood. "Give it time. You're still young." She pointed over to the lodge. "I see two free rockers on the porch. Would you like to join me?"

The pair hurried to the porch, narrowly beating out two other people vying for the coveted chairs.

After rocking silently for several minutes, Winnie said, "Save my seat? I'm going to put my name down for a dinner table. Care to join me?"

"Oh, Winnie, I would love to, but I do not have the money. The food here is so expensive."

"Don't be silly. You're my guest, and I'd love the company. What do you say?"

"Then I say yes!"

"Great. I'll put my name down for a table for two and be right back."

Winnie came back and the two continued rocking. The view wasn't spectacular, overlooking the gravel parking lot, but being outside rocking away was very comforting, and Winnie could see why the chairs were so popular. Soon their table was ready.

Winnie's stomach growled harder than ever as she looked at the menu. "I'm starving. You work here. What do you recommend?"

"People really like the trout, and they say our chuck wagon

corn is very good. I have not tried any of it yet. I mostly eat peanut butter and jelly sandwiches."

"Shall we both try the trout, then?"

Anita's face beamed as she placed her napkin across her lap. "Yes. Thank you for being so kind."

"It's my pleasure. Most of the time it's just me and Patches."

"What is Patches?"

"Nothing but the cutest dog in the world! Patches and I have gotten really close over the last year. I rescued him from the pound, and he rescued me from my depression."

Anita took a sip of water. "Why were you depressed? You seem so happy."

"I am happy—now. A year ago I filed for divorce and it recently became final. I'm glad I got divorced, but it was hard at the same time. Patches helped me over it, and that's when I decided to become an explorer."

"And you have money to just explore?"

"For now." Winnie smiled. "I sold my house and bought a used motor home. It took me over six months to fix it up, but I love being in it. Patches and I call it home, and this is our first trip in it. I was a newspaper reporter, and now I work as a freelance journalist, but I don't take on a lot of work. I've got customers that don't need too much, and I'm happy for the occasional paycheck. I'm content to explore."

Winnie caught herself from going into details about her failed marriage. It was too easy to go down that rabbit hole.

"Enough about me," Winnie said. "Tell me about you. What made you travel from Ukraine here for the summer? Seems like you're an explorer, too."

"Well...kind of. I come here for the summer when college is out. A lot of us do that. Plus, it was good to get away. In my village, there is not so much to do. But here, there is everything. And the people. They are so friendly. Well, most of them." Anita looked down and fumbled with her silverware.

Winnie took Anita's hand. "Hey. It's okay. We'll stick together."

"You are right. I am happy to be here, most of the time."

"With friends."

"With friends." Anita smiled again.

The server came over and greeted them. "Hi, Anita! You're back. This time as a customer." She lit the candle in the center of the table.

"Hi, Gretchen. I made a new friend today, and we are having dinner. Winnie, this is my friend Gretchen. She is from Germany."

"Nice to meet you, Gretchen. Wow, Germany, Ukraine. Are all the servers from different countries?"

"A lot of us," Gretchen said. "Some are from the States. There's an application you fill out, and if you get selected, you get to come and work for the summer. It's a great way to meet people and see a new part of the world. When I'm done here, I'm going to tour around the U.S. Maybe see Los Angeles and New York. I hope, anyway. So, are you ready to order?"

Both Winnie and Anita ordered the trout, with sides of Roosevelt beans and chuck wagon corn. The lodge was packed, and the sounds of clinking silverware mixed with the conversations throughout the dining area. Winnie took in the smells of different foods as they mingled in the air and hungrily dug into a dinner roll when they were brought to the table. The maple butter melted into the warm sourdough rolls, and Winnie took a big bite, savoring the wonderful taste.

The lodge was as rustic-looking on the inside as it was on the outside, with exposed, log cabin beams, but the ceiling wasn't vaulted or as high as Winnie expected. It was redone at some point and looked a little out of place. But overall, she could picture explorers from long ago happy to find this oasis in the middle of nowhere.

The evening was cool, so both fireplaces were running, the crackling of logs and the occasional shower of sparks announcing their presence. Winnie wished their table was closer to the heat, but she enjoyed looking at the wonderful stone lit up from the fire inside. The fireplace showed signs of use but was still a beautiful complement to the surrounding wood. While looking fairly traditional, the lodge had a few modern-day amenities, too, like a bar and gift shop, and several kids busied themselves looking around at all the things they'd beg their parents to buy.

When the food arrived, both Anita and Winnie attacked their meals like they hadn't eaten in weeks. The food looked and smelled delicious.

Taking a fork full of trout, Winnie closed her eyes and took in the wonderful taste. "You made an excellent recommendation." She scooped a load of beans.

Each one took turns learning about the other between bites.

"Boy, that was good." Winnie rubbed her stomach when she finished. She was full, but in a good, *I earned it* way, reminding herself that she'd played with Patches for a long time that afternoon.

Anita nodded, her mouth still full of food. Before long, she was rubbing her stomach, too. Both passed on dessert, opting for a short stroll before it got too dark. Winnie offered to walk Anita to her dorm, but Anita seemed hesitant to leave, wanting to sit on the rockers.

Winnie looked at Anita and knew. She had seen that look before, too. In the mirror. It was the look of fear. *I've got to get her to talk.*

"Winnie, if you need to go, I understand. I do not want to keep you. But it is nice having you to talk to."

"I should go check on Patches. If you're feeling up to it, we can take a ride out to my campsite. I've got a cheesecake I picked up in Cody, Wyoming, on the way here, and I'm dying to dig into it."

Anita looked uncertain. "I do not know. I would like, but it is getting late. I do not wish to bother."

"And you can meet Patches." Winnie tried to convince her. "He's the closest thing I have to a man in my life right now. Not that I need anyone else. It's only eight. You'll be back before you know it."

"How can I say no to Patches and cheesecake?" Anita's smile returned.

"I love your car," Anita said as they reached the Mini. "And that is you on the side, yes?"

Winnie laughed. "A friend of mine's an artist, and she painted it on for me. Maybe she overdid it, but I like it."

"I like it, too. It suits you."

The two chatted their way back to the Pebble Creek Campground, and Winnie pulled into her space.

"This is your camper? It is bigger than I thought it would be. I think it is bigger than my house in Ukraine! And you are on the side here, too. I love it. It is so happy and free."

A gust of wind took the lawn chair she had rested against the picnic table and tossed it into the brush. Winnie jumped out and told Anita she'd be right back. She tucked the chair under the RV, then walked back to the Mini.

As they stepped inside, Patches greeted Winnie, wagging his tail as he raced to the door, excited to see his owner return. At the shelter, they told Winnie Patches didn't bark much. They suspected he was partially deaf, and a trip to the vet confirmed it. Winnie would have taken Patches anyway, but she was relieved. A loud dog and a small camper didn't mix.

"Hi, Patches! I brought a new friend."

Anita was barely in the door before Patches almost knocked her over in his attempt to greet her. Patches was a whirlwind of activity—sniffing and jumping, all the while zipping around Anita like she was the center of a racetrack.

"Slow down, buddy!" Winnie said.

"I do not mind." Anita giggled as she bent down, letting Patches lick her face. "I love dogs. I came here more for him than the cheesecake. But a piece of cheesecake would be nice, too."

Winnie offered her guest a seat at the booth dinette and went to get the cherry cheesecake out of the refrigerator. Putting on a pot of decaf, Winnie cut two oversized pieces, reminding herself she had hikes planned for tomorrow and needed the extra energy.

"Here you go." Winnie set the slices on the table. "I'll get the coffee. Decaf, so we can both sleep. Or would you prefer something else?"

"Coffee would be great, Winnie. Thank you."

Bringing the coffee over, Winnie noticed Anita wasted no time in digging in. *Oh, I wish I had a youngster's metabolism.* Winnie took a more measured approach to her piece.

Patches kept vigil, hoping something would fall onto the floor, where he would gladly take care of it.

Winnie took a sip of coffee. "Do you want to talk about it?"

Anita shook her head. "It is like I said before. He is a creep, but I can deal with him." She bent down and scratched Patches's head. "I would rather think about other things."

Winnie nodded. She made a mental note to check on Anita over the next few days.

After they both finished, Winnie gave Anita a quick tour of the motor home and then opened the door to take her back. Patches bounded out of the RV thinking he was going along. Anita waited in the Mini while Winnie corralled him back inside.

When they arrived, the parking lot was nearly empty. Anita

got out of the Mini and bent down to talk through the open window.

"Thanks, Winnie. I had so much fun. I hope I can see you again before you go."

Just then a park ranger's car slowly approached. Taggart. "Evening, Anita. You're out late. Everything okay?"

"Fine." Anita was already walking away.

Winnie sensed Anita's anxiety and got out. She locked the car and hurried to catch up. "I'll walk you to your room."

"And who are you?" Taggart glared at Winnie.

"I'm Anita's friend." Winnie took out her phone and started recording, but it was too dark to see anything clearly, especially the inside of the ranger's car.

"See you later, Anita." The ranger drove away.

Winnie took a picture of the car, hoping the license plate would come in focus, especially with it being so dark outside. Adding the caption "Officer Taggart, car 7120," Winnie tucked it away in case she needed it later. She was seldom without her phone, and her honed reporter skills told her to collect as much information as she could.

"That guy gives me the creeps," Anita said as they hurried down the path to the dorms.

"Anita, you should report him. If you don't want to, I will. He needs to be stopped."

"Who is going to stop him? He is the police. Besides, he is harmless, I think. I just ignore him and he goes away."

When they reached the dorm, someone caught up to them, smiling and waving her hand. "Hi, Anita! I missed you at dinner."

"I met a new friend, and we had dinner together. Winnie, this is my roommate Olga. Olga, this is Winnie."

Just like Anita, Olga was a petite blonde with blue eyes, but that was where the resemblance ended. Olga's hair was in a short, pixie cut instead of Anita's straight, shoulder-length hair.

Anita didn't seem to use makeup, while Olga was wearing deep red lipstick with matching fingernails. A pair of red tassel earrings flopped around as Olga moved her head.

"Nice to meet you." Winnie tried not to stare at the earrings as they moved. "Are you working here or just visiting?"

"No, I'm working here for the summer. I work at the stables. Yellowstone is absolutely beautiful, and I get to work with horses."

"You have such a great place to work. Are you from Ukraine, too?"

"Yes. I worked here last year and told Anita about it. We go to school together. Luckily, she got to join me this year and we're roommates. When we came this summer, we decided it would be a good time to practice, so we made a pact to speak only English while we're here. Right now, I'm trying to learn American slang."

Laughing, Winnie said, "Well, don't learn it too well. I think we could do with a little less slang."

Winnie made a step back to her car. "I have to be going. Thanks for the company, Anita. I hope we can do it again before I leave. Olga, it was nice to meet you." She waved goodbye as the two turned toward their dorm.

It was dark when Winnie pulled out of the parking lot. As soon as she got onto the road, Winnie noticed lights behind her. She wasn't sure, but the car that followed her back looked like the ranger's car, and it kept right on her tail. Winnie reached for her phone, just in case she had to make an emergency call.

There was no service.

3

Winnie awoke with a start, hearing a loud noise. On edge after being followed home last night, almost any peep seemed to jolt her up. Thankfully, the car following her sped past as she turned into the campground. But she didn't sleep well, finally drifting off after being up most of the night. Thinking the noise was Patches scratching against the door to go out, she lifted her head, only to find him stretched out next to her.

Just as she put her head back down, Winnie heard four loud bangs on her door, followed by a booming voice calling, "Park ranger."

Winnie slipped on a robe and went to the door, peering out the window. A ranger stood there, her right hand resting on her sidearm. She was tall, maybe five-foot-ten, with brown hair pulled into a tight bun. Toned and athletic, she looked like she could outrun a bear. And her body language left no doubt who was in charge. Winnie was intimidated.

Winnie opened the door a crack, her face crinkled up in concern as a cool morning breeze swept past her. She tightened the robe against her chest. "Can I help you?"

The ranger pulled out a business card. It had Winnie's name on it. "Are you Winnie Hackleshack?"

"Yes. What's going on?"

"Ma'am, I'd like to speak to you for a moment. Can I come in?"

Winnie felt that the ranger wasn't asking, so Winnie held the door while she entered, the ranger's hand still on her sidearm as she took in the room. Winnie watched the ranger's eyes probe the room without turning her head, taking everything in.

"Winnie's Winnie and Winnie's Mini. Cute." The ranger smiled, taking her hand off her holstered pistol. "You certainly do stand out."

"Thanks. My name's Winona, but Winona's Winnie didn't have the same ring, and everyone calls me Winnie anyway. Well, except for my mom when she's upset, so I do still hear Winona a lot. And, as you might have guessed, blue is my favorite color. Please, sit down."

Patches came up to sniff the new visitor. He seemed to like the ranger, or at least the way she smelled.

"He likes you." Winnie pulled Patches away. "You must have a dog he's smelling."

"No, but I'm around animals a lot. Ms. Hackleshack, I—"

"Winnie, please." She extended her hand. "And this is Patches."

"Winnie, I'm Ranger Jennifer Malone." She shook Winnie's hand. "Do you know Ms. Anita Tataryn? We found your card in her room."

"Anita? I didn't know her last name, but I met her yesterday. We had dinner and she came back here for dessert. Is something wrong? Is this about that ranger who's been pestering her?"

"What ranger?" Jen asked. "I don't know anything about it. Was Anita involved in an incident with another ranger?"

"I went to Roosevelt Lodge yesterday for dinner. As I was getting out of my car, a ranger practically mowed me over getting to his car. I looked at his name tag and it said Taggart."

"Taggart? I've been here over ten years, and there's no Taggart working here. At least not as a ranger."

"Well, maybe I got the name wrong. Anyway, he seemed to be in such a hurry and was very unpleasant. After he forced his way around me, I noticed Anita looking upset, so I went over and talked to her. She said he had been harassing her, threatening to deport her. We talked for a while, then I suggested she join me for dinner. We had dinner at Roosevelt Lodge, and she came here to meet Patches and have cheesecake. I drove her back, and she met up with her roommate. I came home and went to bed. That's all I know. Now, what's this about?"

"What kind of car did Taggart drive?"

"It looked like a ranger's car." Winnie went to the window and looked out. "Like your car."

"I'll check it out, but I'd be surprised if it was one of our cars."

"What are you saying? You think I'm making it up?" Winnie folded her arms, narrowing her eyes.

"Not at all. It's just I've never heard of a Taggart, and access to official vehicles is controlled. It might have been one of ours, or it might have looked very similar to one of ours. Either way, we now know the basic car type to look for."

"Okay, but can you please tell me what's going on with Anita? Is she okay?" Winnie kept her arms folded as she studied the person in front of her. She couldn't figure out if the woman standing there was playing her, trying to goad her into something. Maybe Winnie was just being defensive after being barged in on. Plus, it was before coffee, and Winnie's cognitive abilities were severely lessened before caffeine.

"I'm afraid not. Ms. Tataryn was found this morning near her dorm, face down in a clump of trees. I'm sorry to tell you this, but she's dead. We suspect foul play, but we're waiting for forensics to get back to us. It looks like it was staged to make it appear she slipped and fell, but there are some odd things that don't fit."

"Oh my goodness." Winnie's hand covered her mouth as she took in the news. "What odd things did you find?"

"I'm afraid I can't go into details, but I can tell you her roommate is missing, and when we searched their room, we found your card. I came here hoping you might know something about what happened or where her roommate is. Anything you know puts us that much further ahead."

"Anita, murdered?" Winnie stammered. "And her roommate's missing? I can't believe it."

"These things happen, even in Yellowstone. Not often, but they do. I need you to come down to the station so we can get a description of the gentleman you saw."

"Of course," Winnie said. "Can I take Patches for a quick walk first? He hasn't been out yet this morning."

"You can take him with us. There's a nice place around the station. The sooner we get this description the better. I can take you, or you can follow me."

Winnie thought about it for a moment. It occurred to her the ranger in front of her might be an imposter and Taggart the real ranger. Something just didn't seem right.

"I'll follow you," Winnie said.

"Fine. I'll be going with my lights on, so stay behind me."

"Got it. I'll be ready in a minute."

Ranger Malone waited in her car while Winnie pulled on a pair of jeans and a red Wisconsin Badger's sweater. She shook her head as she tried to tame her hair, deciding it wasn't worth the effort. She turned to Patches. "Come on, boy. Let's go for a ride."

Patches jumped, twirled, and wagged his tail so hard he fanned Winnie's work papers off the table. A normal occurrence when Patches thought he was getting a treat or going for a walk. After getting Patches secured, they took off, trying their best to keep pace with the speeding police car. Patches loved sticking his head out the window, and his tail wagged the whole time.

At the rate they were going, the normal hour-long drive took about thirty minutes, and soon they reached the Mammoth Hot Springs area of Yellowstone. Ranger Malone escorted them on a quick walk and then directed them into the police headquarters, where they were brought to an interview room. Winnie was allowed to keep Patches with her, and they both sat quietly while they waited.

She surveyed the room, a small box with a closed window on one side. *One-way glass.* A metal table and two metal chairs completed the furnishings. The table was bolted to the floor, with hooks on it to handcuff prisoners during interrogations. The chairs moved, but there were shackles on the wall to secure a prisoner's legs. A camera was perched in the corner, the lens staring at Winnie. She folded her hands and rubbed them against her arms, trying to shake the cold away.

The stiff chairs were uncomfortable from the start, and, after a few minutes of waiting, Winnie was shifting around, trying to find a spot that didn't hurt too much. *I see why people confess, even when they didn't do anything*. Winnie shuddered as she shifted again.

Soon, Ranger Malone came in, carrying a folder under her arm and two steaming cups of coffee. Another ranger followed her with a dog dish full of water, placing it down near Patches. Patches looked up, gave a "what, no treats?" look and skulked over to the corner.

"Thank you." Winnie took the coffee, taking a sip. The coffee tasted awful, and she must have made a face, because Ranger Malone laughed.

"Sorry. What passes for coffee here is sometimes a little...

lacking. Here, maybe some sugar will help. And please, call me Jen. There's no reason to be formal."

Winnie took four packets of sugar and dumped them in. *Not enough sugar in the world can fix this stuff.*

"I just can't believe what happened to poor Anita," Winnie said. "She was so happy yesterday when we were together."

Jen nodded and pushed a button on the table. The surveillance camera in the corner started to blink, its flashing red light catching Winnie's eye.

"Winnie, I'm going to record our session. It's standard procedure."

Winnie looked at the camera, its blinking like a warning beacon. Suddenly, she was afraid of saying something that might be misunderstood. *Plenty of people say the wrong thing and end up in hot water, right?* Her face warmed, and Winnie folded her arms and stared at the table.

Jen seemed to sense Winnie's apprehension. "Winnie, we don't consider you a suspect. Not in the least. We're just following up on any leads we come across, and since you were with Anita the night before she died, you may be able to give us information that may help us find who did this terrible thing."

Winnie looked over at the rings used to restrain prisoners. Then up at Jen.

"I know you're in an interview room, but we need to record this."

Winnie unfolded her arms and sighed. "Fine. I'm just not used to being in a room like this, that's all."

"It's perfectly understandable to be nervous. Most people would be. Now, shall we get started?"

Over the next hour, Winnie described everything she knew, including the mysterious Officer Taggart. It really wasn't much, and Winnie almost felt guilty for wasting precious time when the officers could be out looking for Anita's killer. Nevertheless, Winnie was polite and cheerful. Patches, on the other hand, was bored and occasionally wandered around the small room, sometimes stopping to lap up some water from the bowl, but mostly he just pouted in the corner.

When they finished, Jen offered to take Winnie and Patches on a tour of the area. It was bright and sunny as they stepped out, and Winnie put on a pair of sunglasses. On the lawn in front of them were a herd of elk, sitting or grazing, enjoying the sunshine, and not paying any attention to the people around them. But Patches noticed, and he clung close to Winnie.

"Wow, they're big," Winnie said when one stood up.

"Yes, they are. The females, or cows, like the one that stood up, weigh about five hundred pounds and are about eight feet long." Looking down, she scratched Patches's head. "But don't worry, Patches. Elk only eat plants."

That didn't seem to quell Patches's anxiety, and he stayed close to Winnie as Jen showed them the area.

After the tour, Winnie and Patches got in their car to explore the Mammoth Hot Springs area. Patches seemed relieved to be in the car and away from the elk, jumping into the back for the ride. Winnie was excited, too, to be done with the interview. She wanted to enjoy the sights, but her mind kept drifting back to Anita. She could picture Anita's smiling face when she played with Patches, and the thought of her murdered sent a chill down Winnie's spine.

Trying to shake the thought, Winnie drove along the Upper Terrace Drive, a beautiful one-mile loop that highlighted the terraces formed from minerals being pushed up and deposited, leaving each formation a different shape. Since they couldn't get out and explore, Winnie cracked the back window open just enough to let Patches get some air without letting him stick his head out. The New Highland Terrace, with its long, flowing trail of white bumps, looked like a ski slope, while the White Elephant Back really looked like an elephant. Winnie's favorite was the Orange Spring Mound. Unlike the other ones, it wasn't mostly white. As the name implied, it was a round formation which had deep hues of orange in it.

By the time they were finished, thirty minutes later, both Winnie and Patches were getting hungry, and since Winnie couldn't take Patches inside any of the restaurants, they left to go back to the motor home.

"I'll give you a proper walk when we get there." Winnie pulled onto the road. "After our walk, we'll have some lunch. Okay, boy?"

Winnie was rewarded with a bark, and the two took off, with Winnie putting on more Christmas music, wailing an off-key version of "Deck the Halls." Her tune was festive, but her mind was busy thinking of Anita and why Anita's roommate couldn't be found. And whether the killers saw Winnie's card with Anita.

Could they be looking for her, too?

4

Five Christmas songs after they left Mammoth Hot Springs, Winnie and Patches turned into Pebble Creek Campground. As they got near their site, Winnie noticed a car parked next to their spot, and someone was sitting on the chair Winnie left outside.

"Who's that, Patchy?" Winnie slowed down to evaluate the situation.

Winnie's brain set off alarms, and Winnie parked short of her campsite. Part of her thought she had nothing to fear, that the campground was too crowded for anyone to attack her. But the alarm bells got louder the longer she sat in the car, wondering why anyone was there.

Maybe it's that creep who asked me about my motor home yesterday.

Checking for cell service, she had two bars and was ready to dial 911 if she needed to. She slipped a leash on Patches and got him out. Approaching her motor home, Patches started growling and barking when the person seated looked up and over. Winnie recognized a familiar face.

"Olga?" Winnie said. "Are you okay? Where have you been? The rangers are looking for you."

Olga started to cry, running to Winnie and putting her in a death-grip hug. "Oh, Winnie! Have you heard? Anita, she is... she is..."

"I know, and I'm so sorry. Are you all right?"

"Yes, I'm fine, but I can't go back to my room. The police have it sealed. I'm afraid to go back anyway. What if the killer comes back?"

"The police want to talk to you. Come on inside. I'll make some tea and we can call Ranger Malone."

"No!" Olga shouted. "No police. I don't trust them, not after that one kept coming back to bother Anita. No police or I'm leaving."

"Settle down, Olga." Winnie took Olga's hand. "I promised Patches a walk. Why don't you go with us, then we'll go inside and decide what to do."

"Okay, but no police."

Winnie kept Patches focused and they were back in the RV in five minutes. After going inside, Winnie put out a plate of cookies and a pitcher of iced tea.

"Cookies always make things better." Winnie bit into a snickerdoodle. "Mmm, these are my favorites. They always make me think of Christmas."

Olga stirred some sugar into her iced tea and took a cookie. "Oh, these are really good. Did you make them?"

"Yes. I was in Cody for a couple of days. They have a popular rodeo there I wanted to see. At night it was cool, and I thought I'd bake. I love baking and probably miss that the most about not having a house. The oven in the Winnie is just too small to bake much."

"Why do you live in your camper?"

Winnie sighed. "I needed a change after my divorce, and I decided a great way to get my feet back on the ground and see the country was to get an RV. I've been living in it for a couple of months, but this is my first real trip. It's good for now, and we'll see where it goes. One thing I found out is I love my freedom, and this lifestyle is about as free as you can get."

Winnie stayed quiet while she waited for Olga to finish her cookie. When Olga reached for a second one, Winnie spoke up. "Olga, I know it's difficult, but what happened after I left you and Anita?"

"Nothing. We went back to our room and talked. We both went to bed, and when I woke up, she was gone. I thought she went for a run or something, but after a while, when she didn't return, I tried calling her phone. It kept going to voice mail, so I went out looking for her. When I came back, I saw the police and knew something was wrong. I panicked and slipped out the back."

"Why didn't you talk to the police?"

"I told you. I don't trust them. You seemed to want to help Anita, so I thought I'd find you."

More alarm bells started going off inside Winnie's head after she realized Olga hadn't been with Winnie and Anita last night when they went to Winnie's camper. Something didn't seem right. "How did you know where I'm staying?" Winnie started to wonder whether Olga was being honest.

Did I just invite a killer into my camper?

"When Anita and I were talking last night, she told me about you, Patches, and the cheesecake. She mentioned the campground where you were staying, so I borrowed a friend's car and drove out here. Your camper is hard to miss, and the picture on the side looks like you."

"You have a very good memory." Winnie still wondered whether Olga was telling the truth.

Winnie refilled their glasses and helped herself to another cookie. She took Olga's hand. "You need to tell the police what happened."

Olga looked down. "I know, but I didn't see anything. There's nothing I can tell them."

"That's okay. Maybe they can help you remember something. A clue that helps them solve the case. You've got to try. I'm going to call Ranger Malone."

Winnie picked up her cell phone and called. Olga alternated between pacing in the small living room or sitting with her hands churning. Within an hour, they heard the gravel stir as a car parked, and Jennifer Malone knocked on the door shortly after that. The loud thumps startled a clearly nervous Olga.

"It will be fine, Olga." Winnie reached for the door. "Ranger Malone is really nice."

After Winnie told Jen how nervous Olga was about meeting with the police, she changed out of her uniform, arriving in blue jeans, a sweatshirt, and tennis shoes. Her hair was back in a simple ponytail. She still had her sidearm, but it was unobtrusive next to dark jeans. Much less G.I. Jane than when Winnie first met her.

Winnie smiled at the changed appearance, nodding in approval. "Come on in, Jen. I've got tea and cookies. Help yourself."

"Thanks, Winnie." Jen entered, smiled warmly, and looked at Olga, who was standing and wringing her hands. "Hi, Olga. I'm Jennifer Malone. I understand you're nervous, but I need to find out who killed your friend, and I need your help."

Olga nodded but didn't say anything, so Jennifer sat down and grabbed a cookie while Winnie poured her some tea.

"Thanks," Jen took the glass, drinking it down. "I didn't get lunch today, and I guess I was thirstier than I thought."

Winnie refilled Jen's glass while she dug in on the cookies, mumbling "delicious" between bites. Finishing, Jennifer turned to Winnie. "I think it might be best if I interviewed Olga alone.

I'll take her back to the station and then bring her to her dorm."

"No!" Olga stood, folding her arms. "I'm not going to the station. We do it here or we don't do it."

"Calm down, Olga. I'm not trying to upset you. If it's all right with Winnie, we can just sit here and talk. But, at some point, I may need you to come to the station."

Winnie motioned to the table. "Of course it's all right. I've got plenty of cookies and tea, or I can make something else. Please, everyone, sit down."

Olga's arms dropped and she took a seat, looking at the floor. She started sniffling, and Winnie went to get a box of tissues.

"How can I help?" Olga asked. "I didn't see anything."

"Maybe not," Jennifer said, "but there may be other information you know that can help us. Let's start with a few questions."

Jennifer reached over and helped herself to another cookie. Stuffing it in her mouth, she took out a pad of paper and a pencil. She also started a voice recorder, putting it on the table and turning it on.

"I understand Winnie met you when she dropped Anita off. Do you remember the time?"

Olga looked at her watch. "I guess it was about nine thirty last night."

"After Winnie left, what did you and Anita do?"

Olga shrugged. "I don't know. Maybe we went to our room. That's what we do most nights. I don't remember doing anything."

"That's fine. What time did the two of you go to bed?"

Olga seemed to be considering the question for a while.

"I think it was about midnight. Oh, now I remember. When we got back to the dorm, we went over to see Anita's boyfriend, Seth. He has video games, and we stayed there for a while, playing. After that, we came back to our room and talked then went straight to bed. I remember getting a text from my mother as I got into bed. It was a little before twelve."

At the mention of a boyfriend, Jennifer looked up from her notepad then scribbled something down.

"After you went to bed, did you hear anything or did anything wake you up?"

"No, but I'm a heavy sleeper. Anita snores, although she denies it. Some nights I wake up from all the noise, but I don't remember doing it last night." Olga ran her hand through her blonde hair and started twirling a few strands around her fingers. She took another cookie and nibbled on it.

Jennifer wrote a few things in her notepad. "What time did you wake up?"

Olga thought about it. "I'm not sure. I didn't have an early shift, so I didn't set the alarm. Maybe nine-ish. When did she, umm, you know?" Olga put the cookie down. Her eyes became teary, and Winnie handed Olga a tissue.

"We're waiting for more results to come back, but based on what we know now, the time of death was between four and five this morning."

"Was she, you know...messed with? Did that creepy officer do something to her?"

Jennifer looked up from her notes. "Have you met the ranger that was giving her problems? Can you tell me his name and give me a description?"

"His name? I think it begins with a T. Tag something, maybe."

"Taggart?" Jennifer asked.

"That's it! Taggart. I think he said his first name is Scott."

"Can you describe him?"

Olga tapped her finger on her lips, her eyes looking up. "It's been a while since I saw him. He usually tries to get to Anita when she's alone. I think he's average height. Maybe a little overweight, but not much. Dark hair. He's not bad looking. If he wasn't such a creep, Anita might have gone out with him. Did he do this to her? If he did, I'll kill him myself."

"Hold on, Olga," Jennifer said. "We don't know what happened to Anita yet. We can't afford to make any assumptions."

Olga stood and pointed a finger at the ranger. "You're just sticking up for him because he's one of your own, aren't you?"

"He's not a ranger, Olga. At least not one here. We're checking to see if he's a ranger at another park, or a former park ranger, but so far no one has heard of him before. Even if he was, I wouldn't stick up for someone that committed murder."

Olga slumped back into her seat. "Okay. How can I help?"

"We have a sketch artist coming in from Billings. We need you—and you too, Winnie—to work with the artist to come up with a composite sketch. Then we can canvas the area and see if anyone recognizes him."

"I'm happy to help," Winnie said. "Just tell me when and where."

"Thanks. I expect her to arrive sometime tomorrow morning. Can you two meet me at the station at ten?"

"I'm sorry," Olga said. "I have to work then."

"If you give me the name of your supervisor, I'll make sure you get the time off, with pay. This is important, Olga, and we need all the help we can get."

Olga nodded. "Fine, I'll be there."

"Me, too," Winnie said. "Your dorm is on the way, Olga, so how about I pick you up at nine thirty and we can go together? I'll treat us to lunch at the Mammoth Hotel afterward. I hear they make some great sandwiches. Jennifer, can you find a place where I could keep Patches? Just for a while when I'm with Olga."

Jennifer raised her eyebrows. "I suppose, if you bring his

crate, we could keep him in an interview room for a couple of hours. It's the least I can do for all of your assistance."

"Winnie," Olga said, "if you come by early, I can look after Patches, and you can have breakfast at Roosevelt Lodge. I miss my dog at home."

"Perfect!" Winnie beamed. "Olga, I'll see you at eight thirty."

After Olga and Jen left, Winnie plopped on the couch and Patches jumped up. Winnie shook her head. "Here's another fine mess I've gotten us into."

5

Winnie arrived right on time and found Olga in the Roosevelt Lodge parking lot, waiting. Patches bounded out of the car, pulling on the leash, causing Winnie to practically run over to Olga. Olga giggled as she bent down to greet her guest, scratching his ears. Then she unfolded a napkin, which held two sausage patties. Olga looked at Winnie, who nodded, and then held out the patties for Patches, who didn't need to be asked twice. Within seconds, they were gobbled up, and Patches was licking Olga's hand, looking for more.

With Patches in Olga's care, Winnie went into the Roosevelt Lodge. The smells were different than they were two nights ago, but they were no less enchanting. She wanted some time alone to think without any distractions, and what better thinking catalyst than a stack of huckleberry pancakes covered in syrup, combined with an endless supply of coffee. Not having to do the dishes was a definite bonus, too.

Winnie reached into her purse and took out her iPad. She rarely went anywhere without it, and today she sat and organized her thoughts, trying to make sense of what happened over the last few days. There was practically no Wi-Fi throughout Yellowstone, but she didn't need it. She had expected a nice vacation and a chance to get herself away from Madison, Wisconsin, where her ex-husband was probably canoodling with some new floozy. Instead, she found herself wrapped up in a murder, and all the people, including the murder victim, were complete strangers. Drawing circles lazily as she pondered, Winnie was startled when her phone rang. She looked at the caller ID and frowned. Cell phone reception was spotty, but just Winnie's luck this call came through fine.

"Hi, Mom. Is everything okay?" Winnie always worried when her mother called unexpectedly.

"Yes, dear, everything is fine. I haven't heard from you in a few days, and I wanted to see how you were. Did you make it to Yellowstone?"

"Oh, I made it all right." Winnie recounted the story of what happened so far.

"A murder? In Yellowstone? Well, what's that got to do with you?"

"Like I said, I had dinner with the victim the night before, and the police found my business card in her room. Her roommate managed to find me, and she's leery of the rangers, so I got stuck in the middle. I'm sure I'll be done with it today, then I can get back to my vacation."

Winnie heard her mom sigh. "Winona, you have a knack for getting into mischief. You always have. Why don't you give your statement, pack up your things, and get out of there?"

"That sounds like a plan, Mom, except I haven't even seen Yellowstone yet. Not really, anyway. I've been through Lamar Valley, and I stopped to take pictures of a couple of black bears and a herd of bison, but I haven't been to any of the thermals or the stinky sulfur areas yet. I can't leave Yellowstone without seeing those. I haven't even seen Old Faithful. Maybe you're right, though. Maybe I should move to a different campground within the park."

A huge plate of pancakes arrived, along with a refill on her coffee. "Mom, can I call you back? My breakfast just arrived."

"Okay, dear, but please be careful. I worry about you, Winona."

Again with the Winona.

"I'll be fine, Mom, and I'll talk to you soon."

The food and coffee must have fired a few synapses in Winnie's brain, because she began alternating between her fork and her stylus. On the notepad app she wrote Events: followed by Met Anita (she was upset), Had dinner with Anita, Took Anita to motor home for dessert, Drove Anita back to Roosevelt Lodge, Encounter with Taggart, Met Olga and said goodbye, Anita found dead the next morning.

After Events, Winnie wrote Persons Involved: Anita, Olga, Unknown Ranger, Me. She wrote Seth (boyfriend), then circled his name because he was an unknown. Anyone else?

"Shoot," Winnie dribbled some syrup on her iPad. Wiping it off with her pinky, she pushed the tablet aside and focused on the important things—that plate of pancakes and a freshly refilled mug of coffee.

Winnie was pleasantly full as she stepped onto the porch of Roosevelt Lodge. It was 9:15 and still a bit chilly, but she took a rocking chair and opened her iPad, studying what she'd written so far. The crisp morning air felt good but did nothing to help Winnie make sense of anything. At a little after 9:30, Winnie saw Olga walking up with Patches with a big smile.

"Patches is so much fun!" Olga handed the leash over. "We both had a great time."

"I can see that," Winnie said. "And you look much better this morning, Olga. A good night's sleep seems to have worked wonders. Where did you stay?"

"I was able to stay with a friend. They brought in a spare

bed. I feel much better. I want to help find who killed my friend."

"Me too. We better get going."

Winnie opened the passenger door and Patches jumped in, followed by Olga. When the car started, the stereo started blasting out "Here Comes Santa Claus."

"Sorry." Winnie quickly turned the volume down.

"You listen to Christmas music this time of year? My mom does that, too."

"Yeah, I know it's silly, but I like them all year. They make me happy."

They drove in silence for a while, and Olga seemed to be content staring out the window. Finally, Winnie asked a question she'd thought of at breakfast.

"Olga, you mentioned Anita had a boyfriend. Was it serious?"

"I don't think so. They met right after she got here, but he isn't from Ukraine, so I don't think either one expected it to last. She liked him, and he seemed nice to her. I don't think they got 'involved,' if you know what I mean. Anita wasn't like that."

Before long they reached the Mammoth Hot Springs area and pulled up to the ranger station. Winnie got out and stretched, looking at the elk still sitting happily on the lawn. Olga was holding onto the leash, but Patches was keeping very close to her.

"When Patches and I were here last, he was afraid of the elk, too. I guess he still is."

"Is it hard for Patches to be inside the camper while you're gone?"

"He doesn't seem to mind. I think he likes being alone sometimes. Besides, we went for a long walk this morning, and the motor home's air-conditioning comes on automatically when it gets warm. I don't like to leave him alone all the time, so I wanted to take him with us this morning. We'll definitely need to play for a while when I get back, though. After all those pancakes, we'll both need it!"

Ranger Malone came outside to greet them, shaking each of their hands. She was back in her standard uniform but kept her hair in a ponytail and still had a welcoming smile. "Hi, Olga. Hi, Winnie. Thanks for coming. Right this way."

Winnie walked next to Jen while Olga stayed a few feet behind, watching the elk. Before they got to the door, Winnie leaned into Jen. "Do Anita's parents know?"

Jen nodded. "We couldn't contact them directly. Our embassy handled it. But I heard they took it about like you'd expect. Sadness, anger, and confusion all rolled into one. And we have the autopsy back. Blunt force trauma. They think she was hit with a pistol, then fell and hit her head again. The marks on her skull leave no doubt. This was murder."

Jen led them into a small conference room. Winnie noticed that this room had a nice wooden table with comfy swivel chairs and no rings to secure criminals.

"This is Patty Amherst. She'll be developing the sketch from both of your descriptions. Would anyone like coffee or water?"

No one accepted the offer, so they sat down and got to work. Winnie was glad she'd filled up on coffee at the Roosevelt Lodge after experiencing the swill the last time she was there.

Ninety minutes later, they had a composite sketch of the ranger that had been harassing Anita. Winnie seemed to recall more details about his face, while Olga's description was more generic.

"I guess I didn't pay much attention to him," Olga said. "I just wanted him to go away."

"Maybe Winnie has a better eye for detail," Ranger Malone replied. "As long as you agree with the final sketch, Olga, Winnie's details will be more than sufficient."

"It looks good to me," Olga said. "I'm sorry I couldn't be more helpful."

"Nonsense." Winnie stretched her arms. "Our descriptions matched. I just got up close when he nearly shoved me aside, so I remembered the mole on his left cheek and the color of his eyes. I didn't remember the tattoo on his arm. That was a good catch of yours. Between the two of us, we have a good likeness of him."

After receiving confirmation from the sketch artist, Jen said, "I think we have what we need. I want to thank both of you for taking the time to do this. It was very helpful."

"My pleasure," Winnie said. "I just need to get Patches's crate and then we can go."

Jen added, "We talked to everyone staying at your dorm, and we found the boyfriend. He said he didn't hear anything either and gave us an alibi we're looking into."

Olga looked over. "He's nice. I don't think he did anything."

Winnie went downstairs to get the crate. Jen caught up to her. "One more thing. Anita may have been going for a run. She was dressed for it, and some of the people we interviewed said she liked to run early. What we don't know is whether this was a crime of opportunity—wrong place, wrong time—or a crime of passion. Or something else. Maybe they knew her schedule. We don't have enough of the facts, yet. I didn't want to say anything in front of Olga because she's upset enough already. But if you notice anything, or if she says anything else when you drop her off, let me know."

Winnie nodded as Jen opened the door to the conference room. Upon seeing his crate, Patches jumped for joy.

"I have never seen a dog want to get in his crate before," Jen said.

"Yeah," Winnie smiled. "I don't know why, but he's really at home in it."

After getting Patches settled, the three went outside.

"We're going over to the Mammoth Hotel for lunch," Winnie said. "Would you care to join us?"

"Thanks, Winnie. I appreciate the offer. Right now, I need to get the sketch out to as many law enforcement offices as I can. I want to find this guy and see what's going on."

Olga and Winnie walked the short distance to the hotel. Since it had just turned 11:30, the lunch rush hadn't started, and they were able to get a table right away. They each ordered a soup and sandwich combo, with Winnie ordering the Alaska salmon club and squash soup, while Olga ordered the grilled cheese and squash soup.

"This soup is delicious." Winnie dunked a piece of bread into her bowl.

"It sure is," Olga tried to say with a mouth full of bread from her own dunking. What came out instead was more of a muffled "mit mur miz," causing them both to giggle.

After their meal, they went on a short hike around the Mammoth Hot Springs Terraces. Winnie had taken the drive around it before but couldn't really experience it with Patches. A boardwalk wound its way along different layers of the terrace, allowing visitors to get an up-close view. Although the boardwalk didn't cover the entire terrace area like the drive did, Winnie was able to get much closer to the formations than she could from the car, and she could see the ridges and subtle streaks of color that were formed over time. As they walked along, Winnie crinkled her nose at the sulfur smell, which got stronger as they moved deeper into the terraces.

"You better get used to that smell," someone said when they saw Winnie. "This area is mild compared to others in the park."

The terraces towered over them as they walked along, built up by the steaming water that flowed over the top, leaving deposits of different-colored minerals. The colors varied from an off-white to deep red, with hues of orange and green in various places. It looked like a bunch of candles where the wax overflowed, leaving a bumpy, colorful surface and pools of hot wax. The pools overflowed onto more candles and more pools, each leaving a slight change to the appearance.

The minerals continued to build the terraces, constantly changing the landscape. As the water flowed down, the terraces cascaded into pools of steaming, cloudy water, which looked like acid baths from a horror movie. The baths overflowed into more pools until the water reached the ground.

Winnie snapped a bunch of pictures of the mounds, including selfies with her and Olga. After posting a few to Facebook, the two returned to the station, where they collected Patches and left.

When they arrived at Roosevelt Lodge, the parking lot was packed, and Olga directed her to a service road which led to her dorm.

"Would you walk me to my room? After what's happened, I don't feel safe without an escort."

"Sure. I'd be happy to." Winnie exited the car.

In a few minutes, they were up the stairs and standing in front of Olga's room. The police notices were gone, and Olga unlocked the door.

Turning to Winnie, Olga gave her a big hug. "Thank you for everything. You really helped me."

Winnie turned to leave when she heard Olga open her door and gasp.

"Oh my," Olga exclaimed as she peered in.

"What's wrong?" Winnie turned back. She looked inside, her mouth dropping like Olga's.

The room had been torn apart. Clothes, books, food, everything was on the floor, with doors and drawers opened wide.

"I'll call Jen," Winnie said. "The room is now a crime scene —again."

6

Jen Malone arrived with three other rangers. "Wow." Ranger Malone peered into the room. "Somebody was looking for something. Did either of you go inside?"

"No," Winnie said. "When Olga opened the door and saw the mess, we called you."

"You did the right thing. Why don't you two go over to the lodge and we'll come and get you when we're finished. Olga, I'll talk to the manager about moving you to another room. You can come back and pack up your things after we finish processing. Anita's belongings will be sent to her family except for the items in evidence. Do you have any idea what they were looking for?"

Olga was silent for a moment. "I can't think of anything. Neither of us had anything valuable, except for our phones, and I have mine. Is this why Anita was killed? They were looking for something she had?"

"It's hard to say. Hopefully, we'll know more when we're finished. We didn't find Anita's phone, either with her or in this room yesterday. Do you know where it is?"

"No. She always had it stuck in her back pocket."

"Come on, Olga." Winnie took Olga's hand, pulling her away from the room. "We'll go back to my motor home and dig into that cheesecake while they work. A slice sounds good right about now. What do you say?"

"Okay, I guess. Anyplace is better than here."

After Olga and Winnie got back to Pebble Creek, they took Patches for a walk around the campsite and then settled down for a slice of cheesecake with cherry topping. Winnie took out her iPad and began to make notes.

"What are you doing?" Olga asked.

"Oh, it's kind of a hobby of mine. Back in Madison, I helped solve a murder there, and I liked it. Not the murder, of course, but the challenge of following the clues that led me to the solution. Well, led the police and me to solving it."

"So, you're like a private detective?"

Winnie laughed. "I'm not a detective. I'm just a reporter... well, ex-reporter. I'm just curious, that's all."

Olga laughed, too. "Well, I'm glad you're on this case. Between you and the police, I'm sure you'll find the bad guy. Do you have to go back home to work after this?"

"Nope. At least not for a while. Right now, I work when I want to. I have a few clients, and they give me enough work to keep me busy. Besides, I made out pretty well in the divorce settlement, not that I didn't deserve everything I got. I've got enough money to last me a long time. If it runs out, I'll just take on more clients. I'm resourceful, especially when I'm hungry."

"I can believe that." Olga peered out the window. "Look, here comes Ranger Malone."

Winnie got up to open the door, and Jen walked in with another ranger and sat down.

"I tried to call, but my phone didn't have service. Unfortunately, we didn't learn anything," Jen said.

"There are too many kids going in and out of these rooms to get a decent DNA sample. We took a few prints, but I doubt that they'll tell us much. They're probably Anita's and yours, Olga." She looked at Olga. "Now that we've photographed everything and dusted for prints, I need you to come back and see if anything's missing. Can you do that now?"

Olga nodded and stood up.

Winnie reached into her purse and pulled out a business card. "If you need anything, or just want to talk, here's my number."

"Thanks, Winnie. You've been really kind. I'm going to miss you."

Giving Winnie a hug, Olga turned and followed Jen and the other officer to their car.

Winnie watched the car leave and then breathed a sigh of relief, hoping the ordeal was over, at least for her. She was curious, of course, but this was a police matter, and she was on vacation. Winnie took another look at the notes on her iPad, but with no new revelations, she put it away, finished her coffee, and went outside for some fresh air. She was getting low on fuel and groceries, and Winnie decided to drive into the nearby town of Cooke City. "Come on, Patchy. Let's go for a walk and then we'll go into town and get some food."

They went for a quick walk, and Patches jumped into the car as soon as Winnie opened the door. He looked at Winnie and gave his "I'm ready, let's go" bark.

"Patchy, you really wanted to get out!" Winnie laughed at her dog, who was wagging his tail with reckless abandon. Winnie was feeling upbeat at finally being able to relax, and she put on a hip-hop version of "Rockin' Around the Christmas Tree," singing with the music and tapping the dash to keep rhythm.

They made their way to Cooke City, Montana, which was only four miles outside of Yellowstone. A small town which catered to tourists, Cooke City had an assortment of gas stations, restaurants, and shops. Many of the places had an "old-time" feel, and Winnie was waiting for Wyatt Earp to come down the road with tumbleweeds and dust billowing behind him. At a minimum, she expected every man she saw to tip his hat and offer a "Howdy, ma'am."

After getting gas, Winnie pulled up to the Cooke City Holistic Grocery store. "Look, Patchy, they even have a 'good dog' area for you to play in while I'm in the store." Patches didn't need any encouragement. He tore off for the play area and began the ritual of sniffing (and peeing on) everything around. An attendant was there to watch the dogs, and the first hour was free for customers, so Winnie took her claim ticket for Patches, said a quick goodbye, and made her way into the store. She stepped out a little while later carrying two arms full of grocery bags. After putting them in the car, she went to collect Patches, who was reluctant to leave his new friends.

"Come on, Patch! I've got a comfy chair and a big glass of wine waiting for me. I think we both need a good rest."

Patches gave Winnie a bark and wagged his tail but still didn't move. The attendant handed Winnie a few doggie treats, and Winnie used those as a bribe. That seemed to be enough motivation for Patches.

When they got to the car, Winnie open the back door and Patches jumped in. In his hurry, Patches knocked a notebook onto the floor. It was a black notebook sitting on the back seat, and Winnie hadn't noticed it before.

"What's that, Patch?" Winnie picked up the notebook. "Have you been writing back there?"

Winnie didn't recognize the notebook, and there was no name on the outside. She leafed through it, but it was written in a language she didn't understand. When she got about halfway through, a flash drive fell out. "Are you taking pictures, too?" Winnie's mom worked with immigrants and had borrowed Winnie's car before she left. Thinking one of her mom's patrons left it, Winnie put the notebook and flash drive on the passenger's seat and took off for the Pebble Creek Campground.

Along the way, Winnie pulled over to look for wildlife. She parked next to a group of people that had set up cameras with tripods and long telephoto lenses. There were about twenty people tucked into a small parking lot. Most were sitting on chairs, idly chatting. Others were eating, but none were looking into their cameras.

"Do you see something?" Winnie asked.

"We're waiting until dusk. There's been a pack of wolves roaming out there, and we're going to try to capture them—on camera, of course. If you wait here or come back later, we're happy to let you look through our equipment. I have to warn you, though, the wolves are elusive. We've been out here a few nights and only caught a quick glimpse."

Winnie shook her head. "Thanks for the offer, but I've got a date with a big glass of wine and a whole lot of nothing."

"That sounds great, but if you change your mind, feel free to come back. By the way, I love your car. I take it you're Winnie?"

"Yes, that's me. Thanks again for the invite. I just might take you up on it." Taking one last look at the area, she got back into her car.

"I'm definitely keeping you on a short leash, buddy." She turned to Patches. "Wolves, black bears, grizzly bears, and who knows what else are out there. And you're just too curious to stay away from any of them. Well, except for the elk, which you're scared of, huh, Patchy."

When they got back to the campground, Winnie noticed the door to her motor home was open. She stopped short of her site. "That's strange, I'm sure I locked it before we left."

Winnie checked to make sure the doors to the Mini were locked as she thought about what to do. Maybe it was nothing. Or Olga coming back. *But why would she go inside, or what if it's someone else?* Her hand shook a little as she put the Mini in drive, creeping her way forward, ready to leave in a hurry at the first sign of trouble.

As she arrived, Winnie saw a tall figure run out of the door, ducking between the other campsites. By the time Winnie stopped and got out of her car, the person was long gone, and Winnie could hear tires squealing in the distance. She pulled out her phone and dialed a now-familiar number.

"Hi, Jen, this is Winnie Hackleshack. I think you better come out here. Someone just ran out of my trailer as I pulled up."

7

When Jen Malone arrived, Winnie was sitting on a chair outside, eating cookie dough ice cream with her fingers.

"You told me not to go inside," Winnie looked at her sheepishly. "It was going to melt, so I had to eat it."

"Sure." Jen smiled. "It relieves stress, too. Wait here while I check your motor home."

Ranger Malone drew her weapon and peered inside. The RV was cleared in under a minute, and soon Jen came back outside. She was carrying a spoon and a napkin.

Handing the spoon and napkin to Winnie, Jen grabbed a bag of groceries. "Let's put these groceries away before you have to eat anything else."

Winnie licked the cookie dough off of her fingers, wiped them with the napkin, and grabbed a bag, following her inside.

While they were putting things away, Jen asked, "Do you think this was the same person as our make-believe ranger?"

Winnie thought for a moment. "He was wearing a baseball cap pulled low and kept his head tucked. I couldn't see his face, but who else could it be?"

"It could be anyone. A robber, or someone looking for food. A lot of hikers come through with no money and no resources. We need to keep an open mind until we have all the facts."

"Maybe, but I think it's him. I might have bad luck, but to stumble across a murder and an attempted robbery? My luck's not *that* bad."

"Was there any writing on his shirt? Or on the baseball cap he wore?"

"Not that I noticed, but he was gone so quickly I couldn't really tell."

"Well, if he was wearing gloves, we probably won't find anything useful for DNA or prints, so I won't bother to call the forensic team in. Do you have any idea what this guy was looking for?"

"None."

Patches started giving Winnie that "take me out or clean up my mess" look, a look Jen seemed to recognize.

"I don't want to jump to any conclusions, but you're probably right, this has something to do with Anita's death. Go ahead and take Patches for a walk. I shouldn't be more than a half hour."

When they came back, Jen was sitting in her car, writing down notes. "Perfect timing. I just finished my incident report. Let's go inside and you can tell me if anything's missing."

As soon as the door was opened, Patches bounded inside, scooting past Jen and running around to see what the fuss was about.

"Patches!" Winnie exclaimed. "Sorry, Jen, we're working on his manners."

"No worries. When I was a kid, my dog was the same way."

They both went in and found Patches on Winnie's bed. He looked up and gave Winnie a look that seemed to say, "All clear. You're safe. Time to relax."

"This dog has it made." Winnie checked the motor home

over. “They were looking for something, but it doesn’t look like they took anything. Quite honestly, I really don’t have anything valuable enough to steal. Except my computer and my iPad. My iPad I keep with me, and my computer is in the back pocket of the camper’s driver’s seat.” Winnie reached into the seat pocket and pulled it out.

“That’s a good hiding spot. They probably didn’t think to look there. If you notice anything missing, please give me a call. I’ll make the rounds and ask the other campers if they noticed anything, but I don’t think we’ll have a lot of luck. If I find something, I’ll let you know.”

“Okay. Thanks. I’ll ask around tonight when more campers are here.”

Winnie walked Jen out to her car.

“Be careful, Winnie. I don’t think any of the campers here are involved, but I don’t recommend going into anyone’s RV until we get this resolved.”

“I’ll be careful. Take care.”

Winnie went back inside her motor home and started to clean up the mess. Before she knew it, two hours had passed, and it was time for dinner. Patches came strolling out from the bedroom, stretching.

“Just in time for dinner, huh? I think we need to play first, mister lazy lump.”

Winnie picked up Patches’s favorite toy and held it out. It had the desired effect. Patches jumped up to retrieve the squeaky cactus, tugging at it while Winnie held on tight. Finally, Patches “won” the tug-of-war, running away with his prize cactus and chomping on the squeaker. After a while, Patches brought the cactus back to Winnie, and the process started all over again until they both had had enough.

“Okay, Patches, are you hungry?” Winnie got his bowl. She really didn’t need to ask because, at the sight of the bowl,

Patches worked himself into a frenzy, running in circles and jumping up.

Winnie fed him and watched for a moment as Patches practically inhaled his food. Shaking her head at the way he ate, she started the grill and made a veggie pizza with the dough she bought in Cooke City. While the pizza grilled, she prepared a fresh salad and then washed some fruit for dessert. The whole time, Patches was on high alert, waiting to see if anything fell onto the floor, ready to do his part to keep the place clean.

Winnie took Patches outside and secured his leash then pulled down a swing-out table attached to the motor home. She stepped back into the RV and grabbed her salad, along with a corkscrew and a bottle of wine. She picked a Chardonnay, something the clerk at the store in Cooke City recommended. Winnie was never very particular about the wine she drank. Not that she had too much, but she wasn't afraid of imbibing, either. Especially after a day like she had today.

Winnie checked the pizza. It had taken her several tries of burnt crusts, but she finally had a process for cooking the pizza just right, using indirect grill heat as the source.

"Perfect." Winnie removed her pizza from the grill. Putting it on the table, she sat down and dug in.

As usual, Patches sat close by while she ate, hoping something would fall to the ground. Winnie hadn't realized how hungry she was until she started eating, then her *I have food* receptors took over and suddenly she was famished.

"I'm eating as fast as you tonight, Patchy." Winnie grabbed another slice of pizza. "I need to slow down." After she finished, she looked at a clearly disappointed Patches. "Sorry, Patches. No second meal tonight." Winnie cleared the table.

After doing the dishes, Winnie and Patches made the rounds among the other campers, asking if they saw or heard anything about her uninvited visitor. No one noticed anything unusual, so Winnie returned home.

"You know what, Patches?" Winnie said when she got back. "Let's go back out to where the people were watching for wolves. What do you say?"

Winnie was rewarded with a bark and a tail that threatened to wag off Patches's body. They made their way back to the wolf watchers, pulling in as quietly as they could. It was cool enough that Winnie could leave Patches in the car while she stood with the group, and she would stay within a few feet of her car.

"Patchy, you wait here—just for a few minutes." Winnie got out of the car. "I'll be right back."

Patches curled up in the back seat and Winnie gave him a dog bone.

"Winnie, You're back." The same woman that Winnie talked to before had come up to her car. "And you're in luck. We're tracking a few wolves."

"Hi." Winnie extended her hand. "It's nice to meet you again."

"Doris." The woman took Winnie's hand. "We have to be quiet. We don't want to spook the wolves."

Doris motioned Winnie over to a pair of binoculars set on a tripod. Winnie bent down to look. At first, she couldn't see anything, but after her eyes adjusted, she thought she could make out something in the distance.

"I see them!" Winnie shouted.

"Shhh!" came a chorus of people standing behind cameras.

"Oops," Winnie whispered. She went back to looking through the binoculars for a while, but, with the fading light, it was difficult to see anything clearly. It was really just some grainy shapes moving around. Winnie turned over the binoculars to Doris, thanked her for her hospitality, and quietly chatted with a few of the people milling about. After a few minutes, she decided it was time to leave.

Patches was glad to see her when she approached the car, and Winnie smiled when she saw the tail wagging ferociously.

She opened the back seat and sat with him for a moment, gently stroking his fur. "Time to go." When she opened the driver's door, the interior light reflected on something on the passenger's seat. "The notebook!" She'd forgotten about it when she returned to find her motor home ransacked. She also found the flash drive and put it into her pocket.

It was now dark outside, and Winnie drove slowly back to the campsite, afraid an animal might wander into the road. There were just a few other cars out, and Winnie trudged along, finally reaching Pebble Creek Campground. "Whew." She breathed a sigh of relief as she pulled into her spot. Taking the notebook, she and Patches started to go inside.

"Howdy, camper. Care to join us?" a voice called out from a nearby campfire.

Winnie could see a person waving. Next to him were a number of people sitting in a circle.

"I'd love to," Winnie said. "Can I bring my dog?"

"Of course," the voice called back. "The more the merrier."

"Be right over." Winnie stepped into her motor home. She put the notebook and flash drive down, promising to look at it later. Getting some treats for Patches, she grabbed a flashlight and a folding chair as she made her way over to the group.

"Welcome," the same voice said. "I'm Carlos, and this is my wife, Juanita."

"Nice to meet you." Winnie shook their hands. Moving around the campfire, she introduced herself to everyone there. Some she had met before when she made the rounds looking for anyone that had information about the break-in of her motor home, but most were new to her.

The group chatted about everything but centered around the things RVers liked to talk about the most—where they'd been, where they were going, and what type of camper they were in. When Winnie told them it was her first real trip in her motor home, she was flooded with advice on where to go next, what gadgets were "essential" for her motor home, and what basic maintenance procedures she should be doing.

"I'm planning to head to Yellowstone's sister park, Grand Teton," Winnie said, "after I leave here. After that, though, I may mix it up and head north to Glacier National Park instead."

"Glacier is beautiful," a woman sitting across from Winnie said.

The conversation quickly segued into things to do at Glacier and, of course, the best way to get there from Yellowstone.

"But before you go anywhere else," the woman's husband interrupted, "you need to see the rest of this park. Lamar Valley is great, but it's only one area. You need to see the rest of it—the thermals bubbling mud, the stinky sulfur pots, forcing you to hold your nose as you get close, and the terraced wonders at the Mammoth Hot Springs area."

"I can't wait to see the rest of the park," Winnie said. "I've seen some of the Mammoth area, but only because of the incident I've gotten myself in the middle of."

Winnie recounted the events of the last few days, eliciting gasps and murmurs from the group. When the subject of the break-in at her motor home came up, everyone was interested to find out more, especially because they were worried their campers might be next.

"I don't think there's a reason to worry," Winnie said. "This wasn't random. They were looking for something. As far as I can tell, they didn't take anything."

The conversation reminded Winnie of the notebook she found in her car. She looked at the people sitting next to her. Could one of the people around the campfire be involved? She didn't think so, but there was always a chance. There was also a chance that whoever did break into her car was watching her now. There were lots of hiding places in the campground. Especially at night. She stood up and took another look around. Nothing obvious. "I'll be right back."

Winnie's head was on a swivel as she walked back to her RV. Patches was busy sniffing the ground. She didn't notice movement, but she jumped when a fire crackled, which caused Patches to bark. She stood at the entrance to her motor home and waited. All quiet. Her hand shook a little as she opened the door. No one was there to greet her, and she breathed a sigh of relief.

Winnie debated whether to show the notebook to anyone. On the one hand, she had no proof that the notebook was even related to the break-in. On the other, it could expose her to another break-in. Or worse. She looked at Patches for guidance. He was shaking his tail. "Good enough for me."

Moments later, she returned with the notebook. "I found this in my car. It could have been left when my mom borrowed it, but I've never seen it before. I wonder if Anita left it there, either by accident or for safe keeping. Do any of you recognize the language?"

Winnie passed the book around, but no one knew the language. The conclusion was the words were Slavic, and there was a good chance it was Anita's notebook written in Ukrainian. Winnie put the notebook aside and made a mental note to call Jen first thing in the morning, while the group continued to discuss all things camping.

When Winnie and Patches returned home—it was still a new concept to Winnie that her RV *was* her only real home—she settled Patches down and decided it was time to put her reporter skills to work. After inserting the flash drive and checking for viruses, she copied the contents onto her hard drive in a folder marked Anita. Using her phone, she took a picture of each page in the notebook with writing on it. After that was done, Winnie connected her phone to her computer and transferred the pictures she took to the same folder. Then she sent it all to her mother with a quick note saying she'd explain everything in the morning. By that time, it was late, well past 1:00 am, and Winnie was having a hard time keeping her eyes open.

"You just can't pull an all-nighter anymore," Winnie said to herself as she yawned. Checking to make sure the door and windows were locked, she dragged herself to bed. Even though she was exhausted, sleep didn't come easy, and Winnie listened for anything that sounded like someone outside. Every creak, rattle, or wind-blown leaf caused Winnie to jump.

8

After tossing and turning a good part of the night, Winnie finally fell into a deep sleep until a car backfired and startled her awake. Dogs throughout the campground started barking. Patches, who was sleeping on Winnie's bed, joined in, trying to protect Winnie from whatever evils awaited outside. After hearing the car sputter down the road, Winnie reached over and scratched Patches's head. "You're a good guard dog, Patchy. But I think we're safe. How about a few more minutes of sleep?"

It didn't take much to convince Patches that more sleep was in order. The two of them dosed off for about thirty minutes before Winnie's internal clock forced her to get up. She trudged into the kitchen and put on a pot of coffee. As the aroma of French Roast wafted throughout the motor home, she plopped down at the table and blew the hair in front of her eyes away. Her phone was there, reminding her she promised to call her mother. But not before caffeine.

Patches strolled in, looked at his empty food bowl, and offered Winnie a scowl.

"Don't give me that look, Patchy. I just got up and you know I need my coffee."

Patches came up to her and put his head on her lap, looking up with big eyes.

Winnie laughed and shook her head at her dog's sad expression. "You're spoiled, you know that?" The coffee maker gurgled. Winnie could almost taste her first sip, but she got up, gave Patches his breakfast, and then poured a big cup of coffee. After finishing her second cup, Winnie picked up her cell phone, pressing 2 to speed dial her mother.

"Winnie, what on earth was that email you sent last night about?" her mother asked as she answered.

Winnie rolled her eyes. "Good morning to you, too, Mom."

"Sorry, dear, but I didn't expect to get an email full of Russian notes and boring pictures waiting in my inbox this morning. Where did you get these, anyway?"

"I'm not sure, but I think Anita may have left them in my car. I don't know if she did it on purpose or not. Either way, the notes are probably Ukrainian, not Russian, but I suppose they're similar."

"Was she the one that got killed? You need to get this to the police right away. Now, Winona, don't try playing amateur detective. You're there for a vacation, and you're not part of the police."

Again with the Winona.

"Yes, Mother, I'm handing over the originals to the police this morning. I just thought you might be able to send these to Professor Mellon at the university. You still keep in touch, don't you?"

Winnie's mother retired from the University of Wisconsin, where she worked for over thirty years in the admissions office. She had a long list of contacts at the university and continued to socialize with many of them.

"Yes, but I haven't talked to him recently. He's been retired for years."

"Maybe you could send him the notebook pages I photographed and just ask him if he has any idea what it's about. It could be just some talk about boyfriends or what she wants to do in college, or it could be something that got her killed. I was hoping someone could help decipher it."

"Okay. I'll give him a call, but I thought you were letting the police handle it. Please don't tell me you're getting involved."

"I'm not getting involved, *Mother*. I'm just curious."

"No need to get into a tiff, dear. I just don't want to see you get hurt. Not like last time."

"Mother!" Winona stood for emphasis, as if her mom could see her. "You promised you'd let that drop. And if you recall, the police found me before anything happened."

Her mother couldn't keep from reminding Winnie about her events of the past and her near-death experience the last time Winnie got involved in solving a murder.

"Oh, I remember, all right. You call a three-day stint in the hospital nothing? If the police hadn't shown up when they did, I'd be talking to your tombstone right now. How am I supposed to let that drop, Winona?"

Winnie sighed. Her mom always seemed to want to temper her curiosity. "Mom," Winnie said softly, "I just want to know what was in the notebook I found in my car. That's it."

"I'll let you know when he gets back to me. And, Winnie, please be careful."

"Not to worry, Mom. I'm heading to a new campground this morning. Yellowstone has so many areas to camp, and I haven't seen nearly enough of it yet."

They said their goodbyes and Winnie took a deep breath, trying to calm down. Deciding some yoga was in order, she put her mat on the floor. The RV wasn't huge, but it was big enough she could stretch out without banging into too many things.

Winnie started with the cat pose because it stretched her back and forced her to relax. She cycled through her various poses, ending with downward facing dog.

"This one's for you, Patchy," Winnie called out.

Patches gave her a look, but since there wasn't food or scratching involved, he lost interest quickly.

After yoga, Winnie had a breakfast of yogurt, granola, and fruit. The air was still crisp as the morning dew hung to the grass, but Winnie went outside, enjoying the view as she ate under her awning. She'd brought Patches out, but it was too chilly for him, and he retreated inside. Patches stood at the doorway looking out, waiting for Winnie to come to her senses and go back in.

"Wimp," Winnie called after Patches.

After breakfast, Winnie called Ranger Malone, but the call went to voice mail. She left a message to call her back then went about packing up to move to a different campsite. Before she left Madison, her friends teased her that she wasn't really camping. They told her she was "glamping," a much more glamorous form of camping than the images of a rustic tent, outhouse, and campfire most people thought of. "I'm not glamping. I'm just living comfortably while exploring the great outdoors."

She got the motor home ready for travel. She retracted the slides, secured everything inside, and raised the levelers. Then she hitched the Mini back on and headed to the final stop at the site.

"It's not all glamp, is it, Patches?" Winnie pulled into the campsite's dump station. This was the worst part of her version of camping. Her motor home had a regular bathroom, but when she was out, everything got stored in tanks, which had to be emptied. By her. Which wasn't fun. The dump station was where the waste from the motor home was placed. It was a dirty, smelly end to each campsite visit, and Winnie hated doing it. But it was part of the experience, so she put on her long, thick rubber gloves, strapped on a pair of goggles, and got to work. She connected the hoses and triple-checked to make sure they were secure. The last thing she wanted was to have a hose come off, spewing a mess everywhere. Winnie opened the valves and emptied the tanks. It didn't take too long, but it seemed like an eternity as Winnie finished flushing the remains from the tanks with a special water hose just for tank rinsing. Coiling her hoses back up, she removed her goggles and gloves, washed her hands—twice—and was ready to leave. Patches stayed in the RV the whole time. As adventurous as he was, he didn't like the dump station much, either.

As Winnie pulled out of the Pebble Creek Campground, her phone rang. Pressing the talk button on the RV console, Ranger Jen Malone's voice was broadcast through the speakers.

"Hi, Winnie. I got your message. What's up?"

"I'm just leaving the campground, on my way to Fishing Bridge. I wanted to let you know I found a notebook and flash drive in my car. It certainly isn't mine, and I think it belonged to Anita. The writing looks Slavic, so it could be Ukrainian or Russian. I wanted to hand it over to you."

Winnie heard a drawer being opened and a pad of paper hit the desk. "When and where did you find it?"

"I found it yesterday in my car, but with the excitement of someone breaking into the RV, I forgot about it until late last night. I didn't want to disturb you that late, so I waited until this morning to call."

"I understand, but I want to get that book and flash drive as soon as I can. Which campground did you say you're heading to? I'll meet you there."

"I was able to get a reservation at Fishing Bridge. I'm looking forward to using full hookups for a few days."

Full hookups included power, water, and sewage, which

meant no dump stations. A definite plus for Winnie, and much closer to her idea of glamping.

"Great. I'll leave in a few minutes and meet you there."

"Sounds good, Jen. Patchy and I will be waiting."

Winnie had no sooner gotten off the phone when the traffic in front of her stopped. Ahead in the road was a herd of about ten bison, all meandering along without a care in the world. There were a few bison calves being directed by their mothers, and the group of them had both sides of the road completely blocked. A ranger was parked on the shoulder, making sure visitors stayed a safe distance from the animals. Sitting up high in her motor home, Winnie had a great view of the action. She took a drink from her coffee tumbler as she watched the herd move slowly down the road.

"Look at the baby bison, Patchy! Aren't they cute?"

Patches wagged his tail as he looked out the front window, and Winnie scratched his head. After a fifteen-minute delay, the bison moved off the road, the traffic began to flow, and forty-five minutes later, Winnie pulled into the Fishing Bridge RV Park. Jen was waiting in her patrol car when Winnie arrived, and Winnie slid her window open to talk.

"I spoke to the manager here." Jen got out of her car. "I told him you're a friend of mine, and he's giving you the best spot available."

"Thanks. I really appreciate that."

"And I appreciate all of your help in the investigation. Tell you what. I'll follow you to your site and then we can discuss your latest find."

Soon Winnie was parked at her new campsite and Ranger Malone was sitting at the dining room table. Winnie retrieved the notebook and flash drive, handing them over.

"I looked through it," Winnie confessed, "but it didn't make any sense. I made a copy of the notebook with my camera and sent it to my mom, who knows a retired linguistics professor at the University of Wisconsin. I'm waiting to hear back, but I don't know how long it will take."

Jen pocketed the flash drive and flipped through the notebook. "Well, I certainly don't understand the writing, either. Did you show it to Anita's roommate, Olga?"

"I considered it, but it's not really my place to have her look at it. Besides, I don't even know her. As far as I'm concerned, at this point, she's as much of a suspect as anyone else. That's why I sent it to a professor that has no connection to the case."

Jen nodded. "You're right. No one has been eliminated yet. But I don't know if we can wait until we get results back, especially when a killer is on the loose. I'll take it over to Olga and see if she can make sense of it. Do you know what's on the flash drive?"

"I'll show you, but as far as I can tell, they're just landscape photos." Winnie booted up her computer and moved over so they could sit on the same side. They went through each of the ten photos, but none showed anything but terrain.

"Do you know where this is?" Winnie asked.

"It could be a lot of places. If I had to guess, I'd say it was in northern Yellowstone. It could be somewhere in Montana, too. When I get back to the office, I'll put them on our projector and see if anyone can locate the area. But Yellowstone is so big, I'm not sure how we're going to narrow it down. Once we get these photos enlarged, we might be able to find clues—the location of the sun, a landmark we can't see now, anything that might help us pinpoint the location. You said you found this in your car, but you didn't notice Anita or anyone else putting it there?"

"No, I didn't notice anything. Although, it wouldn't be too hard to drop it while getting in or out. Or when I had to get Patches back in the RV before we left to go to Roosevelt."

At the mention of his name, Patches came striding up, his tail wagging furiously as he waited in anticipation of a treat, or at least a much-needed petting. He was soon rewarded with a belly rub from Jen, while Winnie got up and made coffee. She returned with two mugs and a dog biscuit, and they finished their conversation about the new information. Then Winnie asked about what she should do with the rest of her time in Yellowstone. “There are so many things to do here. I don’t know where to begin.”

“I know. Yellowstone is so big it can be overwhelming. Since you’re at Fishing Bridge, go to the bridge and watch the fish. It’s a great spot to see many different species. You can’t fish there anymore, but it’s a good place to bring Patches. Just keep him on a leash.”

“I promise he’ll stay on a leash.”

“Good. After the bridge, take Patches back for a rest and go to Sulfur Cauldron. It’s very acidic, and the smell of sulfur is almost overpowering, but it’s amazing to see. Across the street is the mud volcano, where you can watch thick mud bubbling. Close your eyes and take it in—the smell, the sound of gurgling mud. Imagine what the first explorers thought when they encountered this. Afterward, go over to the Dragon’s Mouth Spring, which is a steaming hot spring. Don’t just watch. Too many people ignore their other senses. Feel the mist, listen to it. All of these are in the same area, and you really don’t want to miss any of them. If you go at two o’clock, there’s a ranger tour.”

“Thanks. I now have the rest of my day planned.”

“Great. After that, check out Old Faithful and some of the other thermals. But don’t try to do it all in one day. I’ve been here ten years, and I haven’t seen everything. I don’t think it’s even possible to see everything, but I’ll keep trying.”

Jen stood up, collecting the notebook and flash drive. “Thanks for these, and thanks for another cup of coffee. If you hear from your professor, please let me know.”

“Will do. If you get anywhere with Olga, could you let me know? I’ve gotten myself involved in this, and I’d like to see it through.”

"Fair enough. I owe you that much. But please don't do any snooping on your own. Enjoy the park, take lots of pictures, and leave the investigating to us."

"Don't worry about me. Patches and I have plans for the day. When I get back from Sulfur Cauldron, he'll get a much-needed bath, then he'll curl up for a nap while I read a book I've been wanting to start."

"I'll leave you to it, then." Jen turned to leave. "Take care."

Winnie heard the patrol car's door shut and the sounds of gravel crunch as Jen drove away. "It's just us now, Patchy. What do you say we go for a walk?"

As usual, Patches jumped up in a spastic frenzy while Winnie got the leash ready. The campground was big, and Patches pulled Winnie all the way through both loops of RV sites and on to the store. The store featured an outdoor ice cream counter, and Winnie couldn't resist getting a double scoop of mint chocolate chip.

"Don't look at me like that, Patchy." Winnie looked at Patches frown. "You dragged me all over the place. The least you could do is let me have a little treat." She reached into her pocket and pulled out a couple of dog biscuits. That caused Patches to perk up. Winnie dropped a treat, and Patches caught it before it hit the ground. She did the same with the second biscuit, and the two seemed to satisfy Patches, at least for a while.

On the way back to their campsite, Winnie stopped to talk to different campers, comparing stories and asking for recommendations of things to do and places to eat. Winnie tried to cook in her camper most days, staying with Patches, but she enjoyed a meal out, too. They kept walking back to their spot. As they neared the Winnebago, Winnie paid close attention, looking for any signs that someone had once again broken into her motor home. Or worse, that someone was still in it. Relieved that everything looked intact, she made her way to the door. Just as she reached for the handle, Winnie's phone rang. She looked at the caller ID. Her mother.

"Hi, Mom." Winnie stepped inside her motor home.

"Winona," her mother started.

Oh no, we're back to Winona.

"I just got off the phone with Professor Martin. He looked through the pictures of the notebook you sent, and he said its mostly gibberish. He thinks it might be a code of some sort. He likes puzzles, so he's going to keep working on it. Did you get out of there yet?"

"A code? Why would she write in code? None of this makes any sense. And yes, Mom, I moved to a different campsite. I'm at a place called Fishing Bridge, and there are lots of people here. I'll go out and meet my neighbors when they get back to their campers."

"And, Winnie, you gave the notebook and flash drive to the police there, didn't you?"

Good, we're back to Winnie. "Ranger Malone has them. She's going to ask Anita's roommate, Olga, about it, but if it's in code, she probably won't be able to decipher it, either."

Patches barked, nudging Winnie's pant leg. "Mom, Patches is thirsty. Let me take care of him and I'll call you back."

"No need, dear. I've got a date to get ready for. Just promise me you'll be safe."

"I'll be safe. Whoa. A date? With whom?"

"When I called Martin—Professor Mellon, he suggested we get together to catch up. At first, I thought it was just a friendly meeting, but then he told me he's been thinking about me and wanted to ask me out for a while. He just didn't have the nerve to do it, so when I called, it gave him the opportunity."

"Good for you, Mom. See? This notebook may be good luck after all."

Despite Winnie's efforts, her mom hadn't gone out much since Winnie's father passed away. A date here and there, but nothing serious. Winnie knew her mom was lonely. She hoped Professor Mellon might help fill some of that emptiness. At sixty-seven, Sabrina was still in good shape, and the silver hair that most women dreaded seemed a natural fit for her tall, slender figure.

The two said their goodbyes and hung up. After giving Patches food and water, they set off for Fishing Bridge. It was a nice walk, but there wasn't a lot going on, and she really couldn't see any fish, so they came back. After lunch, Patches sauntered into the bedroom for a nap, while Winnie left for Sulfur Cauldron.

Sulfur Cauldron lived up to its name. Even from the road, the putrid smell permeated the Mini Cooper, and Winnie crinkled her nose as she found a parking spot and got out to explore the area. It looked like something out of a Halloween movie, with steam rising from the ground in many places. Mud was bubbling in large pits. Next to one of the larger vats, a bison was soaking up the warmth, oblivious to the fact that one misstep on the fragile soil could mean instant death. Somehow, it didn't mind the smell, either, just standing there like it was out in a field. The bison attracted tourists, and the combination of bubbling, steaming mud next to a buffalo made for some great photos.

Winnie lined up for the ranger-led tour at 2:00. The ranger took them to an area closed to visitors not with a ranger, and, after a short hike, Winnie understood why. She was immersed in a small clearing between two large pools of boiling mud, each one competing for the smelliest location. The group was led onto a narrow strip between the two ponds, both the size of a swimming pool. The thick gray mud made big bubbles that popped as the ponds churned. The noise sounded like large pots of pasta boiling. The ranger was explaining the history and geography of the area, but Winnie wasn't really paying much attention. Her mind kept drifting back to the notebook she found and what its meaning might be.

After the tour, Winnie got in her car and headed back to Fishing Bridge campground. Forsaking the Christmas music, she put on Miranda Lambert's "Gunpowder & Lead," belting it out for all she was worth. Miranda seemed to understand what Winnie had gone through, and she thought of the two as kindred spirits. Winnie approached her campsite cautiously, breathing a sigh of relief that no one had broken in. Her most prized possession was Patches, and she'd be devastated if anything happened to him.

Patches rushed to greet her as she opened the door, but he stopped short, sniffed, and turned away. Winnie wondered what was going on until she pulled her sleeve up to her nose and realized she smelled like sulfur. After being immersed in it for so long, she didn't notice the smell. She started a load of laundry, another reason Winnie was grateful for hookups, then took a shower and changed her clothes. That seemed to satisfy Patches's sensitive smell, and he came out from the bedroom.

"Okay, buddy, I'm cleaned up. Now it's your turn." Winnie gave him a quick bath. Patches hated baths, and Winnie struggled to get through it. Even dog treats didn't help much.

After that ordeal was done, Winnie combed Patches's fur, making it smooth and shiny. "I wish my hair could do that." Winnie sighed as she stroked Patches's back. "And you don't even need a straightener." While most people saw her curly, flaming-red hair as a blessing, Winnie thought it more of a curse. In her youth, she had much longer hair and spent a lot of time trying to tame it, using straighteners, irons, and enough hair care products to handle a thousand heads. But no matter what she tried, her hair curled and frizzed—a lot.

"The hair wants what the hair wants," her stylist had once said as she struggled to force a comb through Winnie's mane. Now, at forty-five, she kept it short and let the curls wander.

Patches was still frumpy from his bath, and he curled up for a nap on the couch while Winnie grabbed her Kindle and continued reading a book she started before she left Wisconsin. It was a cozy bake-shop mystery, and it was just starting to get to the part where it all came together.

After about an hour of reading, the Kindle started to feel heavy in Winnie's hand, and she drifted off into a nice late afternoon nap. Her snooze was cut short by a shrill sound. It took her a moment, but she finally recognized it was her cell phone, and she stumbled around until she found it. It was beginning its sixth ring before she answered.

"Hi, Winnie, it's Jen Malone. I called to check and see how you're settling in. Did you make it out to Sulfur Cauldron?"

"I just got back a couple of hours ago. It was just like you described—smelly, bubbly, and totally fascinating."

"That's good. And I take it no new visitors?"

"Nope. All quiet. Just the way I like it."

"I was also calling to see if your professor friend had any luck with deciphering the notebook."

"No, not yet, but I didn't expect anything this soon. I'll let you know as soon as I hear back."

"Thanks. We sent it off to the FBI for them to take a look. Unfortunately, that will take a while."

"Was Olga able to help with the notebook?"

"Only to deepen the mystery. She knew Anita kept a journal, but Anita was very secretive about it and wouldn't let anyone see it. We asked her boyfriend, but he didn't even know Anita had a notebook. Right before Anita's death, Olga noticed Anita was writing in it a lot. And she started hiding it in strange places or taking it with her. Olga assumed Anita was writing something personal about her boyfriend and didn't think much of it."

"So, you think Anita was killed because of the notebook?"

"I don't know. What I do know is she didn't have anything of value in Yellowstone, so she wasn't killed for something she owned. I don't think her boyfriend had anything to do with it. That leaves me with two realistic options. The first is she saw something she shouldn't have."

"And the second?"

"That there's a predator in Yellowstone. One far worse than a bear."

Winnie let out a low whistle. "We need to find Taggart before he has a chance to do this to someone else."

9

Winnie sat outside and looked around at the activity of the Fishing Bridge campground, but her mind was trying to cope with two competing thoughts. First, there might be a predator on the loose, one that was after Winnie. Was it just her, or were they after others, too? The second thing was that everyone around her was having fun. Children were running around, yelping and screaming with an energy only kids could muster. Adults were chatting and talking with neighbors in a carefree manner. Their world seemed safe. Could that be an illusion? It was bad enough to know someone was after her, but terrifying to think there might be a madman stalking campers.

As soon as Winnie was able to set the thought of a predator aside, she started thinking about her mother. The thought of her mother seeing someone filled Winnie with different emotions. She wanted her mom to be happy, but she never pictured her with anyone but her dad. Until his death, the two were all each other needed. Winnie had hoped to find a relationship like that, too, but instead found herself with someone who really didn't love her. Worse, he used every opportunity he could to cheat on her.

"But I've got you, Patchy." Winnie petted her friend. "And you smell good, too. At least for the moment." She took Patches for a walk, and soon he was sniffing and peeing on all the rocks and trees he could find. He didn't waste any time rolling in the grass, either, trying to undo the effects of the bath. Winnie shook her head as Patches managed to get himself dirty in about two seconds. After a long walk, the two felt refreshed, and Winnie was ready for dinner.

"Let's cook in tonight." Winnie took out the ingredients for tacos. Patches and Winnie both loved Taco Tuesdays, even if it was Sunday, but for different reasons. Patches loved the scraps of cooked meat Winnie would toss down, and Winnie liked the spicy Mexican flavors. And the gooey cheese, tortillas, and salsa. What neither of them liked, though, was the smell it made in the motor home, which wanted to linger from Sunday until Wednesday. Winnie set up the portable grill and cooked everything outside.

The Fishing Bridge campsite was much bigger than Pebble Creek, and with the increased size came a lot more noise. With bears in the area, Fishing Bridge didn't allow tents, so the campground was a sea of hard-shelled campers like hers. And having over three hundred campsites, the place was packed with row after row of motor homes and trailers. It was a little cramped, and Winnie missed the openness of Pebble Creek, but the hookups meant she had plenty of water and electricity, and the long, hot showers felt great. Especially when she was used to a shower consisting of about three minutes of running water, total. And that was with the shower head set to "water miser," which meant more of a drip than a flow.

Winnie sliced an onion and added it to the ground beef she took out of the freezer, putting both in a skillet with water and seasoning to simmer. She got out the lettuce, cheese, salsa, and tortillas then grabbed her Kindle while she waited for the tacos to finish. "I knew Jake did it," Winnie said out loud when she finished the book. "I didn't like him from the start." By then, the tacos were nearly done and Winnie made two tortillas, adding the salsa on the side to dip into. Patches took up his usual spot, hoping for something to fall from Winnie's plate.

"Tacos and wine, Patchy." Winnie had finished the last one and heaved a contented sigh. "It really doesn't get better than this, does it?" Patches wagged his tail, but he was still on alert for food to fall down.

After dinner, Winnie sat down at her computer and posted to her blog. She decided when she started her adventure that she'd keep a travel log of her journeys on her website, winniehackleshack.com. Her mother thought a blog was a great idea but made her promise two things. First, she didn't want Winnie to post pictures of herself or Patches on the site. "Too many weirdos." It was hard for Winnie to argue that one. Second, Winnie had to delay her postings until she moved to another site and not to post where she was going next. "You don't want some weirdo trying to track you down."

What's with all the talk of weirdos, Mom. But both rules made sense, and Winnie had agreed to keep them. More grateful now than ever, considering what she'd been through.

After uploading her latest blog post, Winnie checked her email, hoping she might have something from Professor Mellon, but there was nothing other than junk mail. She put her computer away and got out a box filled with maps. Winnie loved to unfold the maps, waiting in anticipation of the places that would appear once the map was opened. She had a map of each state and the provinces in Canada, but right now she was interested in Wyoming. She found where she was in Yellowstone and then started looking for her next park. Grand Teton was the closest one to Yellowstone. The two parks were connected by the Rockefeller Parkway, and it would be a simple drive from Fishing Bridge to her next campsite. Even though the two parks were connected, both parks occupied so much land that it took almost three hours to get between the two campsites.

Winnie sat on the couch and put her feet up, yawning as she picked up her Kindle to start a new mystery, but she couldn't concentrate. She had a mystery of her own she was living in. And, unlike her Kindle, she couldn't just put it down. She racked her brain trying to make sense of what she knew, but she couldn't. Because it didn't make sense.

~

THE NEXT MORNING, Patches sauntered out of bed and made his way to his food dish, nudging it toward Winnie in an attempt to hurry her up.

"Patchy," Winnie said in a fake scolding tone. "You know coffee comes before anything."

But Patches looked at his dish then back to Winnie, wagging his tail in anticipation. Winnie sighed, put the coffee back on the counter, and picked up the dog food. After filling the bowl, Winnie went back to her coffee. A cup of coffee followed by some yoga and she was ready for the day. Or at least another cup of coffee, which she was making when the phone rang. She looked at the caller ID. Instead of her usual angst over the caller, Winnie was excited to answer. She wanted the scoop on her mother's first real date in a long time.

"Hi, Mom." Winnie didn't wait for an answer. "How was your date? I hope you didn't get back too early."

"Winona," her mother started.

Oh boy. We're starting off with Winona.

"How could I have a nice time when all he wanted to talk about was your notebook. Goodness, he was like a schoolboy, giddy and excited. And not over me, mind you. Heavens no. I don't think he even knew I was there."

"Sorry, Mom," Winnie said sheepishly. "I didn't know that would happen. Did you at least have a nice meal?"

"Yes, the food was wonderful. Not that my date noticed. He picked at his, taking a bite between more random thoughts about the notebook."

"Sorry, Mom." Winnie felt bad she was responsible for dampening her mother's evening. "But, umm, did he figure anything out?"

Her mother sighed. "No, he didn't. Not yet anyway. But I have no doubt he was up all night working on it. And yes, to answer your question, I got home way too early. After dinner, I suggested he take me home."

There was a tense moment when nobody spoke.

Finally, her mother caved. "It's all right, Winnie. To be honest, I was really nervous about the date anyway, so it worked out okay. I actually enjoyed parts of it, and I think Martin realized he needs to make it up to me. He already called this morning to apologize and asked me out again for this weekend. Which I accepted, on the condition there'd be no talk of codes and secret messages."

Now Winnie sighed. Her mother loved to string her along, just to let her off the hook.

"And," her mother's her tone changed completely, "he promised to take me dancing at the VFW. I'll have to buy some new shoes."

"He sounds nice. Tell me about him."

Sabrina was quiet for a moment. "I guess he's what you would imagine a stately professor would look like. He's about my height, which I guess is a little shorter than average for a man. A little paunchy, but I think most men his age are. Short, wavy salt-and-pepper hair, the kind that always looks scruffy, even when it's combed. He even wore a tweed jacket with elbow patches. All-in-all he passed muster."

"That's quite a compliment coming from you."

Sabrina liked to "dress for success," as she called it, and expected everyone else to do the same.

By the time Winnie got off the phone, her coffee was cold. Her actions ruined her mom's date. Decoding the notebook seemed a bust, and what was supposed to be a nice day turned into a downpour, with dark clouds and thunderclaps that rocked the motor home.

And the rest of the day didn't get any better.

10

Having spent yesterday stuck inside her RV while a spring storm raged, Winnie was happy to see the sun shining. The storm gave her an opportunity to get caught up on a monthly newsletter she prepared for an accounting company in Indiana. But because of the murder mystery she was involved with, her sightseeing agenda fell behind. With nothing new about the notebook, and no new work, she concentrated on another item on her sightseeing list —Old Faithful. All of the travel sites described Old Faithful as a must see, but, because of the crowds, they also advised seeing it either early or late in the day. Winnie got up at six to make sure she could get a good view, giving Patches breakfast before they left and packing a muffin and banana to eat in the car.

"Guess what, Patches? You can come with me to see Old Faithful spew its plume into the air. Isn't that great?"

Patches seemed less than impressed, but when he saw his leash, he got very excited.

"Come on, boy. Let's go!"

Before long, they made their way out of Fishing Bridge. Winnie kept an eye out for anyone following her, but no one seemed to pay much attention. Instead, the Mini Cooper sped along on U.S. Highway 14, which traveled along Yellowstone Lake, offering a scenic view of the pristine water. There were no boats on the water, but a blue heron stood on a log, looking for breakfast. Winnie preferred her muffin.

While the majority of Yellowstone was wide open spaces, the area surrounding Old Faithful was the most built-up in the park, and Winnie was glad she came early. Several big parking lots lined the area, and tourist buses were already starting to arrive when she pulled in at seven. Many of the buildings were modern, but the most impressive, Old Faithful Inn, was the oldest. Built in 1904, it loomed over the newer structures. A huge, three hundred twenty-seven-room log-cabin-style hotel, it was purported to be the largest log building in the world. Winnie wandered in with Patches, buying a cup of coffee while she looked around.

The lobby and first-floor seating areas were open to the floors above, providing a view of the wood logs all the way to the fourth floor. Each of the guest levels had chairs overlooking the lobby, and guests above her sat and talked. A massive stone fireplace featured a hearth on each of its four sides, and a large fire was being stoked by a burly man who looked like he could split logs with his bare hands. On one of the fireplace sides an antique clock rested, its pendulum rocking back and forth.

After touring the inside of the hotel, Winnie and Patches walked around the outside, marveling at the peaks of the roof and seeing the changes over the years where the inn had been modified or expanded. The cedar shingles had a pleasant, weathered look, and the shape of the building was just as impressive on the outside.

Even this early, more people were out than Winnie expected, braving the morning chill to get a good look at the famous geyser. Taking Patches over to the boardwalk surrounding the area, Winnie found a sign with the expected eruption time. Old Faithful erupted about every seventy-five minutes, and the next one was expected at 7:50. The times were approximate but usually accurate within a few minutes.

"We've got about thirty minutes to wait, Patchy. Let's go for a walk."

Winnie found a few others milling about, some with their pets, too, and Winnie was soon in a conversation about what sites to visit and when to go. Before long, Winnie heard the steam as Old Faithful was getting ready to put on its show, and she and Patches went up as close as they could.

Dogs were only permitted to a certain point, and Winnie stopped at the sign. "It's still a good view."

Patches seemed more interested in the dogs next to him than the hissing, steaming geyser about to erupt.

Winnie reached for her phone to take a picture. "Shoot, Patchy," Winnie frowned. "I forgot my phone. No selfies for us this morning."

Instead, she pulled out an old point-and-shoot camera from her purse and snapped a few pictures. Winnie managed to capture the plume of steam at its peak then took a snapshot of Patches, who was looking around, probably wondering where the noise was coming from and why the ground was shaking. After Old Faithful quieted down, Winnie decided it was time to get back. "Let's get something to eat, Patchy." Patches was busy exploring the other dogs, and Winnie had to tug him along to get him moving.

When she got back to her camper, Winnie picked up her phone and the screen lit up. It showed one missed call and a voice mail, both from a Madison area code. She listened to the voice mail, which was from Professor Mellon, but the message just said to call him back when she could. Winnie started to dial, but Patches hadn't been on a walk since they left Old Faithful, and his pacing told Winnie he needed to go out—soon.

After a quick walk with Patches, Winnie returned and dialed the professor's number. "Hi, Professor Mellon. It's Winnie Hackleshack."

"Hello, Winona. Thanks for calling me back, and please call me Martin. Professor is only for students and other stodgy old has-been teachers like me."

Winnie conjured up an image of a man in a library, wearing a tweed jacket, with a pipe in one hand and a magnifying glass in the other. But his tone was jovial, and Winnie also pictured a warm smile on the other end of the conversation. She could see why her mother liked him. Winnie took an instant liking to him, too.

"Tell you what, I'll call you Martin if you call me Winnie. Winona is reserved for my mother, mostly when she's scolding me."

"Deal. Well, I suppose you know why I called. I've made a little progress on the notebook you found. It seems to be a journal. Parts of it, especially in the beginning, were written in Ukrainian, but with some substitutions. These were easy to decipher once I found the key."

"Key?"

"Yes, a cipher needs a key to be able to unscramble the message. In this case, Anita, and I'm sure it was Anita, used what's called a simple substitution cipher. Using..."

"Wait," Winnie interrupted. "How do you know it's Anita's notebook?"

"I'm getting to that. Just be patient a little longer."

"Sorry. It's just that now I know for certain I found a dead girl's notebook in my car."

"I understand. The reason I know this is Anita's notebook is because her name is on it. At least the name she used in code. I believe her real name is Anita Tataryn. When I figured out her substitution cipher, that's what I came up with."

"I know her first name is Anita. I don't remember her last name."

"Well," Martin continued, "I believe I have deciphered the text correctly. At least as far as I've gotten, which isn't too far."

"What have you learned so far?" Winnie reached for her iPad to take notes.

Professor Mellon chuckled. "So far, I've learned Anita was a typical teenage girl. I'm only a little into the notebook, but the opening is mostly about boys, school, and how her parents don't understand her, and how once she turned eighteen, she was going to be on her own. But that was a few years before her last entry, and I haven't gotten anywhere near through it yet."

"Oh," Winnie said. "I didn't realize that this was going to be so difficult. Maybe we should wait for the FBI to analyze it."

"Hold on, Winona," Professor Mellon said.

Jeez. Another with the Winona.

"While you're right it would take me a long time to decipher this by hand, I do have access to faster means. I'm planning to bring the scanned pages to the linguistics lab at school. Since I know the cipher key, or at least I think I do, it should be a fairly straightforward matter of letting the computers do their thing. Assuming, of course, she didn't change the key at some point. Then we'd have more work to do in finding that key."

"That sounds great. When do you think you'll be able to work on it?"

"I've got a call into a friend that works there. Once he calls me back, I'll know their backlog and when I can get in. Hopefully, it won't be too long of a delay. Then I can send a copy to you and your ranger."

"I really appreciate your help. I don't know how I got involved with this, but hopefully your findings will help identify at least why she was killed, if not the killer."

"You're welcome, Winnie. But you could do something for me in return."

"Name it." Winnie was grateful for not being called Winona.

"You can put in a good word for me with your mother. I'm afraid my curiosity got the best of me with this notebook, and I didn't give Sabrina the attention she deserved. I'm hoping she'll give me another chance, and a kind word from you would help."

"No problem, Martin. But I don't think you really need my help. My mom seems to care for you. Just keep the conversation more balanced next time. Here's one more tip, and it's the most important one I can give you. Flowers and chocolates work wonders as an apology. Especially hand-delivered ones."

"Gotcha. Some flowers, chocolates, and a little groveling coming up. I'll let you know how I make out in the lab. It shouldn't be more than a day or two."

"And I'll be your inside source to Mom. Take care, and thanks for the help."

"You too, Winnie."

After clicking off, Winnie went back to her iPad. She added some notes, but there was only a little new information to go on. Winnie tried to think about it from Anita's point of view. At first, the idea of her being harassed and then dead seemed clear-cut. As creepy as it was, it didn't take a large stretch to imagine an infatuated person in a fit of rage after being constantly rejected.

But why put the notebook in a stranger's car? Winnie and Anita had just met and were not likely to see each other again. Was it simply a mistake? Winnie dismissed that notion. Anita sat in the front, so, to put something on the back seat had to have been deliberate, didn't it? She went over the events in her mind, trying to determine when Anita could have put the notebook into the back. There was no time... except when they arrived at Winnie's motor home and the chair blew away. Winnie got out and stowed the chair, then came back for Anita.

Or, it could have been when they were leaving to head back to Roosevelt and Patches bounded out of the camper.

"It must have been one of those times." She looked over at Patches, who was curled up on the couch next to her.

Winnie had been lost in her thoughts about Anita for over an hour when she finally decided to put it aside. She grabbed a cookie and poured a cup of coffee, then checked her email, where she found a request from a regular client for a corporate brochure. Winnie looked it over, accepted the job, and was going to start an outline when her phone rang. She looked at the caller ID, but it said private. She considered rejecting the call but thought it might be another customer, so she answered. Before she could say hello, Winnie heard a low voice that sounded like someone had chewed gravel for breakfast.

"We know you have the notebook, and we want it back."

"Who is this?" Winnie put the phone on speaker to get the voice away from her ear. "Is this Taggart?"

"Who is Taggart? No, I am someone who can cause you a lot of trouble, Miss Winona Hackleshack of Madison, Wisconsin. I want the notebook returned. Now."

Winnie cleared her throat. "First, this isn't your notebook. It appears to be from Anita, but since it was found in my car, it's now mine. Second, I already gave it to the rangers, and they forwarded it to the FBI. So, I can't get it back, even if I wanted to. Which I don't. So just leave me alone."

Before Winnie could disconnect, she heard the voice on the other end say, "you'll regret this, Miss Hackleshack."

11

Winnie sat and wondered what to do. Whoever it was knew about the notebook and knew Winnie had it. But she didn't have it, and there was no way to get it back. She thought about the events of the last few days and wondered if she'd make things worse by calling Ranger Malone. Or, should she just pack up and go? No, that wasn't an option. Winnie didn't run from a fight—not anymore, anyway. Those days were over.

"I've been on the defensive this whole time." Winnie looked at her phone. "It's time to go on the offensive and get to the bottom of it."

Winnie took a deep breath to steady herself, then called Jen Malone. She picked up on the first ring.

"Hi, Winnie, I was just thinking about you. Have you heard from your professor friend?"

"Yes. He figured out that it was written in code. He found a way to break it, and he's working on a translation now. Martin said the first few pages were normal teenage girl diary stuff, but he hadn't gotten very far with it. He's waiting for a time slot to use the university's computer, which he thinks will be just as accurate and a lot faster."

"Okay. Thanks for the update. The FBI still hasn't started looking into it yet. I guess a young woman killed in Yellowstone doesn't grab their attention."

"There's something else, Jen. I just got a call from someone. The caller ID said private. It was someone who knew I had the notebook and wants it back. Somehow, he got my name, number, and even where I was from. Though, I suppose, if it is the same guy who broke in, he could've gotten my information from one of my business cards in the RV, or when he rummaged through everything. To be honest, I'm a little scared."

"Winnie, that's horrible. Are you all right? Maybe I should come over there."

"No, I'll be fine. It's just unnerving to get a call like that."

"Did the voice sound like this mysterious Taggart?"

"The voice was very low and raspy. It sounded like someone trying to disguise their voice. But when I asked if it was Taggart, the person seemed genuinely confused. It could all be a ruse, but I don't think this was Taggart."

"Okay. We still haven't located our ranger Taggart yet, but we're looking. There's nothing in the database about anyone by that name working as a ranger anywhere. We'll find him eventually."

"Hopefully before he finds me," Winnie added. "I told him I didn't have the notebook anymore, so maybe he'll just go away."

"I really wish I could agree with that, Winnie, but the reality is somebody wants that notebook. They went through Anita's room and your motor home looking for it. I bet he hasn't figured out where you moved to, or he would have come back to your RV and searched again. And maybe your car this time, too. You should consider going to a different park and coming back when this is all over. In the meantime, if you're okay with it, I'll ask the phone company to check their records to see who called your cell recently. Maybe we can at least get a location narrowed down."

"You can check my records, and I thought about leaving, but it seems to me I've been running away for quite some time now. A woman I met was killed and I've been threatened, and no one knows why or who's responsible. Nope, they picked the wrong person to mess with. The sides of my motor home may feature me with a big smile, but don't let that fool you. I may be small, but I'm a big bundle of trouble when provoked. Or, to put it in Yellowstone terms, they poked the bear. Now the bear's going to poke back."

"Just so long as the bear doesn't get hurt, Winnie," Jen said. "Please be careful."

"I will. Oh, I went to see Old Faithful this morning. Where else should I go?"

"Ah, good question. Well, if you're going to leave Patches in the RV, then I have the perfect spot. Tell you what. I need a break, so how about I pick you up in an hour and I give you a private tour. Are you up for it?"

"Are you kidding? Of course I'm up for it. Thanks, Jen."

"My pleasure. See you soon. Bring comfortable shoes and some water."

After they hung up, Winnie got Patches's harness. "Come on, boy, let's go for a walk and then you can have a nice rest."

RIGHT ON TIME AN HOUR LATER, Winnie heard a car pull up. She said goodbye to Patches, grabbed her backpack from the counter, and opened the door to see Jen smiling.

"It's a great day, Winnie," Jen said. "I think you're going to love this."

Jen drove them back to the Old Faithful area. Just as Winnie suspected, this time of day the entrance to Old Faithful was jam-packed and the area was filled with tourists, tour busses, and cars.

"Wow!" Winnie said. "This is why Patches and I came early."

"Yeah," Jen sighed. "This time of day it gets very crowded. But you ought to see it in winter. There are very few people and the view is spectacular."

"Sounds amazing."

"Unfortunately, you have to be brought in on a special snow coach because all the roads are closed and there are no pets allowed. So, if you ever want to leave Patches with your mom for a few days, come back at winter. You won't regret it."

"I'll put that on my to-do list, which is getting longer by the day."

Jen's patrol car could park almost anywhere, and they pulled into a spot marked "Official Vehicles Only." After calling in her location to the office, she and Winnie made their way past Old Faithful to an area that was currently closed to visitors. Jen stepped past the closed sign and motioned for Winnie to do the same. "This area is called Geyser Hill. We're going to reopen the area soon, but I can take you back now and give you a private tour."

As they began their walk, she explained a bit about the area. "This trail is short. It's just over one-half mile. But don't let the distance fool you. The area is abundant with thermal features. After that, I thought we'd walk part of the Upper Geyser Basin trail. It's over two miles each way, so I thought we could walk to the crossing of the Firehole River and then come back. The view of the river is better there, and the hot water from the thermals meet up with the cool river water, making it look like the river is burning."

Winnie looked around and saw several spots smoldering.

Small pools of bright turquoise contained steaming water just under the boiling point. "This place is absolutely incredible."

"No other place like it. And it's always changing. That's why we had to close this area off for a while. The thermal activity was high and unpredictable, and we were concerned for everyone's safety. It's more stable now, so we can open it up again."

As they approached Giantess Geyser, one of the biggest geysers in the world, Jen stopped and closely examined it. "This geyser is sporadic in its activity. The last time it was active was several years ago, but when it starts, eruptions can last for days and shoot up over two hundred feet. We thought that since the whole area seemed to be more active, the Giantess might start again, but so far she's been quiet."

The next stop was Grand Geyser. "This one erupts about every seven hours or so and lasts about ten minutes. More predictable, but less spectacular than Giantess."

As they continued their walk, Winnie took a lot of pictures, including selfies with her and Jen. Winnie was starting to warm up to Jen. The gruff exterior she presented when she was banging on Winnie's door was her business persona. Winnie guessed she needed that to survive in her line of work. Jen was a federal law enforcement officer—essentially, a traditional park ranger and a police officer combined. A job like that required a tough exterior.

But Jen had a different persona, one that she was showing now. Kind, warm, and friendly. The type of person you would instantly like.

WHEN WINNIE and Jen returned to the motor home, Jen went inside first and checked it out, just as a precaution in case someone was in there, but they found only Patches, who ran to the door looking for Winnie.

"Thanks for the tour, Jen. I really had a good time."

"My pleasure. You needed to get caught up on your sightseeing, and I appreciate your help. If you hear back from your professor friend, please let me know."

"I'm going to fix dinner. Nothing fancy, but you're welcome to stay."

"I appreciate the offer, but I need to get home tonight. I've missed too many dinners lately."

As soon as Winnie sat down to dinner, her phone rang. Checking the caller ID, she saw it was Professor Mellon. "Hi, Professor, I mean Martin." Winnie talked around a mouth full of pasta salad."

"I must have caught you during dinner. I'm sorry. I forgot the time difference."

"That's okay. Patches and I don't mind. Did you find anything?"

"No, not really. I wanted to tell you that I have time scheduled for the supercomputer at the university. Unfortunately, it's not for two days. In the meantime, I went through a few more pages, but, so far, it's been nothing but adolescent angst. I won't be able to work on it tomorrow because I'm sculling all day with friends."

"Skulling?" Winnie crinkled up her face in surprise. "Is that some sort of hunt for bones?"

Winnie heard so much laughter on the other end she could almost see the tears that must be falling.

"Heavens no, Winnie," Martin said after he was able to speak again. "Sculling with an 'sc' and not an 'sk,' although I can see how you'd get that impression. Sculling means to propel a boat with oars. In my case, I row a single-person shell on Lake Mendota. I love being out on the water, and it's great exercise."

"Oh, you mean crew?"

"Yes, exactly. That's a common name for it. Sometimes I even row in a four-person boat, but not often. At my age, I just don't have the skills I used to. Or the stamina."

"Well, I hope you have fun, Martin, and thanks for the update."

Winnie had no sooner clicked off when the phone rang again. Assuming it was Martin forgetting to tell her something, Winnie didn't look at the caller ID.

"Hello." Winnie expected to hear a familiar voice on the other end. She did, but not the voice she was anticipating.

"Winnie?"

"Olga?" Winnie looked at the caller ID. The display read caller unknown. "Hi. Is everything all right?"

"Oh, Winnie, I just got a call from a horrible man." Tension emanated in Olga's voice. "He's looking for Anita's notebook. He told me to find it, or he would come after me and warned me not to contact the police. I didn't know who else to call, so I called you."

Great. Going from the sidelines right back into the fire.

"Calm down, Olga. I got the same call. I told the person I already handed the notebook over to the police, so I'm not sure why he would have called you. Did he say anything else?"

"He told me not to leave or he would find me. His voice was so low and mean, it gave me the creeps. And the accent may have been Ukrainian. I couldn't tell. I'm frightened, Winnie. What should I do?"

"Well, since the police have the notebook, I don't think there's anything to worry about. I would call Ranger Malone and tell her what happened. Maybe she can relocate you or something. Or maybe you should go home."

"Home? I can't go back there. What if the person was Ukrainian? He could find me there. I'm just not safe anywhere."

"Olga, he's probably the one that went through your room and the one that called me. You need to call Jennifer Malone. She can help, and you can trust her."

"You don't understand," Olga said.

The call disconnected. Since the caller ID didn't provide a number, Winnie couldn't call her back. Instead, Winnie gave Jen a call.

"Hi, Winnie," Jen said. "I didn't think I'd hear back from you so soon. Did Professor Mellon have an update?"

"Yes, kind of. He said he has the computer booked for two days from today. He deciphered more of the text, but so far it was normal teenage girl stuff. But that's not why I called. Olga just called and she sounded in tears. Someone called her demanding the notebook. She was frightened and wanted to know what to do. I told her to call you, but she hung up before I could convince her."

"Do you have her number? I can give her a call."

"No, the caller ID said unknown. I thought maybe you had it."

"I should in my case notes. I live close to the Mammoth office, so I'll stop in and see. I'll also have a ranger stop by her room. We moved her out of Roosevelt and over to Mammoth so she could be closer to us, she's just a few minutes away by car. Let me take care of that and I'll call you back."

Winnie tried to go back to her dinner, but all she could do was pick at it. She put it away for later and grabbed her Kindle, plopping down on the couch and hoping to get distracted away from her own mystery into someone else's. The title was cute—*Add, Subtract, and Die*—and the story was about a bookkeeper that found a discrepancy in the accounts and she was killed for it. Winnie asked Patches whether the mystery she was reading was similar to the one she was living in, but Patches merely offered a tail wag.

"You're no help." Winnie scratched Patches behind the ears.

Winnie was concentrating on the book when the phone rang, causing her to jump off the couch and onto her feet.

"Winnie, it's Jen. One of the rangers went to Olga's room, but he can't find her anywhere. He checked with her work, and she didn't show up for her shift. He went through her dorm, asking everyone that was around, but no one had seen her recently. Olga is missing."

12

Thirty minutes of yoga couldn't clear Winnie's head as her brain switched between thoughts of Anita's death and Olga's disappearance, trying to make sense of it all. She wanted to call Jen to see if they'd found Olga, but Winnie didn't want to be a pest. Instead, she took a fresh look at the notebook pages and photos, but after pouring over them, she didn't find anything new.

After putting the copies away, Winnie looked at Patches. "Today is a Winnie and Patches day. I've got a route planned that we could take to see some sights. Let's get ready to go."

The two spent the morning together, enjoying the scenery and a pleasant drive. Yellowstone was carefully planned for tourists, and they could see many of the attractions right from the road. Her favorites were the areas of bubbling mud. The sulfur-reeking pools were everywhere, and the ground surrounding them was thin and fragile. People had literally fallen through the earth when they strayed from the paths. Winnie couldn't take Patches near the thermals, but they both got a good view—and smell—from the road.

At lunchtime, Winnie set everything out from the cooler

she'd packed. Leftover pasta salad and a chicken sandwich for Winnie, and Patches got his usual dog food, which he seemed to consume faster than Winnie could pour out. They sat on a picnic table at a pullout between Old Faithful and Mammoth Hot Springs. To her left was Mount Holmes, the snow-capped jagged peaks in sharp contrast to the forest below. To her right was Obsidian Cliff, the volcanic rock shining in the sun. In the distance, Winnie could see buffalo wandering around, casually grazing, and thought it would be nice to see a buffalo run, or at least move a little. The ones she saw seemed content to just eat, barely taking a step. But the view was great, and Winnie enjoyed sitting there with Patches. After lunch, she snapped a few photos of the area to post to her blog and then spent an hour working on a travel piece she'd been writing while Patches sat in the car snoozing. The windows were open, and the constant breeze kept the car nice and cool. Eight hundred words and a few more photos later, Winnie was ready to keep exploring.

Winnie was on the lookout for the many birds found in Yellowstone. She had seen a few that were too small to identify, but she hadn't seen the bigger birds that frequented the area. As she pulled into another picnic spot, this one along the Gardner River, Winnie was rewarded with what she most wanted to find—eagles. Taking Patches on a leash, Winnie grabbed her binoculars and watched as both bald and golden eagles made their way overhead, each moving in wide arcs near the river, their trained eyes looking for fish they could pluck out of the water. Winnie was in awe of the birds, captivated as they floated gracefully, seemingly without effort. Minutes passed and Winnie still had the binoculars up, fixated on the show above her head. Patches couldn't see what all the fuss was about and found sniffing the ground much more exciting.

Before long, a golden eagle swooped down, dive bombing for the water in what appeared to be a sure plunge to its death, only to snatch a fish out of the water with its claws and pull up hard, soaring into the air and away, the fish hopelessly flapping in a vain attempt to get free. Winnie snapped a photo. As the eagle flew away, Winnie felt a sharp tug as a squirrel caught Patches's attention, pulling hard at the leash and barking loudly. The squirrel climbed the tree next to the picnic table as Patches continued to bark.

"Oh, hush, Patchy. You'll scare everything away."

The squirrel scampered out of the area, and Winnie tugged Patches over to a picnic table, dropping a few treats to make him forget about the squirrel. Patches curled up next to Winnie, satisfied he'd done his part to keep them safe, as she continued to watch the show overhead. Winnie was still mesmerized by the eagles, looking up as the majestic creatures continued to gracefully soar their aerial ballet. She snapped a few photos of the birds in flight, watching as they flew away.

Winnie and Patches got back in the Mini Cooper and started to turn back toward Fishing Bridge when a ranger vehicle with lights and sirens blaring sped past. For a moment, Winnie thought the patrol car would pull into Winnie's picnic spot and Jen would rush out, delivering more bad news or an urgent request. Instead, the car sped past and was soon out of sight.

Winnie was relieved she wasn't involved, but then she felt guilty. It wasn't like her to walk away when someone was in trouble, and she wasn't going to start now. "Nope, Patchy," Winnie sighed. "Good or bad, we're in this 'til the end. Are you with me?"

Patches licked Winnie's face.

"I'll take that as a yes." Winnie laughed from being tickled. She returned the favor by scratching his belly. "We're pretty close to the ranger station in Mammoth. Why don't we drive there and see if we can find out anything. Then we'll take another look through Lamar Valley and do some animal watching."

Before Patches could object, Winnie had turned back around, heading for Mammoth Hot Springs and the ranger station. It wasn't far, but traffic was heavy, and it took nearly thirty minutes to get there. Winnie wished she could have arranged a police escort, like when she followed Jen, but she had to follow the herd of cars like everyone else. Winnie stopped at reception and asked for Ranger Malone. After a few minutes, Jen walked down the hallway.

"Winnie," Jen said. "What a pleasant surprise. I didn't expect to see you today. Did you hear back from your professor friend?"

Winnie had forgotten about Professor Mellon, and it took her a moment to remember the status of the notebook deciphering. "Um, no. I was just in the area, and I was a little worried about Olga. Patchy and I were enjoying the eagles along Gardner River. Well, I was enjoying them. Patches was busy treeing a squirrel."

"It's great that you saw the eagles. They love to hang out there. It must be a good fishing spot for them. Unfortunately, we haven't found Olga yet. The whole thing is very strange. I mean, she's just a kid, who doesn't have the notebook and doesn't seem to know much."

"Unless she's lying," Winnie mumbled.

"What?"

"It's just that we don't know her. Not really, anyway. And there's no proof she's telling the truth. I've been a little suspicious ever since she showed up at my RV unannounced. Would a kid, who's in a foreign land, really have the presence of mind to seek me out? And why me and not the rangers? Or someone in the dorm, like whoever manages the kids staying there."

Jen smiled. "You think like a detective. Actually, we've been mulling over the same thing. Her behavior certainly doesn't seem to follow what we would have expected. We've given her the benefit of the doubt, but, after this latest disappearance, we're treating her as a person of interest and not just a witness. When we find her, she will be remanded to our custody until we can get to the bottom of it."

Winnie nodded but kept quiet for a moment. "I hate to think Olga was involved with Anita's death, but I suppose anything's possible. If I see her, I'll let you know."

"Winnie," Jen's tone was soft. "She might be dangerous, so please, if you do see her, or hear from her, let me know immediately. And stay as far away as you can."

"I will."

"Good. And no heroics, okay? Patches needs a travel partner, and I'd hate to see anything happen to you."

"Got it."

13

It was a long, silent trip back to Fishing Bridge. Patches seemed to sense Winnie was troubled, so they both rode quietly. The usual Christmas music was off, and there was no off-key singing as Winnie's Mini chugged along. There weren't many roads in Yellowstone, and during the summer, at least some of them were being repaired. Winnie was lucky when she came up to Mammoth that the construction crews were on a break. This time, however, she wasn't as fortunate. A string of cars, motorcycles, and motor homes were lined up, and Winnie stopped next to a construction sign that warned of delays lasting up to forty-five minutes. With nothing else to do, Winnie shut off her engine and reached for her iPad, patting the passenger seat and inviting Patches to join her up front. Which he did, but Patches was much more interested in putting his head out of the window than anything Winnie might have to say.

"I know, Patchy. It's not much fun just sitting here, but let's make the best of it." Winnie handed Patches a dog biscuit.

Patches gobbled it up, giving Winnie the wide-eyed "sad dog" look and putting his paw out.

"Okay, one more." Winnie gave him another treat.

Grabbing a handful of pretzels, Winnie began munching as she went over the notes she had on the case so far. As she always did, she talked out loud, using Patches as her sounding board.

"So, where are we? I meet Anita. She's being harassed by a man dressed in a ranger's uniform that no one seems to know. She comes to my motor home for dessert, and the next day she's dead. Somewhere along the way, Anita leaves a cryptic notebook in my car.

Winnie looked up as a group of cyclists sped past, able to dodge the construction. Patches offered a bark of encouragement to the last rider, who was huffing and puffing trying to stay with the group. After they were out of sight, Winnie went back to her notes.

"Her roommate, another girl from Ukraine, comes to my campsite. How did she get there? She said she drove, but surely, she didn't have a driver's license valid in the U.S., at least not at her age, would she? And whose car did she borrow?"

Winnie chastised herself for not taking note of the car Olga drove when it was parked next to her motor home. It didn't seem important at the time, and, once she saw Olga, she forgot about it.

"Come to think of it, Patchy, how did Olga even know how to get to the campsite? I guess she could have used Google Maps, but it seems to be a stretch that she would have sought me out instead of calling home to her mother or talking to another friend she worked with. Maybe that's what's bothered me from the start about her. Something just doesn't seem genuine."

Winnie continued to flip through her notes about the interviews and the notebook.

"What do we know about this Taggart, except that he's rude? No one seems to know anything about him. Of course, his description could fit a lot of people. But why hasn't he appeared again? Is he a part of all of this or just a creep at the wrong place? And why pretend to be a ranger? Why did he choose Anita to pick on? She's pretty, but there must be a lot of pretty girls around."

Winnie heard the engines around her starting to turn on, signaling they were about to move. She got Patches in the back seat and started her car as traffic began to flow. Instinctively, she reached for the entertainment system, turning on a CD of Dolly Parton's *Home for Christmas*, and soon she was belting out a version of "Joy to the World" that very few people would recognize, even if they unplugged their ears long enough to listen. Winnie felt good to be singing, and her smile showed it. Patches was more active, going between sides in the back seat. Their moods seemed to be in sync.

Several songs later, Winnie pulled into her campsite, her mind cleared and back to her cheerful self. After taking Patches for a long walk, Winnie pulled up a lawn chair and took her iPad out again. She thought about trying to find Olga on Facebook, but without Olga's last name, she wouldn't be able to find her. Instead, Winnie decided to concentrate on why Anita was killed.

"We still don't know much. She could have been killed for something she did or saw here or back in Ukraine. But since she was killed here, I'll focus on that. Now, where does this Taggart person fit in?"

Talking out loud helped Winnie think. But no revelations hit her, and the notes she had were so skimpy she couldn't draw any conclusions. Making sure Patches was fed and comfortable, Winnie decided to go back to the Roosevelt area and see if she could spot Taggart. Or Olga. "At least I know I'll get a great meal." Winnie waved goodbye to Patches.

On the way back to the Roosevelt area, Winnie came across

a row of cars parked along the side, with people hurrying down the road, a telltale sign there were animals around. Winnie pulled over, grabbed her phone, and rushed out to join them.

"What's up there?" Winnie asked when she caught up to another woman.

"There are a few grizzlies, a little back from the road."

Winnie slowed down. "I hope they're not too close."

"Don't worry. With all these people around, the bears will want to leave the area soon."

Sure enough, as Winnie got to the spot where people were looking, the two grizzlies started to wander off. Winnie got a few good pictures with her phone and watched them until they were out of sight, then she followed the crowd back to the line of cars. Before she continued on to Roosevelt Lodge, Winnie decided to look through her photos. That was when she realized it. In the excitement and confusion of the recent events, Winnie forgot she had taken a photo of Taggart's car the night she took Anita back to her dorm. "You idiot," Winnie said to herself. "Some reporter you are."

Winnie looked up to find she was the only car parked on the side of the road. Worried that the grizzlies might come out to greet her, she decided to get going.

"No cell service anyway." Winnie pulled onto the road.

The rest of the drive was uneventful. Winnie could see some bison along Lamar Valley, but they had become so common they weren't special anymore. Instead, Winnie tried to remember the first time she met Anita and her encounter with Taggart. After pulling into the parking lot, Winnie took ten minutes and wrote down everything she could remember. Looking at her phone, Winnie had no data service and two bars registered for signal strength. She tried to call Jen, but the call wouldn't go through.

In her motor home, Winnie had installed a cell signal

booster, and she was almost always able to get a signal, at least enough to send email and make calls, but, without the booster, she was lucky to get anything, especially while roaming around the park. Putting her phone in her pocket, Winnie went to the hostess at the lodge and was told there was a thirty-five-minute wait. With her name on the list, Winnie stepped outside, hoping to rock the time away while enjoying the scenery. Sadly, the rockers were full this time, so she decided to go for a walk, trying to catch a glimpse of this mysterious Taggart or maybe spot Olga.

Winnie walked past the dorms where the summer workers lived, but, other than a few kids, she didn't see anyone. After getting back to the lodge, Winnie still had fifteen minutes to kill before her table was supposed to be ready, so she decided to walk around the parking lot and look for Taggart's car. It took about ten minutes to walk up and down the rows of cars, but she came up empty. Tired and hungry, Winnie went back to the hostess stand, where she was told she was next in line.

A few minutes later, Winnie was enjoying a White Zinfandel and studying the menu, a welcome distraction from all the mayhem that occupied her time lately. She decided on the Mesquite Smoked Chicken. Her mouth watered at the thought of food, and she was grateful when the server brought some warm bread. Slathering a generous amount of butter, Winnie made quick work of the roll, feeling a little guilty as she crammed the last bite into her mouth.

While she waited for her food to arrive, Winnie glanced around the dining room. As she scanned the faces of the other patrons, her mind always raced with ideas about their lives and what they might be thinking about. It was a game she liked to play, and it helped in her creative writing. She came across a young couple that couldn't keep their hands—or their feet—off of each other. Basically, the two were twisted like a pretzel. Winnie wondered if they were on their honeymoon, all smiles and giggles. She remembered the unbridled passion that came from youth and chuckled at the thought of her own past trysts.

Maybe I can relive some of those memories. But I don't think I can move like that anymore.

Winnie continued to look until she found a familiar face. Jennifer Malone was sitting at a table with another woman, and they were both engaged in what appeared to be a happy conversation. Jen looked different sitting there, as if she was finally able to relax and be herself. Her hair was down, instead of in the ponytail or bun she'd always seen, but she still didn't seem to wear any makeup. Not that she needed it. Winnie noticed how happy Jen looked, and it made her smile.

As if she sensed something, Jen looked over at Winnie and returned the smile. Then she said something to a server, who looked over at Winnie and nodded.

Jen got up and walked over to Winnie's table. "Hi, Winnie. I asked our server if you could join us, and they were happy to free up a table, so I hope you don't mind having dinner with us."

"I'd love to, Jen, but I don't want to intrude."

"Nonsense. Grab your drink. The server will bring your food over to our table."

Winnie took her things and followed Jen.

Jen's friend stood and extended her hand. She was shorter than Jen, standing a few inches below Winnie. Her sandy-blonde hair hung mid-shoulder, with waves that framed her face. Smiling broadly, her blue eyes were soft and gentle.

"Hi, I'm Sally," Sally Claire said. "I'm Jen's partner."

"Oh," Winnie said. "You two work together?"

Sally smiled. "No, I'm a teacher. Jen is my life partner. We've been together almost five years now."

"Oh," Winnie's face warmed. "I'm sorry, I..."

"It's OK," Jen said. "An honest mistake."

Winnie smiled but didn't say anything, and the conversation seemed to lull for a moment. After what seemed like an eternity, she told them of the bears she saw on the way in. "They were cute." Winnie was glad to have something to talk about.

"From a distance," Jen said. "There was chatter on the radio about it when Sal and I were driving over. Another ranger was on his way to make sure that everyone, including the bears, stayed safe."

Sally took Jennifer's hand and smiled. "Always a ranger."

Just then the server came over with three plates of food.

The conversation lulled as they dug in, but Jennifer brought up Winnie's motor home. "You should see it, Sal. It's a pretty blue with Winnie's likeness on it. In bold letters it says Winnie's Winnie."

Sally looked at Winnie. "Did you buy it because it was a Winnebago?"

Winnie laughed. "No, I bought it because I could afford it. The brand was just a coincidence, and the name came after that. The car, on the other hand. Well...I couldn't resist that one."

"Oh," Jen said. "Winnie's car is painted the same color. It's a Mini, and it says Winnie's Mini on it. It's cute."

The talk of cars made Winnie remember the picture she took. Taking her phone out, Winnie flipped through until she found the one she was looking for and handed it over to Jen.

"Sometimes," Winnie said, "I wonder where my mind goes off to. When I first met Taggart, he nearly ran me over. When I came back to drop Anita off, I took a photo of the car he was in, but, in the excitement and confusion of everything that happened, I forgot about it until I was driving over here. Sorry."

Jen barely acknowledged Winnie. She had already pulled her notebook out and was taking notes.

"Can you send this to me." Jen finally looked up.

"As soon as I get a good enough signal. It will probably have to wait until I get back to my RV."

"Reception is spotty throughout Yellowstone," Sally said. "The same spot can get good signal one minute and horrible the next."

Jen stood up. "Excuse me. I'll be right back."

She walked away, already dialing numbers on her phone. In a few minutes, she came back.

"They're running the information now." Jen sat back down. "Hopefully, we'll know something soon."

It didn't take long before Jennifer got a call back. All Winnie and Sally could hear were a lot of "uh-humms" and "okays," but after she hung up, she filled the two in.

"We've identified Taggart's car. That car belongs to Lisa Stewart, a ranger over at Grand Teton National Park. They're looking for her now."

"It was definitely a man harassing Anita, though," Winnie said.

"Yes, but if we can track down the car, we might be able to see who's been driving it. Besides Lisa, that is. Either way, the car might have DNA or other evidence in it that can help us."

After dinner, they shared a Yellowstone sundae, which consisted of a crumb cake supporting a generous serving of huckleberry ice cream, followed by mixed berries. Three spoons clanked away as the trio chitchatted about all kinds of things.

"Where do you two live?" Winnie asked as they were enjoying some coffee.

"We have a small house over in the Mammoth area," Sally said. "It's government housing, but it's nice. I teach in Gardiner, which is just a few miles away. We'd love to have you over sometime. We can go into Gardiner and show you around."

"Yes," Jen added. "We don't get to meet many people, and we'd love to have you come over. Patches, too, of course."

"Thank you both." Winnie smiled. "I look forward to it. But right now, I'd better get back to my RV and see how Patches is doing."

After splitting the check, the three made their way to the parking lot and said their goodbyes. On the way home, Winnie thought about how happy Jen and Sally seemed and whether she could ever be that happy with someone ever again. *Do I even want that?*

The ride was uneventful, but, since it was dark, Winnie drove very slowly, mindful of anything that might wander out. Arriving at her campsite, she found Patches waiting by the door when she opened it. It was clear he was ready for a walk, so Winnie took him out for a quick one around her parking loop, not wanting to stray too far from her motor home at night. After settling in, Winnie went over what she knew about the events surrounding Anita's death. She was still waiting to hear back from Professor Mellon, and Winnie was grateful Jen hadn't brought up the subject. He was due to call tomorrow, and Winnie hoped he could shed some light on what got Anita killed.

Looking over her notes, Winnie wondered again about Olga's role in all of this. Was she really an innocent bystander, or was there trouble lurking behind that teenage smile? It still bothered Winnie that Olga showed up at her motor home. It didn't seem plausible that Olga would have the ability to find her.

And what about the mysterious caller warning Winnie to turn the notebook over? Was that Taggart, or was someone else involved? And what about her phone number? It was on the park reservation and sign-in, but who had access to that? Winnie couldn't wrap her head around any of it. Patches had already gone off to claim his spot on the bed, and Winnie was soon following his lead. Outside were the sounds of people bustling about, even at night, and Winnie found the noise comforting. Fishing Bridge was a big and crowded RV park, and, while some people might be disappointed with its wall-to-wall campers, Winnie suddenly found it very reassuring.

"If there *is* a killer on the loose, looking for me, he's not going to risk it by showing up here."

But with a park as big as Yellowstone, there were plenty of other opportunities.

14

Winnie was up before dawn. Wednesday's weather was supposed to be partly cloudy and cool, a perfect day for sightseeing. After an early morning yoga session, she went outside with her coffee and iPad, hoping to get a little work done while it was still quiet. She checked her email, but there was nothing new about the case. She wondered what Martin would find after he used the university's computer.

A breeze picked up, and Winnie shuddered in the cold morning air. Putting her iPad down, she held her coffee cup with both hands as she watched a few clouds taking shape in the morning sky.

Winnie looked over at her camper. Her smiling face painted on the side stared back at her. But was that smile a façade? She was a long way from home, both physically and emotionally. Why was she here? What was she really doing? The questions danced around in her mind a lot. When her mother asked, it was easy to dismiss it as parental meddling, and even a woman in her forties didn't like to be harangued by her mom. But Winnie asked the same things about herself.

Patches peered out of the door, his paw scratching as he beckoned for Winnie to come. She knew the thoughts she was having wouldn't go away, but, for now, she had more pressing matters. *The big questions in my life will have to wait.*

The two went for a long walk around the RV park. It was still early, and a lot of the campsites were quiet. Winnie enjoyed the chill in the air. It reminded her of mornings in Wisconsin. With all the water surrounding Madison, mornings were often chilly, and the air seemed to be full of moisture. It was almost like walking through a fine mist.

They had been out for a while, and Winnie got twisted around trying to find her RV. It was a bit like trying to spot a ship in the ocean, and even the distinctive blue paint couldn't be seen from very far away. Reminding herself to use the "Find My Car" app next time, Winnie continued to look around as Patches tugged her in a zig-zag pattern. Until he came to an abrupt stop.

"Whoa there, buddy."

Winnie turned to see a man in a cowboy hat stooped down, giving Patches a back rub. Patches was normally wary of strangers but seemed to have warmed up to this person. Then he stood, and it was Winnie's turn to warm up. Standing over six feet, Winnie looked up to see a mesmerizing smile under the ten-gallon Stetson.

"Howdy, ma'am." He extended his hand. "I'm Cal Miller."

Winnie took the proffered hand. Warm and secure. She looked at the big smile and big blue eyes and a tingle ran through her. Until she saw a woman coming toward them, wiping her hands on a towel. Cal turned and smiled as she approached.

That tingle didn't last long.

"Looks like you made a new friend." The woman tucked the towel into her apron. Her expression looked more curious than dubious.

Still, Winnie felt a distinct chill in the air.

Winnie let go of Cal's hand as a new one was thrust in front of her. She was surprised at how firm the woman's handshake was.

"I'm Regina, Cal's wife, but everyone calls me Reggie."

"Hi, Reggie, I'm Winnie. Nice to meet you."

"Winnie's dog found me irresistible," Cal said.

"Sorry. I was looking for my motor home when Patches wandered over to Cal. He must have smelled another dog. Or food."

"Guilty on the food, and it's no trouble at all. Don't have a dog, but I love 'em. Where are you from? I'm trying to place the accent. Somewhere in the Midwest or Canada, maybe?"

"Good guess. Madison, Wisconsin. I take it you're not from New York?"

Cal laughed. "The hat and drawl tip you off, did it? We're from Sweetwater, Texas. Grew up together. High school sweethearts and all that."

Reggie looped her arm through his and the two smiled at each other. A little shorter than Winnie, Reggie had curly brunette hair in a bob, with blue eyes that seemed to dance around as she spoke. Her skin was well tanned, as if she spent a lot of time outdoors.

Cal's tanned skin matched Reggie's, and Winnie was suddenly aware at how pale her skin was in comparison.

Winnie nodded and smiled, a slight twinge of jealousy coursing through her as she looked at the two. Then she took a look behind her at the motor home they were by. It looked new, certainly newer than hers. And a lot fancier. Did she look as green as she felt?

"So," Winnie looked back at them. "How long have you been here?"

"About a week," Reggie said. "We decided to see the country and figured this was the best way to do it. We've been going for over a month now. So far, we've been to the Grand Canyon, Bryce, Zion, and Grand Teton National Parks."

"I set out to see the country, too," Winnie said. "I changed careers so I could work on the road. Are you retired? You seem too young."

"Sort of," Cal said. "I grew up on a cattle farm and, shortly after I inherited it, we found a big reserve of oil. It's a little deeper than most, but there's a lot of it. With that much oil, money started pouring in. Reggie and I decided it was time to sell and enjoy ourselves a bit."

"We're taking a few years off, but we have plans," Reggie said. "I'd like to start a soup kitchen. Sweetwater is small, but there are still a lot of people in need."

"Reggie didn't have a lot of things growing up," Cal said. "And she never got to travel. We decided this would be a good chance for us to see our beautiful country before we settled back in Sweetwater."

"That sounds like a lot of fun. Do you have an itinerary planned, or are you just wandering?"

"We have somewhat of an itinerary, but we're free to change it whenever we want. We joined a travel group called Drove There, Did That. It's more of an online thing, but there are a few meetups throughout the year, and we keep in touch with some of the people. It's great for support, and you can find other people staying nearby. You should join. You'll have an instant group of friends."

"I'll look it up. I better get going. It was nice to meet you."

"You, too, Winnie," Reggie said. "Say, we're going on a hike later with another member of the Drove There group. Would you care to join us? It's eight thirty now. How about if we meet at the trailhead at ten. The trailhead isn't far. There's a pullout about two miles from here."

"That's an excellent idea," Cal said. "The more the merrier, especially in bear country. It's called the Elephant Back Mountain Trail. It's a three-and-a-half-mile hike, and it does have an incline to get to the top, but it's a great day and should be a fun hike. Plus, nobody's in any hurry, so don't think you can't keep up. We think we'll be back here before two. Come on. It's a great way to meet new people. The Thurmans are joining us, and they're a lot of fun. We'd offer you a ride, but with the Thurmans, our car is full."

Winnie hesitated, but then she realized she was here for adventure, and maybe a hike with this new group would do her good. "Okay, I'll be there. Do you have directions to the trailhead parking lot?"

"Hang on," Reggie went back into her RV. She appeared after a moment with a slip of paper. "This is my cell phone. Call me if you get lost. The trailhead is two miles away. After turning right onto East Entrance Road, turn left at the intersection onto Grand Loop, which is US-20. The trailhead will be about a mile or so on the right, and there's a small parking area just off the road. We'll try to get there early to look for you. We'll be in the red Subaru Outback over there."

"Thanks." Winnie slipped the paper into her pocket. They said goodbye, and Winnie and Patches turned to find their site. After rounding another bend and walking for what seemed like a mile, Winnie finally saw her motor home. Patches must have found it, too, because he was pulling on his leash in that direction.

Winnie filled Patches's bowls, made her breakfast, and was just sitting down when the phone rang.

"Harro?" Winnie's mouth was still full of yogurt and granola.

"Hello, Winnie. It's Martin Mellon. I hope this isn't a bad time?"

Winnie put down the spoon and swiveled in her chair, reaching for her iPad. "Hi, Martin. Nope. This is a great time. I take it you've been able to run the notebook through the computer at the university?"

"Yes. We started first thing this morning. I just got the results. I haven't had a chance to look at them closely yet, but I thought I'd send them your way so we could both take a crack at it. Are you someplace where you can get email?"

With the cell phone booster, Winnie had three bars for voice and a decent data connection. "Fire away, Professor. It should be fine."

"Very good. I'll send them now. Will you have a chance to look at the document this morning? We could set up a time to go over it."

"I'm going on a hike at ten, but it shouldn't take more than a few hours. Then I'll be able to go over it and be ready for our talk. Is three, your time, too late?

"Perfect. I have another date with your mother this evening, and that will give me time to get ready. I'll call you at three. Until then."

"Bye." Winnie's thoughts were on what she last heard. *Another date with Mom? Already? Am I going to have to call him dad soon?* Winnie brushed off the thought as she waited for the email to arrive. Her iPad sounded the familiar ding of a new email shortly after they hung up. She resisted the urge to read it then. Instead, she put the iPad aside and got ready for her hike.

WINNIE PULLED into the Elephant Back trailhead parking lot just before ten. Reggie and Cal were standing next to their Subaru, waving, and another couple was next to them. Winnie waved back and pulled into the space next to theirs. She grabbed her day pack and got out.

"Winnie," Reggie said. "Glad you could join us."

"Thanks for inviting me. It's nice to do things with other people."

"That's what Drove There, Did That is all about." She turned and pointed to the other couple. "I'd like you to meet Rita and Jack Thurman. Rita and Jack, this is Winnie."

After handshakes all around, the five started on the trail. The trail was called a "lollipop loop" trail—a straight out-and-back section with a loop up to the top. Cal was taking the lead, and Reggie brought up the rear, with Winnie in front of her. The Thurmans were in the middle, talking to each other with an occasional comment to the rest of the group.

The trail started fairly flat and was wide enough for two people, so Reggie stepped up to walk next to Winnie.

"I'm sorry if I was abrupt with you earlier," Reggie said. "Women seem to flock around my husband, and I've been a little protective. Maybe too much, I'm embarrassed to say. Anyway, I apologize."

"No worries." Winnie smiled back at her. "I can understand your concern."

"That's just it. I have no reason to be concerned. Just my own insecurities."

You and me both, sister. "I've got my share of insecurities, too. Maybe we can work on them together."

"Deal."

There were a lot of people on the trail, and Reggie dropped back to keep their group single file and let the oncoming hikers pass. Winnie was enjoying the hike through the dense lodgepole pine forest and got lost in her own thoughts. Squirrels darted around, and Winnie noticed flowers just starting to bud. After clearing the forest, the trail split into a loop. There was a sign indicating the trail went in either direction. Directly below that, however, was another sign. And not a good one. It was a picture of a bear with a warning that bears frequented the area and to be careful.

"Don't worry." Cal took a sip from his water bottle. "There are a lot of people on the trail, and everyone's making noise. Bears won't want to come near."

"Left or right?" Winnie still wasn't sure it was a good idea to be out with bears wandering around, but like Cal said, there were a lot of people, and Winnie felt somewhat safe.

"I read that most people go left, so let's follow the crowd," Cal said.

"Did you know the lodgepole pines have a special cone that needs heat to release their seeds?" Winnie was doing her best to make as much noise as possible without seeming too obvious.

"I'd read about that." Reggie caught up and moved beside Winnie. "They actually need a fire to grow new trees. Something about a waxy coating on their cones needs to burn off before the seeds can be exposed. Mother Nature's way of healing after a forest fire."

The two chatted about their experiences growing up. Reggie's father was a farmhand and her mother worked in the church. Neither made much money, Reggie explained, but the family had an abundance of spirit and love. Winnie was just the opposite. Lots of material things but not enough of real family togetherness.

They continued to talk, and, despite their differences, Winnie felt a strong connection to Reggie, and she wished she had the same connection with her own sister.

As soon as they started the loop, the trail began its steep incline, and it didn't take Winnie long before her lungs started to burn. It was an uphill climb for about three-quarters of a mile, with a series of switchbacks to minimize the steepness. At the top it leveled off again, and, once they cleared the trees, they were rewarded with a great view of Yellowstone Lake. Wooden benches were placed at the top, and they stopped for a break to eat and enjoy the view. Winnie was glad she'd brought some trail mix with her.

"The lake is beautiful," Winnie said between bites, offering the bag to Reggie, who took a handful of trail mix. Winnie noticed a large yellow building along the lake. It looked like it had been there a while, but it appeared well maintained. "And that building—what's that?"

"That's the Lake Lodge. We went to dinner there a couple of days ago, and it was very nice. The food was fantastic. I hear the rooms are like a resort, too."

"Sounds nice, but I don't think it's a place for Patches and me."

"Maybe you could get him in a suit," Reggie teased.

"Or at least a sport coat and tie." Winnie laughed at the thought of Patches dressed up, and she could picture him rolling in the mud as his tie flopped around.

Winnie took a few snapshots of the lake, one of the group, and then a selfie with her and Reggie. Then the group descended the other side through another set of switchbacks then back into the lodgepole forest. Before Winnie knew it, she was back to the trailhead. The group had made good time, finishing the hike in just under two and a half hours.

"Thanks for inviting me," Winnie said. "I had a lot of fun."

"Thanks for coming with us," Cal said. "I hope you decide to join our group. We're heading to Glacier next, and it would be great to see you there."

Another set of handshakes, and Winnie was walking to her car when Reggie came running up. "I almost forgot. We're having people over tomorrow for a cookout. Nothing fancy, just burgers and chicken. Can I count you in? Patches, too. No sport coat required."

Winnie laughed. "We'd be delighted. What can I bring?"

"Just you and Patches. We'll take care of everything else. Come by around six for drinks."

"Thanks, Reggie. I'll see you tomorrow."

Winnie smiled as she got into Winnie's Mini. She'd had a great hike with a nice group and met a new friend. But the smile faded as she pulled into the Fishing Bridge RV Park. She had a report waiting for her, and Anita's killer was still out there.

15

After fixing tuna salad for lunch, Winnie opened the document Martin sent. As she started to read, she found a dizzying array of numbers and graphs, none of which made a lot of sense. It was all about letter frequencies, probability, substitution approaches, and seed letters, whatever that was. After more pages of the same, Winnie finally found a section labeled results.

"Thank goodness." Winnie looked at the first paragraph. It was words she could understand, and, after a few paragraphs of introduction, each page was presented, first with the original writing and then with the translated text. If there was any doubt about the translation, alternate suggestions were placed in brackets.

Sure enough, many of the pages dealt with typical teenage stuff. Anita had an on-again, off-again relationship with a boy named Yegor. From the diary, Anita liked Yegor, but he was making advances Anita wasn't ready for, so she broke up with him. But she missed him and thought about getting back together...teenagers were the same everywhere.

There was a lot devoted to gossip, Facebook posts, clothes,

and makeup, but nothing that would interest many people outside Anita's small circle of friends, and, after slogging through pages of Anita's thoughts and feelings, some of which even a drama queen couldn't have come up with, Winnie thought this might be another dead end. Her tales continued in Yellowstone, with boys from her dorm asking her out, and... Winnie couldn't read any more of this. She put the iPad down to think about what she'd read. So far, Winnie had no idea why Anita left the notebook in her car and was starting to wonder if it was all a mistake. *There has to be a reason.*

After a quick break, Winnie picked up where she left off, expecting more of the same juvenile ruminations. She came across Anita's encounters with Taggart, but they were mostly about her feelings changing from amusement to dread as Taggart's presence began to wear. At least for now, Taggart's harassment had just been verbal.

The next section the computer couldn't translate or decipher, with a bracketed explanation that the text was illegible to read. Winnie heaved a big sigh, wondering if this was going to be a waste of time. But the next page proved her wrong.

The first sentence started with "Today was a bad day." Apparently, Anita was supposed to go with some friends on a hike in Yellowstone. When the friends didn't show up, Anita found a group of strangers going hiking and she went with them.

"Well, that was dumb." Winnie shook her head. But since teenagers weren't known for making the best decisions, Winnie understood. She knew from her own experiences that teenagers made stupid choices sometimes. Getting back to the document, Winnie continued to read about Anita's adventures. After the group arrived at the trailhead, they dispersed, and Anita found herself alone. Assuming she'd come across them at some point, Anita decided to follow the trail. It was a typical hike at first, with a pleasant walk and a few people along the path. Anita felt safe knowing other people were out there, too. After about ninety minutes, though, Anita realized she was lost and no longer on a trail. She tried calling out, but no one answered. Checking her phone, she didn't have cell service, so she kept walking. She continued to wander, using the compass app on her phone. Knowing she needed to go south, and maybe a little west, she started off in that direction, hoping to find the trail or a road or people.

Over an hour later, Anita hadn't found a road or a trail, but she heard voices. She was going to call out, but the voices didn't sound particularly friendly, so she remained quiet. As she got closer, Anita could make out three distinct people talking. To her, it sounded like a few males and one female, but she still couldn't understand the conversation. Moving closer, the dialogue still didn't sound friendly. In fact, the closer she got, the more hostile it sounded, with shouts and threats coming from different voices.

When Anita got close enough to see what was going on, she heard a loud bang, followed by a thump. Shouting followed, and Anita crouched down in the tall brush. After the shouting died down, Anita peered out and could see one of the men dragging the other, while another man was now digging a hole off in the distance. A woman was standing there, staring at the man being dragged away. Close to Anita was a car, and next to that was another hole.

The computer flagged the words car and hole, providing bracketed alternate word choices. Winnie glanced at the original text and noticed that it was smudged, in addition to being written in code, so maybe the computer had had a hard time understanding the meaning. The words did look slightly different, but Winnie didn't understand any of the Ukrainian characters, so she couldn't tell.

Winnie went back to the translated text. The alternatives for car included truck and all-terrain vehicle. Scanning the rest of the text, Winnie couldn't tell which one Anita meant, but if she was on a trail, she might have meant all-terrain vehicle, or ATV.

Going to the next bracketed word, alternatives for hole included cave, cover, or conceal, but Winnie had no idea which one Anita meant. Were there any caves in Yellowstone? There must be in a place this big, but she didn't know where any of them were. Then she reread the translation to see if there were any indications of where Anita had been hiking, but she didn't see any mention of it. She assumed the location was in the part the computer couldn't translate or decipher.

Winnie wondered if Anita took any pictures of who she saw. None of the photos on the flash drive showed faces, just an area that could be any number of places. Anita might have been unable to see faces from where she was hiding. The rangers couldn't find Anita's phone, so maybe whoever killed her took her phone and that's where the pictures of the people were. Winnie shook her head at the thought of someone taking another person's life. None of Yellowstone's treasures could be worth that.

Picking up where she left off, Winnie scanned through the rest of the text. Anita gave a quick account of her running away. Her movements must have made too much noise because Anita heard shouts, but she didn't look back to see if anyone was chasing her. Eventually, Anita found a trail and was able to follow some hikers back to the trailhead. She didn't say how she got back to her dorm, but, once she got there, she decided the best thing for her to do was to keep quiet. Anita knew she should report what she saw but didn't know who to trust.

In the next paragraph, Anita described the people she saw, but the details were so generic, they could apply to any number of people. The only distinguishing remark she noted was that one of the men was particularly big and tall and seemed to have something on his face, like a scar or tattoo, but Anita couldn't see them very well.

"That rules Taggart out," Winnie said to Patches. "Taggart was average height, maybe a little taller. I don't remember any face tattoos or scars, either."

Patches looked up at the sound of Winnie's voice, but since there weren't treats involved, he put his head back down. Winnie went back to Anita's journal, but it really didn't say much else, except for one entry where Anita thought she might have spotted one of the men—the tall one—but wasn't sure and didn't know how he could have found her.

Winnie let out a long sigh when she put the translated notebook down. Someone killed her because of what she saw, at least that was what it seemed, but why? Because Anita witnessed a murder and they were trying to cover their tracks? So now it'd gone from one murder to two? And where was this other one? Too many questions that Winnie couldn't answer. She forwarded the document to Jen and took a deep breath. The RV seemed dark and cold, and Winnie decided to go for a walk to clear her head. She grabbed a tissue to wipe her eyes as she took the leash.

"Come on, Patches," Winnie said, her voice low and soft. "We both need to get some air."

Winnie dropped her phone in her backpack and slung it over her shoulder as she stood on the steps of her motor home. She closed her eyes and absorbed the sun, taking deep breaths in an effort to calm down. When she opened them, she was rewarded with a beautiful spring afternoon. It was good to see so many people around, and it made Winnie feel safe. She had been so preoccupied with solving Anita's death that she wasn't taking much time to appreciate the beauty all around her. Winnie was a little sad she was bogged down in such a depressing situation. But one look at Patches pulling at the leash, tail wagging, not a care in the world, made things better. It seemed Patches could go through anything and come out the same as he always was. He didn't hold grudges, and, other than being more than happy to take food off your plate, didn't want much. Just affection, and Patches seemed to give more than he took.

"Which one of us rescued the other?" Winnie asked Patches.

More tail wagging was the response.

Winnie stopped at the amphitheater, which was close to the park. There was nothing going on, but it seemed to be a peaceful place for Winnie to clear her head. Patches enjoyed being out in the sun and sprawled out, his belly soaking up as much of the heat as possible. Winnie leaned over and scratched Patches's belly, and he seemed to enjoy every minute of it. Among other things, the amphitheater was used for Sunday church services, and Winnie bowed her head, offering a silent prayer. She prayed for strength to get through her troubled times and to help find Anita's killer. She threw in another for her mother, hoping she would find happiness.

Raising her head, Winnie felt better. Patches was still lying there, enjoying the day, and Winnie resolved to be more like him—carefree and in the moment. "You know the secret to life, don't you?"

They sat there another twenty minutes until Patches started getting restless, then they moved on to their next destination, the RV park's general store.

The general store wasn't pet friendly, but Winnie was told that as long as her dog was quiet and didn't jump on the food, no one would mind. Winnie looked at Patches and hoped for the best. She'd never been thrown out of a store before and crossed her fingers this wouldn't be the first time, so she grabbed a few things she needed and left before Patches had a chance to get into any mischief. After they left the store, Winnie reached into her pocket, giving Patches a dog treat for being so well-behaved.

The two made their way back to Winnie's Winnie. The RV

park was so big that Winnie got lost again for a moment, but soon enough she spotted her blue motor home. It was getting hot outside, and the air conditioner was running when they walked in. Patches went straight for his food bowl to see if anything had magically appeared, offering Winnie a disappointed look that the dish was empty. Winnie took the groceries out of her backpack.

"Wow." Winnie picked her phone up from the bottom of the backpack. She must have wandered out of cell coverage because there were four missed calls and three voice mails. She plopped down on her dinette booth as she thumbed through her missed calls. Two were from her mother, one was from Professor Mellon, and the last one was from Jen Malone. Listening to her voice mails, Winnie cringed at the first one.

"Winona," her mother began. "Martin just shared with me the details of the notebook. Another murder? What have you gotten yourself into? Please, dear, call me back as soon as you get this."

Winnie expected a sound scolding when she called her mother back. She pressed delete and moved to the next one. It was from Professor Mellon.

"Hello, Winnie. This is Martin. I thought we had a call scheduled, but maybe I got the time wrong. Anyway, I wanted to go over the email I sent. If you've read through it, you probably noticed a few gaps and alternate meanings. Unfortunately, this is normal. But a lot of it is intact, so I hope it helps. Please call me back if you need anything."

Winnie looked at her watch. It was two thirty. She had forgotten about the one-hour time difference. Oops.

Winnie was just about to press delete when her phone started buzzing with an incoming call. Glancing at the caller ID, she took a deep breath.

"Hi, Mom." Winnie tried to sound cheerful.

"Winona—" her mother began, fury sounding in her voice.

"Mom! It's okay. Everything's fine."

"Don't tell me everything's fine. You've uncovered another murder. That makes two dead bodies! I don't want you to be the third."

"Mom, I'm fine. Really. I'm just helping where I can. I want to see Anita's killer brought to justice. It's the right thing to do. Isn't that what you always told me growing up? Do the right thing."

"Don't throw my words back at me. This is different, and you know it."

Winnie lost that argument. "Yes, Mom. It's different in some ways. But I need to help. Whether you like it or not, I've been thrust into this, and I'm going to see it through, so please stop worrying."

"Worrying is what mothers do, Winnie. It's one of the things we're really good at."

"I know, Mom, and it's one of the many things I love you for. I'll be careful."

There was a long pause before Winnie's mother spoke. Finally, a soft "Okay."

Winnie wanted to change the subject before it turned sour again. "So, how are things with Martin?"

"Oh," her mother sounded a little startled at the new topic. "Things are good. Very good, as a matter of fact. He's so sweet, in a nerdy sort of way. I'm afraid I've become quite smitten with him."

Smitten?

Winnie laughed. "Well, from what I can tell, the feeling is mutual. He's a nice man."

"That he is. When, of course, he's not helping you get into more trouble."

Winnie heard the distinctive tones of another call coming in. "Mom, I've got to go, but I'll call you soon."

"Bye, dear. Please be careful. I love you."

"Love you, too, Mom. Bye."

Winnie switched over to the incoming call. It was from a number she didn't recognize.

"Hello?" Winnie said a little apprehensively. She was afraid it was someone demanding the notebook. Or something else.

"Hi, is this Winnie? This is Sally, Jen's girlfriend. Is this a good time to talk?"

"Hi, Sally. Yes, it's fine. What's up?"

"Jen's in the middle of something, so she asked me to call. Are you free for dinner tonight? We wanted to make good on our offer, and Jen wants to go over your professor's findings. Would six o'clock be okay?"

"Sounds fantastic, Sally. I'll bring over a bottle of wine."

"Great. I'll text the address to this number and we'll see you and Patches at six."

After hanging up, Winnie listened to the last voice mail. She thought it would be from Jen, but instead, it was another one from her mother.

"Winona," the message began. "Are you ignoring me? We need to talk about—"

Winnie pressed delete. She had no desire to relive the conversation she'd just had with her mother, even if it did turn out nice. But what her mom said about Martin. Wow, things seemed to be moving fast.

Smitten? Are there wedding bells in their future? I guess time will tell.

Winnie plopped down on the couch, giggling at the thought of being the flower girl, with Patches carrying the rings in on a pillow.

16

By the time Winnie was finished getting caught up on her messages and other errands, it was after four. She got Patches ready to go over to Jen and Sally's house, giving him a quick bath using pet wipes and brushing his fur. Google Maps showed the route would take about sixty-five minutes, and soon it was time to leave. She took the 2016 Chardonnay from Jackson Hole Winery she bought the other day at Cooke City, put a bow around the bottle's neck, and slipped it into a wine gift bag. Winnie grabbed it as she and Patches left.

Traffic was light, and Winnie made good time, pulling into Jen's driveway right at six. Sally must have heard her pull up because she opened the door as Winnie got out.

"Hi, Winnie." Sally smiled. "I hope you found us okay."

"Google maps is a Godsend." Winnie opened the back door.

Patches came barreling out, running between Winnie and Sally in circles.

"And you must be Patches!" Sally bent down to give her new friend some attention. "Let's get you inside before you find something to chase."

As the two walked inside, Sally said, "Jen should be home any time now. Something came up right as she was leaving, but she said it shouldn't take too long. In the meantime, I've got some appetizers ready. I even found something for Patches."

"Oh, here," Winnie handed Sally the bottle of wine. "This is for you."

Sally took the wine and put it in the refrigerator. "Thanks. I've got some already chilled if you'd like a glass. Or something else? Beer?"

"A glass of wine would be great. Whatever you're having. I'm not picky, especially when it comes to wine."

Sally appeared a minute later carrying a steak bone. Patches was right by her side, waiting to see what happened to it. "Can I give this to Patches? We had steaks last night, and I kept the bone. I think he'd like it."

"I know he would. Thanks."

Sally lowered her hand just a fraction, but that was enough for Patches to take the hint. He grabbed the bone out of Sally's hand and took it back into the kitchen. Winnie could see him through the doorway, happily gnawing on his treasure. Sally came back a moment later with two glasses of wine.

Winnie took a sip. "So, how did you and Jen meet?"

"Through a friend. I was teaching in Gardiner, and my friend worked as an assistant in the ranger's office. She thought Jen and I would hit it off, and we did. We've been together ever since."

Just then, the door opened and Jen walked in. "Hi, Winnie. I'm glad you're here." Jen smiled at Sally and took a sip of wine from her glass.

"Get your own!" Sally swatted at Jen's hand, but it was clear the two were a happy couple, and Sally got up to get Jen a glass of wine while she talked to Winnie.

"Sorry I was late. I was actually following up on two things."

Sally came back into the room. "Jen, you promised to keep

shop talk to a minimum tonight. Winnie's our guest. So, can we save the rest of it for tomorrow?"

"You know how I am when I'm on a case. It'll just take a minute. Okay?"

"Fine." Sally gave Jen a look. "I need to check on dinner anyway."

"I hope I didn't cause trouble," Winnie said when Sally was out of earshot.

"Nonsense. As long as we don't go over it all night, she'll be fine. She knows this is important to both you and me. I'll wait until Sal gets back. She'll want to hear this, too."

Sally came back in carrying a tray of puff-pastry appetizers. Winnie's stomach started growling at the wonderful aroma, and she reached for one when offered. Sally put the tray down next to Winnie.

"Sal, you're not going to believe this," Jen started, her mouth full of crab and cheese. "Mmm, these are great. Where did you get them?"

"The market in Gardiner. Now, what wouldn't I believe?"

"Oh, yeah. Do you remember Dickie from the motor pool group?"

"You mean the creep that was always hitting on you? Even after you told him you were in a relationship? Wait. He's Taggart?"

"Yep. He's the one. He moved down to Grand Teton to work with them. Somehow, he got a ranger uniform and had a badge made up with a fake name. Then he'd take one of the cars, which no one noticed because he was in maintenance, and he'd drive up here to try to hit on women. When that didn't work, I guess he decided to try to intimidate the college kids that came to work here for the summer."

"Isn't he in his mid thirties? And he's going after vulnerable eighteen-year-olds? Yuck."

"Well, he won't be doing that again for a long while, hopefully. But, so far, it doesn't look like he's involved with what happened to Anita. He gave us an alibi for when she was murdered, which we're checking. Plus, he seemed truly shocked to learn of her death. I'm glad we found him, but I don't think he's part of that."

Just then, the timer in the kitchen went off.

"Oh, and we found Olga. She got scared and decided to stay with a friend. She really doesn't trust the police, and when we moved her, she thought we did it to spy on her, not to keep her out of trouble. A manager saw her and tipped us off. We thought it best if she went home, so I arranged for her flight back. She should be in the air right now."

Sally came back and refilled everyone's glass. "I'm glad we're through with business for tonight."

"One last thing." Jen bit her lip as she and Sally exchanged glances. From the looks of it, Jen was pushing her luck. "I know you sent me an email about the notebook, but we've been chasing down Taggart and dealing with Olga all day, and I haven't had a chance to read it. Can we go over it tomorrow?"

"I'd be happy to."

"Okay," Sally got up to get everything ready. "The rest of this can wait until tomorrow, can't it? I need some help with the food."

"I'll help." Winnie headed for the kitchen.

Patches had finished his bone and was coming into the family room.

"And I'll play with Patches," Jen said.

Winnie was tossing the salad while Sally was carving a few slices of roast beef. Three salmon fillets were resting on a platter.

"Jen always had a dog growing up," Sally said. "I think she's been missing that lately, so I thought spending some time with Patches would help."

"I know Patches rescued me more than I rescued him," Winnie said. "I understand how therapeutic a dog can be."

After the table was set, the three sat down to dig in.

"Wow, this is so good. Thank you for inviting me. And Patches."

Sally put some roast beef out for Patches, and, by his noises, he was enjoying himself. There was another bone with it, and he happily started gnawing on the bone as soon as the meat was gone. But he kept looking over, keeping a sharp eye for anything that dropped.

"This is delicious," Winnie said. "Usually in the motor home, I only get to cook simple meals. What's in these potatoes? I've never tasted anything like it."

"They're potato and parsnip gratin. I found the recipe online and just had to try it."

"I'm so glad you did." Winnie picked up another forkful.

After a wonderful meal of salmon, asparagus, salad, and potatoes, Jen took the plates and started doing the dishes. Winnie tried to help, but she was shooed away and told to sit and relax. Instead, Sally took her outside to enjoy the sunset. It was quiet, and a chill was in the air as the sun took its warmth with it.

"I never really enjoyed the outdoors until I met Jen," Sally said. "She taught me how to appreciate it."

Winnie smiled, her eyes never leaving the fiery landscape. There were no bubbling mud pots where they were standing, but the waning light on the mountain peaks gave a beautiful glow. "There's a lot to appreciate here. The area is so different from the horn-honking, concrete-laden, tense environment I'm used to. Looking around is like yoga for the eyes. Relaxing. Plus," Winnie looked at Jen through the window, "you two make a great couple, and being with you makes me feel good."

"Thanks. It's not easy sometimes, especially in a place like this. This part of the country is very conservative, and we don't always fit their idea of a couple. But most people are nice, and we try to keep a low profile."

Jen called out that coffee was ready, and the two went inside for slices of blueberry tart. Patches was ever hopeful something would fall down, but, to his dismay, nothing did, so he went back to his bone. After dessert, the three went into Gardiner, a small town located just outside the park. Sally showed Winnie the school where she taught and the area she grew up in. After the tour, they stopped into the Two Bit Saloon. Winnie went to the bar to order a round of drinks while Jen and Sally played a game of pool.

"I play the winner." Winnie brought the beers over. "I hope you don't mind. I asked the bartender what local beers he had and he poured me a taste of Working Guys Cream Ale. I liked it so I got it for all of us."

Jen took a sip. "We've had this before and both liked it. We just change the name to Working Gals."

After four rounds of pool, they decided to call it a night. "It's gotten late, Winnie." Jen checked her watch. "Why don't you and Patches spend the night? We have a spare room, and you can get up tomorrow and head back to Fishing Bridge. It's dark out, the roads aren't lit, and there won't be many people out this time of night. I don't want to see you getting into an accident. Please stay."

"How can I refuse?" Winnie said. "I'd love to, as long as you're sure it won't be a bother."

"No bother at all," Sally said. "And don't even think about rushing off in the morning like Jen, grabbing a piece of fruit on the way out the door. I'll make you a nice breakfast. Patches, too."

"Hey!" Jen said. "I'm trying to keep the park safe. But I'll stick around tomorrow as late as I can."

~

The next morning, Winnie was still in bed when she heard the front door shut. She assumed it was Jen leaving for the day and decided it was time for her to get up, too. The house seemed quiet, so Winnie thought Sally might still be sleeping. As Winnie changed, Patches simply rolled over, apparently not eager to start his day. But that changed as soon as Winnie opened the bedroom door. She could smell breakfast cooking. Patches must have smelled it, too, because he jumped off the bed and brushed by Winnie. They ambled into the kitchen, where Sally was busy with eggs, fruit, and yogurt.

"Oh, hi," Sally said. "I hope I didn't wake you. Please sit down and help yourself. Coffee? I have tea, too, if you prefer that. And let me take Patches for a walk while you eat. I don't get to play with dogs very often, so it'll be my pleasure."

"Coffee is great. I'm sure Patches would love a new walking partner. And thanks so much for making breakfast." Winnie pulled up a chair as Sally poured a cup of coffee, placing cream and sugar nearby. "I heard the front door open, so I guess I missed Jen."

"Jen went for a run," Sally said as she attached Patches's leash. "She'll be back soon. She wants to talk to you before you leave. I made her promise no shop talk last night, but today is fair game. I think she wants to go over the notebook. Be right back."

When Sally returned, she set out some leftover roast beef for Patches and a bowl of water. His tail wagged appreciatively as she set the food down, and he didn't need to be asked to start eating. Sally gave him a pat on the head and went to the table. Winnie was mixing yogurt, granola, and fruit when Sally sat down.

"When do you have to leave for school?" Winnie asked. "I don't want to keep you."

"I'm fine, but I better get ready before Jen gets back and commandeers the bathroom. I'll be back in a few minutes."

The door opened and Jen walked in, still breathing heavy from her run. She said hi and excused herself, heading for the bedroom. Before long both Jen and Sally were back, each digging into their breakfast.

"It must be nice to set your own schedule," Sally said between bites. "Don't get me wrong, I love my students, but I must admit I'm a little envious of your freedom. Especially at your age. You're still plenty young to get out there and do things."

Winnie smiled. "It does have its advantages. I still work, but I do it on my terms. That's my definition of a perfect retirement."

"Sounds wonderful." Sally took her dishes to the sink. "But for now, I'm happy with teaching. My kids can be challenging but a lot of fun." She slipped on a light jacket. "Well, I'm off to face the little gremlins. Thanks for coming, Winnie. I hope to see you again soon."

Winnie and Sally hugged goodbye. Jen followed Sally to the front door and then returned to the table. She looked at Winnie, and Winnie could see a weary expression on her face.

"I'd love to spend the day here, but I have to get to work soon. So, if it's okay, I'd like to take care of a few things."

"Back to reality," Winnie said.

"We think we have the man calling himself Taggart. He even confessed to it. I'd like to get confirmation on it, though. I was wondering if you would be willing to come down to the station and see if it's the same man you saw. We don't have enough people for a police lineup, but he will be on one side of a one-way mirror."

"Of course." Winnie smiled.

"Thanks. I'm trying not to involve you in any more of this stuff than I have to. You're supposed to be on vacation."

"I like solving puzzles."

"I can see that. Maybe after we're done at the station we can go over your professor's findings. I forwarded the email you sent me to the FBI forensic lab, but with their backlog, I don't expect anything for another week."

"I'd be happy to go over it with you."

"Great," Jen said. "I'll get changed if you want to take Patches for a walk. He can stay here while we're at the station. It shouldn't take long."

On the way to the station, Jen called and asked that Taggart be put into one of the interview rooms facing the one-way glass. "I'm sorry to be taking up so much of your time here in Yellowstone."

"It really hasn't been that much time, and I enjoyed spending the evening with you and Sally. I probably wouldn't have ventured into Gardiner without you two. I'm too young to just sit around and do nothing but too old to go bar hopping. I came on this journey seeking adventure, and that's what I got!"

"Well, remember the old adage—be careful what you wish for."

They entered the station and walked to an empty booth next to the interview room. A curtain covered the window separating the two rooms. Winnie was a little nervous about seeing him again, but Jen assured her she couldn't be seen. "He can't see in, and he'll be kept in there until we leave. I'm going to open the curtain. Just take a look and tell me if that's the man you saw."

When the curtain opened, Winnie took one look and knew. "That's him. Taggart, or whoever he really is."

"You're sure?"

"Positive. I remember faces, and he's still got that same mean smirk he had when I saw him in the parking lot at Roosevelt Lodge. It's him."

"Good enough. I'll take you back to my house and we can look over your professor's notes. Do you mind waiting here for a few minutes while I finish up some paperwork? Would you like some coffee?"

"Take your time. I'll walk over to the hotel's gift shop and look around." Winnie wanted to stay as far away from "cop coffee" as she could. Twenty minutes later, Winnie came back with a new Yellowstone T-shirt and baseball cap.

They returned to Jen's home to find Patches waiting by the door. He seemed relieved to see Winnie again and practically knocked her over when she walked in, excitedly jumping up to her waist.

"He was probably a little worried." Winnie sat on the floor while she and Patches played. "He's in a strange place and I left. He may have thought I wasn't coming back."

Winnie gave Patches a nice belly rub then a treat, and all seemed forgiven. Jen poured coffee, and she and Winnie sat at the kitchen table, with Patches staying by Winnie's side. Winnie pulled out her iPad and her copy of the notebook.

"Oh, I meant to tell you," Jen said. "I asked the rangers patrolling the Fishing Bridge area to keep an eye on your RV. They're driving by as often as they can. So far, nothing looks out of the ordinary."

"Thanks. I haven't gotten another call demanding the notebook, so maybe whoever it was realized that too many other people had it, so terrorizing me wouldn't help."

"Perhaps," Jen said. "Or maybe they left before they got caught. Either way, we'll find them. Now, shall we go over your professor's findings?"

17

For two hours, Winnie and Jen poured over the printout of the notebook's translation. They skipped over the initial entries of Anita's tribulations in Ukraine and went straight for when she arrived at Yellowstone. As it started, Anita wrote about her wonder at being in a new place. With some of the money she earned, she was hoping to travel to New York City and see a Broadway play before she left, along with all the other sites, like the Statue of Liberty and the Empire State Building.

Anita then chronicled her run-ins with Taggart. At first, she was flattered an older man was interested in her. Soon, however, the creep factor set in, and Anita wanted to stay as far away from him as possible. And that was when Taggart got mean.

"From what I can tell, it looks like Taggart went from sweet talker to intimidator after she rejected him," Winnie said. "Further on, Anita writes she's not the only one he's been targeting."

Jen shook her head. "Even if he's not our killer, I'm glad he's locked up."

"What will happen to him?"

"He was arrested on federal property, using a stolen federal vehicle, and impersonating a park ranger. Most people don't know it, but Yellowstone has its own jail and court. He'll either be held until trial or let out if he can post bail. I doubt he's got two nickels to rub together, so my guess is he'll sit there for quite a while. The biggest problem is going to be with witnesses. From what we can tell so far, he was smart enough, or lucky enough, to only pick on the ones that didn't speak English as their native language. That was smart for two reasons. First, he could always claim the girls misunderstood him. Second, chances are these girls were foreigners, which means getting them to testify will be a lot more difficult, especially after they returned home."

"Jen, do you think Taggart, or whatever his name is, had the intelligence to figure that part out? I didn't really see him that much, but my first impression of him was more of a bully than a brainiac."

"I don't know, but either way, I'm going to do everything I can to see he stays in jail for a long time."

Patches started to get restless. It was time for another walk.

Jen smiled and asked if she could take him out. "I could walk him and give you a few minutes of peace, or we can both go, and I can show you around the neighborhood."

"Let's both go. I need to stretch my legs, too."

The three were soon outside, and Patches was leading the way, pulling on his leash while he explored the new area. Jen laughed at Patches as he tried to pee on every rock he found.

"Bears sometimes come into this area," Jen said as they navigated the roads, "but there are so many houses, cars, and concrete, they don't usually stick around. During the day there's always someone around to chase them away. At night, though, they come out, attracted by the smells of food or trash."

They continued to walk, the roads leading them in a circle, until they were back at Jen's house.

"Ready to dig back into the notebook?" Jen asked as they sat back down at the table.

"Sure. We're just getting to the interesting part."

Winnie got out her iPad to make notes, while Jen started to read Anita's description of her being lost and stumbling across the people.

Jen let out a low whistle. "Poor Anita. Wrong place, wrong time. It's a shame she doesn't tell us where she is, but maybe we can figure it out."

"I wonder why she didn't mention any roads or places," Winnie said.

"She probably didn't know any of the places, and most of the back roads aren't marked. Since there are only a few paved roads, she probably didn't need to memorize streets. She didn't give us much to go on, but if we assume she was near caves, that might narrow it down. There are actually caves all over Yellowstone, but they're closed to the public. None of them are safe to enter. They're either too narrow to get into or out of easily, or there's a risk of the cave collapsing. The rangers are stretched too thin to monitor all of them, so we just close the areas around the caves."

"You know where this place is?" Winnie asked.

"No, but I know some of the most obvious places. We looked at the pictures on the flash drive but couldn't narrow it down. The revelation about the cave helps, so maybe we'll have more luck. Let's go through the rest of this, and then we can take a ride out to one or two of them. If you have time, of course."

"I've got nothing but time. Whoever is on this killing spree needs to be stopped. But what's out there that's worth killing for?"

"I don't know for certain, but probably either gold or silver. Maybe both. It's not widely known, and we don't advertise it, but there are a few old mines scattered about Yellowstone. All of them are inactive, or at least they're supposed to be. Mining in Yellowstone has been illegal for some time, and anyone caught is looking at a lot of jail time."

"That might explain what they were doing out there but not why Anita saw them kill one of their own."

"I'm guessing greed, which is a powerful motivator. A deal gone bad, someone wanting more than their share. It could be anything. The answer could be as simple as some friends out drinking got into an argument and it turned deadly. That's happened here more than once."

"Really?" Winnie raised her eyebrows and frowned. "I thought Yellowstone was just families looking at the wonderful sights."

"Don't I wish. Then I wouldn't have to carry my gun. Unfortunately, this is a place where some people, mostly younger males, think they're cowboys and this is the old west. Mix that with alcohol and vehicles and you've got a dangerous combination."

Winnie shook her head at the thought. "I never knew."

"Most of the parks are pretty tame, but the bigger ones, like Yellowstone, get their share of trouble. Now, let's see what else is in the notebook."

They went over the remainder of the notebook quickly, not finding anything useful.

Winnie got Patches ready to leave. "What I don't understand is why she didn't go to the police."

"Taggart. When Taggart started harassing Anita, she was probably too scared to talk to the police. She thought Taggart *was* the police."

18

Winnie followed Jen to the RV park at Fishing Bridge and dropped her car off at her campsite. Even without the lights flashing, it was hard for Winnie to keep up, and she was glad the ride was over.

"We're heading into a primitive part of Yellowstone, and we might have to go into a bear management area. Stay with me and you'll be fine, but it might be dangerous for Patches to come along. If he can stay cool enough in the RV, he'll be better off there."

Winnie scratched Patches's head. "He'll be fine in the RV. The air conditioner will automatically come on if it starts getting hot, and I'll make sure he's fed and has plenty of water. I'll need a couple of minutes to get everything ready."

"No problem. I'll run over to the store and pick a few things up."

Jen came back fifteen minutes later with a bag full of water bottles and snacks. "I was hungry and I thought you might be too." She offered a granola bar.

"Thanks." Winnie tore the wrapper open and took a bite.

"We'll start with a site not too far from here. The road is

going to get pretty rough. The pavement ends just after the turnoff, and the access road isn't well maintained. Your Mini would have hit the bottom in the ruts. Hopefully, you don't get car sick."

"I'll be fine. If I need to, I can roll down the window and stick my head out like Patches does."

"Good. We're actually going to leave Yellowstone and enter the Shoshone National Forest. I don't know if Anita would have ventured out this far, but it does have an area that fits her notebook, and I thought it would be good to check it out while we're here. I've been wondering, though, why she didn't take any pictures of the people she ran into. She's got some landscape pictures, but no people."

"I wondered that, too. Maybe it just happened too fast."

The route followed U.S. Highways 14 and 20 around Yellowstone Lake, heading east. Before long they exited the park and entered Shoshone National Forest. The highway continued on to Cody, Wyoming, but Winnie and Jen left the highway after only a few miles, turning right onto an unmarked road. A sign loomed in front of them, warning they were on an unimproved road and could enter by permit only. An unlocked gate blocked their path. Jen got out and pushed the gate open, and the two continued on.

Almost immediately after leaving the pavement, Jen's car started bouncing around from the potholes and ruts. She had to slow down to about twenty miles per hour to minimize the jarring, but there was no avoiding most of the dips and bumps.

"I can see why this road is unmarked." Winnie's knuckles were white against the armrest. "What do you need a permit for?"

"The forest service allows some controlled logging. There are also some researchers that use the road to study animal migrations. But the sign and the gate are mostly to keep people out."

"If the sign didn't make me turn around, this road surely would have. How far do we go in?"

Jen laughed. "These roads take some getting used to. We'll go about ten miles, then it's a short walk. We're actually catching up to a trail. Very few people go on it, which is why I don't think Anita ventured out here, but this road does lead to some caves. There's also an abandoned mine shaft here, too."

Thirty minutes later, they got out of the car, both taking their time to stretch and work out the kinks that developed along the bumpy route. Winnie was happy to be walking around, and she was already dreading the trip back. After some water and another granola bar, Jen pointed them in the right direction.

"The trail picks up just over this clump of trees. This road used to come all the way to the mine, but after it closed, the road was altered to end sooner, then trees were planted."

"You can't tell the road ever went farther," Winnie said. "How'd you know about this place?"

"I've had to come out here a few times for training. This is one of the biggest mines around, so it made for good search and rescue exercises. We had experts examine the mine and tell us we could safely go fifty feet inside. Believe me, that was plenty far."

Winnie shuddered. "I bet. I'm getting woozy just thinking about it. When was the mine in operation?"

"I don't know. It hasn't been used in decades, but the last time I was here I could tell people had been inside it. Probably kids, since there were beer bottles everywhere."

They picked up the trail, and Jen led the way. It was an old wagon trail, making it wide with not too many sharp turns. As they walked along, they continued to talk, making noise to alert animals to their presence.

"The best way to keep yourself out of a dangerous encounter with animals is to let them know you're here. Most animals want nothing to do with humans, so they leave the area when they hear us. But if we startle them, they react, and their reactions can be unpredictable. Some people wear bells that jingle when they walk, called bear bells. They're great as a gimmick, but they're not loud enough and they don't sound like a human, so they're not very effective."

Winnie looked over at Jen. She was quite a few years younger than Winnie, but she carried herself like a woman who'd experienced a lot and come out on top. She was confident and strong. Someone you'd want to turn to when things got tough. Winnie wished she could have been more like Jen when she was younger. Her marriage left her feeling weak and insecure, and breaking free from that was the start of her recovery.

They came into a clearing, and the remnants of a mine came into view. Winnie expected to see a big structure held up by wooden beams, with lots of mining equipment scattered around. Instead, the area looked barren, with no equipment, and the mine shaft looked like the entrance to a small cave, with maybe a four-foot height and a two-foot width. She could hear a stream running by, but she couldn't see it.

Jen seemed to read Winnie's expression. "It used to look a lot different when it was in operation. There are some pictures in the archives. I think you can find them online. They built a channel to divert water over here for panning. The pictures showed equipment scattered about and about a dozen men. They used this natural cave as the mine's entrance. No one knows why they didn't make the opening bigger. We've speculated they were concerned the opening would collapse, but it's doubtful it would have."

They walked up to the cave, looking for any signs that someone had been there recently. The sounds of the rushing stream grew louder, and Winnie could make out its outline.

The cave seemed spooky to Winnie, and she shuddered as she approached. She hoped Jen didn't suggest they go inside.

Jen was busy looking around, examining the area. "This isn't our spot. No one's been here for a while. I thought this would be a dead end, but I wanted to check it out just to be sure. Ready to get back to the car?"

Winnie didn't need to be asked twice, turning and quickly making her way back.

Jen had to hurry to catch up. "I'm sorry if that made you uncomfortable."

"Was it that obvious? I was hoping I hid it better."

"Your body language was screaming 'get me out of here.' I can drop you off at your camper and check out the other site I had in mind."

"Absolutely not. I just got a little unnerved. I got lost in a cave once. I was a kid, and I ran ahead inside, despite my parents' screams for me to stop. It didn't take long before it was pitch black. I turned to leave, but I couldn't see a thing. I started crying and screaming, and soon I saw flashlights bouncing along as my parents came looking for me, but it left a lasting impression. I haven't gone into a cave since. Even going through tunnels in a car gives me the heebie-jeebies."

"I understand." Jen offered a reassuring pat on the back. "I wouldn't have gone more than a few feet into the cave, but, for the next ones, we'll stay outside. Okay?"

"Thanks. I should have gotten over this phobia by now. I mean, I was six when it happened." Winnie shuddered as she thought about being in the cave.

"Some things stay with us a lifetime. You shouldn't be too hard on yourself. We all have things that bother us. Of the two of us, Sally is a much stronger person. I'll deny I ever said it because I'm supposed to be the tough ranger. And maybe I am physically stronger, but she's stronger every other way."

"It's great you two are so close," Winnie said. "You make a great pair."

"Yeah, I got lucky. How about you? Ready to find Mr. Right?"

Winnie laughed. "I'd probably settle for Mr. Okay. Seriously, I'd rather go into one of these caves than start dating again, at least for a while. I guess I'm on my own version of *Eat Pray Love*, minus the love part and heavy on the eat part. For now."

The two made their way back to the car, and Winnie grabbed another granola bar.

"See what I mean?" Winnie said. "I should call my adventure *Eat Pray Eat*."

"Well," Jen grabbed a water bottle, "at least you didn't give up on the love part. Maybe you'll find another intrepid traveler out there."

"Could be. But he *Must Love Dogs*. Hey! That's the second book I brought up. I'm on a roll."

Jen shook her head as the two got in the car and began the torturous ride back to Yellowstone. The road was just as bad going out as coming in, and Winnie said a silent prayer of thanks when they turned onto solid pavement. As soon as they cleared the first bend, Jen's cell phone started chiming with missed messages. She pulled over to flip through them.

"Sorry, Winnie," Jen pulled back onto the road. "I'll have to drop you off. Something's come up that I need to take care of. Can we do this tomorrow?"

"Sure. Is everything okay?"

"Yeah, it's fine. It has nothing to do with this case. I just have to assist another ranger. Can we say nine tomorrow morning?"

Jen dropped Winnie at her RV, said goodbye, and sped off with lights flashing and siren blaring. Winnie wondered what had happened, but she was glad to be done riding for the day, and when she opened the door, she forgot about everything.

Patches was there to greet her, and he had his leash in his mouth, wagging his tail furiously.

"Okay, buddy. I could use a walk myself."

The two went for a short walk then played a game of tug-of-war at the campsite, which ended with Winnie on the ground, pulling Patches, as the two wrestled. Winnie got up and checked her watch. She was afraid she'd missed another appointment, but it was only five thirty.

"Time to get ready to go, Patchy."

Winnie filled Patches's water dish then went to take a shower. She was grateful the site had hookups and she didn't have to stick to a two-minute, get wet-get soapy-get rinsed routine. Her water heater only had six gallons, so she couldn't lollygag, but it was enough to feel a little pampered.

It was going to be a cool evening, so Winnie put on a pair of jeans, a denim shirt, and a green fleece jacket. She took food and water dishes, along with a doggie sweater with the University of Wisconsin emblem and Bucky Beaver mascot on either side, then left for Cal and Reggie's RV.

As Winnie approached, She expected to hear laughter and maybe some music. Instead, she heard hushed voices, and it didn't sound happy. Winnie wondered if she should turn around when Reggie spotted her and came over.

"Did you forget something?"

"No. You seemed to be having a private conversation, and I didn't want to intrude."

"Oh, yeah, not much of a party, I guess. This morning we received a call that Cal's aunt died. We were talking about it with the Thurmans."

"I'm so sorry. I'll leave and come back another time. Please give Cal my condolences."

"No, Winnie. Please stay. Cal's aunt was the life of any party, and she would have wanted us to celebrate her life and have a toast for her."

Reggie took Winnie's arm and brought her over to the rest of the group. Cal's eyes softened when he saw Patches saunter over, wagging his tail.

"We meet again." Cal bent down to scratch Patches's ears.

Reggie brought Winnie over to the camp seat next to her. A fire was crackling in the fire ring, and the group was gathered around. Patches sat next to Winnie. He was wary of fire and stayed close to her.

"I'm sorry to hear about your aunt, Cal. It's difficult to lose someone, especially when you're traveling."

"Thanks, Winnie. At ninety-three, she lived a long life, but she was still active. At least mentally. She was fighting a losing battle with cancer, but we thought she'd be around for a while longer. I guess you never really know when your time's up."

Winnie nodded. "What are your plans?"

"Tonight, we're going to mourn a little but then celebrate. She was the one that convinced us to take this trip. 'You two need to see the world while you still can,' she told us. She was always upbeat, even when the cancer or the treatments got her down. A truly remarkable woman." Cal wiped his eyes and took Reggie's hand.

"Most of the arrangements were already made. She made sure of that. Reggie and I will fly out tomorrow. We found a place where we can store the RV, and we'll leave our car at the Jackson Hole airport. We'll probably be gone a week, then we'll come back and continue our trip. Aunt Edith would have wanted us to do that."

Cal picked up his drink and smiled. "But tonight, we remember her, and we celebrate her and friends, new and old."

Reggie opened the cooler next to Cal and pointed to Winnie. "Beer, wine, or something a little stronger?"

"It seems like a good night for a beer."

"Beer it is." Reggie rummaged around and pulled out a purple-colored can. "We picked these up at the Snake River

Brewery in Jackson on our way up. I really like the flavor, and I think you will, too."

Winnie looked at the label of the Jenny Lake Lager as she pulled the tab. "I read about Jenny Lake. It's over in Grand Teton National Park. I hear the hike is fabulous. Since it's so close, I'm planning to go there after I leave here."

"The hike is fabulous," Reggie said. "The whole park is wonderful. But I'd like you to consider changing your itinerary a bit. We're planning on going to Glacier National Park when we get back from Texas, and I'd love for you to join us."

"*We'd* love for you to join us," Cal chimed in. "Plus, the Thurmans are going back home tomorrow, so we won't have a traveling partner. I know that sounds selfish, but it's so much more fun traveling with friends. We've only known each other for a short while, but I consider you a friend."

"I'll have to think about it, but it does sound fun."

"That's all I can ask," Reggie said. "We won't be hitched at the hip, but it would be nice to have another gal around, and you can really get into the whole Drove There, Did That experience."

Cal started the grill and Reggie pulled corn out of a pot of water, wrapped each ear in aluminum foil, and placed them on the fire. The water hissed as the corn met the flames, and Cal lined the grill with burgers and hot dogs. Reggie went inside and brought back a bowl of potato salad. Then she broke a hot dog into bits and placed it in Patches's food dish. Winnie poured water into his water bowl and added a little dog food to the hot dog. The burgers were sizzling as Cal flipped them over, and Reggie ushered the group over to a picnic table.

Winnie took a bite of the potato salad as she waited for the burgers to arrive. "This is wonderful."

"Thanks." Reggie smiled. "My mom taught me how to make it."

With the food on the table, the group dug in. The conversations were replaced by mmm's as they enjoyed their food. After dinner, they returned to the fire, and Cal added a few logs to it, fanning the flames until the fire was raging. Reggie brought out a plate of marshmallows, chocolate, and graham crackers, while Cal brought over some sticks.

"I thought we'd make s'mores for dessert," Reggie said.

Everyone loaded their sticks with marshmallows. Winnie kept hers out of the flame and rotated to heat the marshmallow evenly. When it looked done, she pulled the gooey treat off of the stick and placed it on a graham cracker, adding a piece of chocolate and another graham cracker on top. While Patches didn't like the fire, he was very attentive to Winnie's creation.

"Sorry, buddy, but this isn't good for you. It's not good for me, either, but, well..."

"Tell me about the soup kitchen," Winnie said between bites.

"I didn't have much when I was growing up. But I had the most important thing—a great family. We did okay, but we needed help. Heck, a lot of folks needed help and still do. But there really wasn't a place to go for it. That's what I want to do, open a place where all are welcome. It's not about religion, family composition, or what you look like. It's about need. And not just a soup kitchen. You know the adage 'Give a man a fish and you feed him for a day. Teach a man to fish and you feed him for a lifetime'? Well, that's my philosophy, too, so we're going to have a soup kitchen, where we give a man a fish and a community garden and a technology training center, where we teach them how to fish, so to speak. We're going to name it The Benedict Family Center. Saint Benedict is the patron saint of the homeless, and we couldn't think of a better guide than him."

"That's wonderful. When you get it up and running, I'd like to donate."

"Thanks, Winnie, but we have money. We don't need donations. I'm expecting you to volunteer."

"Me?"

"Yes, you. You're a writer and computer savvy, aren't you?"

"I suppose."

"Of course you are. And we're going to keep in touch, aren't we?"

"I hope so."

"Me, too. And while we won't need money to keep the center open, we need people. Smart ones like you."

"But I don't live in Sweetwater."

"True, but there's this thing called the internet. It makes a lot of things possible, like remote teaching. You can even help us by teaching other people how to teach. In fact, right now we're building a curriculum, so once the center is complete, we'll be ready. I've got some ideas, but I'd really like your opinion."

Winnie smiled. "I'd be glad to help in the planning. As far as teaching, let's see how that goes."

"Fair enough. After the funeral, I'll send you my ideas. Hopefully, we'll meet up in Glacier and I can go over them with you in person. If not, we'll do it over email."

The Thurmans stood and thanked Cal and Reggie for a lovely dinner and for being such good traveling partners. They wished them well over hugs, promised to stay in touch, and said goodbye. Winnie said goodbye, too, offering condolences again. She gave Reggie her business card with her phone number and email address.

It was nearly eight when Winnie got back to her RV. After getting Patches settled, she went over her copy of the notebook another time, looking for any clues that might lead them to where Anita found the cave or mine. If it was a cave or mine. The trouble was, no one really knew what she saw, and, without a good geographical location, trying to pinpoint a spot in a place the size of Yellowstone was nearly impossible.

Winnie needed a break from thinking about Anita and was putting her iPad away when the phone rang.

"Umm, hello?" Winnie tried to snap out of the fog she was in.

"Winnie, it's Martin. Did I wake you?"

"Hi, Martin. No, I was just thinking about Anita. It's late there. Is everything okay?"

"Yes, perfect here. I just took your mother home. She's a wonderful woman, but I suppose you already knew that. Anyway, I was wondering how you're doing with the notebook. Any progress on the notes I sent?"

Wonderful woman. Those wedding bells are getting louder.

"We've made some progress, but it's slow. It turns out Yellowstone is dotted with both caves and a few mines. We went to one spot today, but it wasn't where Anita had been. We're going to look at another tomorrow."

"Your mother worries, Winnie, and so do I. You should give her a call to let her know you're all right."

"I will. Tomorrow morning."

"Right then. I'm off to bed. Let me know if I can help."

"Sure thing, Martin. Thanks for the call."

After hanging up, Winnie began humming "Here Comes the Bride" while she played with Patches.

19

Winnie was packing for her day with Jen when the phone rang. A part of her was hoping it was Jen, calling their trip off. But it was only six thirty, and Winnie doubted Jen would call this early. She looked at the caller ID. *Crap*. It was her mother. Winnie liked her mother and enjoyed spending time with her, but sometimes she was a little bossy.

"Winona," her mother began.

"Really, Mom, Winona? It's Winnie. And it's early." Winnie shouldn't have snapped, but she just couldn't help herself. It was too early, and Winnie was still half asleep.

"Oh," Sabrina said. "I'm sorry. I forgot about the time difference. But you seem to have forgotten our deal about calling every few days, and I get worried. And yes, I know you like being called Winnie. Winona is the name I use for you when I'm upset. I'm sorry about that, too. You're a grown woman, and I'll try to remember to treat you that way. But you're still my little daughter and always will be."

"What about Lexi? She's your little daughter."

Lexi Clemens was Winnie's younger sister. Her name was really Electra, but everyone called her Lexi. Winnie felt Lexi was more like Mary Poppins—practically perfect in every way. Doctor, mother to a boy and girl, wonderful husband, nice home in her mother's neighborhood, Lexi was the anti-Winnie.

"I know Lexi's my daughter. But I see her almost every day. And I babysit Jake and Emma twice a week. Martin and I were just over there for a cookout. I wish you were still around so you could have gone, too. Everything would be better."

"Maybe someday, Mom, but right now I'm where I belong." *Am I really?*

"Anyway, dear, I just called to see how you are. Everything okay? How's Patches? I miss him, too. And so do Jake and Emma. They keep asking about 'funny' Aunt Winnie and Patchy."

"I miss everyone there. I wish I could've made it to the cookout, but how about if we Skype soon? I bet Jake and Emma are getting big."

Sabrina huffed in the background. "Skype. I suppose it will have to do."

Mom really has this guilt thing down. "Mom, I need to go. Patches needs to be walked."

"Fine, dear. I'll talk to you later. Just remember to call—"

Winnie clicked off a little too soon, cutting her mom off. She was sure she'd hear about that later, but Patches really did need to go out, so the two of them went for a long walk. Winnie hated being compared to her sister. Her younger sister. But her mom made it a daily event, or at least it seemed that way. A family practice doctor, Electra had a doting husband, handsome and a big-shot corporate executive. Lexi's kids seemed to have inherited the perfect gene, too. They were never a lick of trouble, and Winnie couldn't remember a time when she heard anyone raise their voice at either of them.

Electra's only complaint in life was her name. She never liked being called Electra. Instead, she preferred Lexi, or even Lex, as her husband called her. Yep, it didn't get any better than Lexi. Winnie, by comparison, was a mess. At least in her mother's eyes. Divorced, no kids, and living "out of a trailer," as her mother called it. Oh, and, of course, no steady job.

"Freelancing isn't a real job," her mother insisted when Winnie announced she'd quit the paper.

"What is it, then?"

"A hobby," her mother snapped back. "You're too old to change careers. You need something more stable."

"I'm not changing careers. I'm still writing, I'm just changing how I get paid for it. Besides, I can support myself, so what's the problem?"

Her mother sighed. "I just worry about you, dear. I want you to be happy."

A tug of the leash brought Winnie back to reality. Patches had a way of grounding Winnie. He seemed to know when she was anxious and helped her through it. She pushed the thoughts from her mind and focused on what was really important—the fresh air, beautiful surroundings, and love. Even if the love was from a four-legged kind.

Plus cake. You have to have cake.

By the time they got back and had breakfast, Jen pulled up to the RV.

"Morning, Jen." Winnie shut the motor home's door.

"Good morning. Are you ready for another ride? This one shouldn't be quite as bad."

"That's good. The last road was horrible. My butt's still sore."

"Well, this one won't be great, either, but it'll be shorter and hopefully a little smoother." Jen laughed. "You want to bring a pillow for your sore butt?"

Winnie gave her a smirk and shook her head, and the two took off, heading north.

"What happened yesterday that you needed to leave so quickly for?" Winnie asked.

"Oh, there was a fight over in Grant Village. They were arguing about a parking place, and it escalated to fists. Both of them got a few good punches in, by the looks of their faces. By the time I got there, the ranger had them separated and the fight was over, so I took one of them with me and processed him. He was drunk and kept trying to hit on me on the way to the station. I kept telling him to shut up, but he just rambled on. I'm grateful he didn't throw up or I would have spent the night cleaning my car."

Winnie glanced in the back seat, grimacing at the thought of transporting a drunk. Especially one that was just in a fight, probably bleeding. Then she glanced over at Jen. She really was one tough cookie, and Winnie wished she could be that strong.

But I'm getting there. Stronger every day. "I could never do what you do, Jennifer."

"Sure you could. Most days are pretty boring. I spend a lot of time keeping traffic flowing. The times I need to arrest someone are few and far between. I've been with you long enough to see how tough you are, Winnie. You don't back down. Well, except when there's a cave involved. Or, apparently, a bumpy ride."

Winnie looked over to see Jen grinning from ear to ear. It had been a while since she had anyone to joke around with, and it made her happy she had a new friend. She really liked Jen and Sally and would miss them when she left. That was one of her goals in this RV adventure—to make new friends along the way. People she could call on and visit, not just "Facebook friends" that shared pictures of food or things Winnie knew nothing about.

Jen was a friend. Sally, too, and Winnie hoped they would keep in touch.

"Hold on, here we go," Jen said as they left the paved road, turning onto a service road. She was right. This road wasn't as bad as the one they were on yesterday, but it still had plenty of potholes, and the car bounced along, tossing both occupants as they went.

They were more out in the open on this road, and Winnie was happy she could look around to distract her from the jarring. A mile later, Jen slowed down then stopped, getting out to check a fence leading to another road. When she came back, she didn't look happy, and she got on her radio.

"Just as I thought," Jen said when she finished talking to someone at her office. "This road's off limits to anyone but park personnel, and this gate is supposed to be kept locked at all times. There's no record of anyone being out here recently, so somebody that wasn't supposed to be here went through the gate."

"Maybe someone forgot." Winnie forgot things all the time, so it wasn't hard to believe this was a simple mistake.

"No," Jen said. "The lock's not even here anymore. Someone must have cut it off and taken it with them. Plus, there are checks we go through anytime we enter this area."

"Why?" Winnie's eyes got wider. "Is this place dangerous?"

"A little. The gate is locked for two reasons. It leads to an area where we take roadkill and other dead animals we find in the park. Bears, wolves, and other animals come to that area to feed off the carcasses. With animals and food, the area becomes dangerous, so we keep it closed. The second reason is the caves. This gate is the entrance to both." Jen pointed up at the road. "There's a feeding area on the right and caves on the left. We're going left."

"Wait. You feed the animals in Yellowstone? Don't they just forage for their food?"

"We don't really feed them. We move the dead animals to a few spots we know carnivores go. That keeps the animals from feeding on the side of the road, so it helps them, and it gets rid of the dead animals. We don't want anyone near the animals when they're feeding. If they feel their food source is threatened, they will attack."

Jen called in that she was entering the area, asking for backup to assist. Thirty minutes later, another car pulled up. Winnie looked over, expecting to see another car like Jen's. But what pulled next to them was a smaller version of a monster truck. It stood at least two feet taller than the car Winnie was in, with huge tires that looked like they could plow through anything. The tires seemed taller than her Mini, and Winnie could picture needing a ladder to climb inside. Mud covered the body and the side windows, blocking Winnie's view of the occupants. She couldn't see them, but they must be real cowboys.

"We're here, Jenny," the driver of the other car called out. "And we brought another lock with us. Boss said try not to lose this one."

"Ha Ha, Charlie." Jen smirked. "We're going to head out to the caves and have a look around. Can you take a drive over to the feeding area and then meet us at the caves? I want to make sure nobody broke in to take pictures of bears feeding."

"It wouldn't be the first time," Charlie called out. "We'll be up at the caves soon. Be careful."

"Roger that. You, too."

Winnie watched as the truck sped off, kicking up a cloud of dust.

Jen shook her head. "Those two love these roads. They're great rangers, but when it comes to off-roading and driving that thing around, they jump at the chance. Shall we? We'll take a more civilized driving approach."

"Do you think it's safe?"

"We'll be fine. The feeding area is only a mile or so from here, and they should be back in just a couple of minutes."

Winnie nodded but didn't say anything. *Stronger every day? I guess it's time to show it.*

20

It didn't take long for Winnie and Jen to reach the caves. They both got out and looked around, but thankfully no one was there. Instead, they found lots of tire tracks and trash. A short distance away, a couple pieces of equipment stood next to a small stream.

"Someone's been making a regular visit here." Jen walked over to the equipment. "This stuff is in good shape. It looks like it's been used recently."

"What is it?"

"Mining equipment. The long device going into the water is called a sluice. My guess is they dug the stuff out of the mine and brought it over in these buckets to the stream. They use the pump to force water up and across the sluice. The water and the particles in the bucket mix. The big rocks get caught in the top and the finer particles travel with the water down the chute. Gold and other particles get trapped in the chute's ridges, and the water flows back to the stream. Once that's done, they just pick out the gold."

Winnie looked at the chute and noticed a couple of tiny

flecks of gold. “They dig through all this stuff for a few bits of gold? I can’t believe it’s worth it.”

“It adds up after a while. And sometimes, when you’re really lucky, you can get a bigger nugget. The mine must be producing enough or they wouldn’t waste their time or spend money on gas and equipment.”

“Don’t they need a permit or something to do that?”

“To do it legally, yes. But it wouldn’t be granted. Mining in Yellowstone is illegal. No exceptions. Whoever these people are, they’re not here legally, and if I had to guess, I’d say this is where Anita saw them.”

Winnie thought about that for a moment. Jen was probably right, but something didn’t make sense. “But Anita said she was on a trail. Do you have trails out here close to where you feed the animals?”

“No. The nearest trail is several miles away. Anita must have gotten lost and misjudged how far she strayed from the trail. We don’t come out to this area often—maybe every month or so, and usually only to the feeding drop-off. There are other areas we bring dead animals to more frequently. That’s why nobody noticed the lock was gone until now.”

Jen walked back to her car and came back with the photos from Anita’s flash drive. “Come on. Let’s look around and see if these fit.”

Before they could get far, they heard a car approach. Jen placed her hand on her sidearm while Winnie stood in silence, eyes wide open, staring at the dust trail being thrown up as it approached. Both breathed a sigh of relief at seeing the other rangers.

“Anything?” The ranger asked as he got out of his truck.

“Mining equipment. I think this is the spot.”

“They left the equipment out in the open? They’re either bold or stupid.”

“Or in a hurry,” Jen said. “My guess is they left after the incident with Anita and haven't been back. I noticed drag marks on the ground from the sluice to the cave, so I think they were probably dragging it in and out every day. But I doubt they were trying to hide their tire tracks, so they didn't bother to disguise their operations much. I didn't notice it on the way in, but if we look for it, I think we can find a spot where a lookout sat, watching to see whether any unexpected visitors showed up. By the tire tracks, there was an ATV in the area, so maybe they used it for a quick getaway. We need to get some pictures of this as soon as we can. Jason, stick with me and we'll look around. Charlie, can you go back and get some lights and another camera? We'll take a walk and compare this to the photos, but I'm confident we have the spot. When you get back, we'll check out the mine. You two okay with that?"

"You're the boss." Charlie got back in his truck. "Be back before you know it."

Another cloud of dust kicked up as Charlie left, and Winnie heard a shout of "yee-haw" in the distance. While the rangers examined the area, Winnie took out her phone and snapped pictures of everything.

"You can't take pictures of a suspected crime scene," Jason shouted over to Winnie.

"It's all right, Jay," Jen said. "She's working with me on this case. We couldn't have gotten this far without her help. And she knows not to post them."

Jen smiled and gave Winnie a wink.

"Fine," Jason said. "Just don't touch anything."

Jason went around the perimeter, looking for anything out of the ordinary, while Winnie and Jen got a closer look at the mining equipment.

"Jason seems a bit bossy," Winnie said when he was out of earshot.

Jen laughed. "You must have missed the way he looked at you. He's actually a really nice guy, just shy. I think he likes you."

"Wow. Acting up because he likes me. It's like fifth grade all over again."

"Yeah, kinda. But don't be too harsh. You could miss out on something you didn't expect."

Winnie looked over and crinkled her brow but didn't say anything. Jason was cute, in a military sort of way. His crew cut and squared jaw gave him a rugged, outdoorsy look, and his dark hair contrasted with his fair complexion nicely. He looked good in a uniform. Winnie watched him search the area. A little bit of a beer belly, but his broad shoulders more than made up for it. And there was a fire in his eyes. But was that fire passion, playfulness, or anger?

"This mining equipment looks pretty new." Jen snapped Winnie back to reality. "There's not much wear on it." She took pictures of the serial numbers and manufacturer tags. "I'll contact the manufacturer. Maybe we'll get lucky and find out who they sold it to."

Winnie wiped her finger inside a bucket. "Everything looks caked on and dry. It doesn't look like they've used this in a few days."

Jason wandered back to them. His clothes were dusty, and Winnie noticed a strange expression on his face. He looked away when he saw her. She couldn't tell if he was flustered or nervous. Or if that was just how he was.

Jen looked at Jason. "You okay?"

"Fine. Just slipped." He dusted off his clothes and tried to look casual, but he seemed nervous about something.

Winnie wasn't sure if she believed him, but when Jen nodded and got back to examining the sluice, she let it go.

Maybe this IS like fifth grade. The thought made Winnie giggle, but she stifled it and no one seemed to notice.

After Jen finished photographing the mining equipment,

she pointed to the cave. "Jason and I are going in there to check it out."

Winnie's eyes went wide. "Shouldn't you wait for Charlie? That's what you said, and there's strength in numbers."

"I just want to get a quick look to see what we're getting into. It would probably be better if you wait in the car while we're in there. Jason will give you his radio in case you need anything."

Jen nodded at Jason, who unclipped his radio and handed it to Winnie. Jason's face flushed as their hands touched.

Winnie looked at the car, then the cave, before putting her hands up, refusing the radio. "I'll go with you."

"Are you sure?" Jen asked. "You don't have to. You'll be perfectly safe in the car."

"I'm sure. I'm better off staying with the both of you."

Jen retrieved a flashlight from the car. She looked at Winnie. "Stay close."

"No problem there." Winnie followed the two rangers, taking one small step at a time. Soon—too soon—she was at the entrance.

Winnie stuck her head inside. The cave smelled musty, but with a residual hint of exhaust fumes. And it was dark. Very dark. She looked back longingly then stepped inside.

The cave opening was big enough that Winnie could walk upright. As she watched Jen's flashlight bob farther inside, Winnie saw the cave shrink rapidly.

She froze.

"Winnie," Jen called out. "You stay there and listen for anything outside. Call out if you see or hear anything. Okay?"

"Okay," a meek voice came back. Winnie could see the flashlight come closer, followed by Jen.

"Hey," Jen put her arms around Winnie and gave her a hug. "Are you okay? This must be difficult."

Winnie nodded, her lower lip trembling. "Sorry. I guess this bothers me more than I thought."

"Nothing to be sorry about. Do you want to sit in the car?"

"No. I'm fine here. It's just when I saw how narrow the cave got it brought back some unpleasant memories."

"Just stay where you're comfortable. You'll be fine. I promise."

Jen smiled as she let go of Winnie. "Besides, I don't have enough friends to lose one."

That brought a smile to Winnie, too.

As Jen retreated deeper into the cave, Winnie took another tentative step and another. After a couple of minutes, she stood about five feet inside the entrance. She could still look out and see daylight, which helped calm her nerves. And Winnie occasionally got hints of fresh air, but the damp cave was doing its best to convert all the air to a musty, dreary smell.

What's taking them so long? "Hello?" Winnie called out, almost in a whisper.

Silence. She cursed herself for not taking the radio when offered.

Her heart was thumping, and Winnie wished she had Patches there to comfort her. Just the thought of him seemed to help, and Winnie started to relax, thinking about how excited he'd be to be here, exploring. She tried to take a deep breath, but the dank air made her cough.

Winnie was about to call out again when she heard something. She couldn't tell where it was coming from, so she took a step toward the entrance and listened, turning her head to try to localize the sound. She looked back inside the cave, hoping to see Jen's flashlight, but it was dark. And quiet. And musty.

Another step and Winnie could tell the sound was coming from outside. It sounded like a whine from a chainsaw, only more powerful. Another step. The noise was still there.

Winnie took a final step and was at the entrance. The wind picked up, and she couldn't hear the noise anymore. She took a deep breath, enjoying the fresh air until the wind shifted and the whine was back. This time it was much louder and getting closer.

Winnie stuck her head back inside the cave. "Jen!" Winnie screamed. "Someone's coming."

When Winnie didn't get a reply, she took two steps back into the cave to hide herself. She started shivering, but not from the cold.

The whine came closer.

"Jen," Winnie shouted again.

This time Winnie was rewarded with the sound of footsteps and the flashlight bobbing. "Are you all right, Winnie?"

Winnie pointed outside.

"I hear it," Jen said. "Wait here."

Jen and Jason drew their weapons and peered outside the cave. Winnie couldn't see anything, but the whine was definitely getting closer.

"Cover me," Jen said to Jason as she stepped out.

Winnie leaned out, squinting as her eyes tried to adjust from the darkness of the cave. Jen and Jason had disappeared, so she carefully stepped out. In the open air, she could locate the direction of the sound and spun to her right as a deep blue all-terrain vehicle came into sight, kicking up dust as it made a tight turn around a large sagebrush. There were two occupants, both wearing helmets. They both looked small and lanky, but Winnie couldn't tell with any certainty.

"Stop!" Jen shouted.

Winnie watched Jen chase after the ATV. The driver took another tight turn and the passenger must have seen Jen, because Winnie saw him tug on the driver's sleeve and point in Jen's direction.

The ATV came to a sudden halt.

"Stop, park rangers." Jen leveled her pistol in their direction as she headed toward them.

The passenger of the ATV put his hands up, but the driver

hit the gas and turned. The sudden maneuver caused the passenger to fall off as the driver sped away.

"Stay on the ground." Jen raced toward him. "Put your hands behind your back."

"Don't shoot," the passenger said, but Jen had already swapped her pistol for a Taser.

Winnie watched Jason running off, trying to get to the ATV, which slowed as it ran over a low bush. She didn't know if Jen needed help or not, but Winnie wasn't going to stand by while Jen might be in danger. Winnie ran toward Jen, who was still wrestling with the suspect. Without knowing what else to do, Winnie threw herself on the passenger's legs, receiving a hard kick in the stomach as she got down. But with the suspect's legs now pinned, Jen could secure his arms.

The passenger finally gave up, and Jen quickly got handcuffs around him and asked if he was hurt. The passenger shook his head.

"You can get off him now, Winnie. I appreciate the assistance."

Winnie got to her feet and rubbed her stomach where she was kicked.

Just then, Jason came running up. "Are you okay? I saw you take a nice kick when you got on his legs. That must have hurt."

Winnie smiled and nodded but kept a hand on her stomach.

"I called it in, boss," Jason said. "Maybe we'll get lucky and track that ATV down."

"Good." Jen pulled the passenger up.

The passenger's body style and movements looked strange for a man. Winnie took a step closer and flipped up his visor.

It wasn't a man. Winnie was surprised to see a tall girl staring back at her. She couldn't be older than eighteen.

Jen pointed. "I'm going to take your helmet off, okay?"

"Okay."

Jen tugged the helmet off, releasing the girl's long brunette hair as it plopped downward.

"What's your name?" Jen asked.

"Puddintane. Go ahead, ask me again."

"Winnie, we've got one here with a sense of humor. Thinks she's clever." Jen looked back at her prisoner. "I'm going to search you. Do you have anything sharp in your pockets?"

"Nope."

Jen did a quick search, taking out some money and a driver's license.

"Well, lookey here," Jen said. "This says your name's Shelly Quinn, age seventeen, from Cody, Wyoming. The picture looks like you, too."

"I'm seventeen. You can't touch me. I'll just get a ticket or a warning or something."

"Technically, you're a minor. Unfortunately for you, however, that doesn't give you a free pass. I'm sure when I explain everything, including your attitude, they'll treat you like an adult in this matter. You're in trouble, Ms. Quinn. So, are we done playing games or should we continue?"

The toughness seemed to deflate quickly, leaving a clearly shaken teenager. "I'm done. Look, I didn't mean any disrespect. We were just having some fun."

"Well, your fun is illegal in Yellowstone. And as soon as we find your friend, we'll confiscate the ATV. Now, if you want to help yourself, you'll help me. The more you help, the more I'll help. Got it?"

"Got it."

"I'm going to take the cuffs off, but don't make a run for it. My Taser will reach you before you get far."

"I won't run."

With her hands free, Shelly slipped off her jacket and tossed it next to her helmet and sat down. "What do you want to know?"

"For starters, who was the driver, and where does he live?"

Shelly hung her head. "Mark Connors. He lives near me in Cody. We came out for the day." She shook her head. "He's never going to talk to me again."

"He left you out here to fend for yourself. You shouldn't talk to *him* again. You're seventeen. Are you going to be a senior in the fall?"

"Not after this. My parents are going to kill me."

"Well," Jen chuckled, "they probably won't be pleased. But they kept you around this long, so I think you'll be safe. I'm going to take you over to our station at Old Faithful. We'll call your parents and they can come get you. This will give us some time to talk. I need to put the handcuffs back on for the ride, so please stand up and put your hands behind your back."

Shelly started to cry. "I didn't mean to do anything wrong," Shelly said between sobs. "But he asked me out and I thought it he liked me. Until he left me here."

"We'll talk on the way back. You'll be okay."

Jen put Shelly into her patrol car and shut the door.

"I'm going to take her in and see if she knows anything. Winnie, can you stay with Jason until backup arrives? He'll give you a ride home."

"Sure. What are you going to do with Shelly?"

"Her tough girl stance didn't last very long. She's pretty scared, so I thought I'd take her back and get her to calm down. Maybe she knows something about our miners, or maybe her friend does. After that, I think I might put her in a cell until her parents show up. Maybe she won't do another stupid kid thing for a while. But once her parents show up, I'll let her go with a warning."

Jen got into her vehicle and put the window down. "Thanks for being understanding, Winnie. I'll call you later."

"I really like her," Winnie said as the car pulled away.

"Me, too," Jason said. "She's tough as nails when she needs

to be, but she has a lot of understanding. A great balance for a ranger."

"What do we do now?" Winnie looked around. She wasn't too keen on being there any longer than she had to.

"Jen filled me in on the notebook. Let's look for the body Anita saw being dragged."

"But what if the miners come back before help arrives?"

Jason patted the pistol on his right hip. "This is a nine-millimeter Glock pistol with seventeen rounds. I've got two more clips, each with seventeen rounds. I can hold my own."

"That's great, but what would I do?"

Jason looked over and smiled. "Take cover and hope for the best."

21

Winnie and Jason scoured the area until they found a freshly disturbed mound of dirt. Someone had tried to wipe footprints away, but there was no mistaking the clump was man-made. Approximately the size of a person, Winnie stopped and said a prayer for whoever was under there. Jason marked the location with yellow tape and took the GPS coordinates from his phone. Then they went back to the mining equipment, where Winnie and Jason cataloged each piece, chatting away about their lives and experiences. Jason wasn't the obnoxious person Winnie originally thought. He was a nice guy, and Winnie wondered if something could come of their relationship.

After a long, stressful day, Winnie was glad to see her motor home. She was looking forward to taking Patches on a nice, long walk and relaxing with a big glass of wine. Maybe two.

"Thanks for the ride, Jason."

"Yes, ma'am." Jason smiled. "If you'd like someone to show you around, I'd be happy to."

Winnie's face warmed. It had been a long time since anyone

had paid much attention to her. At least *that* kind of attention. And she liked it.

"I was thinking of eating at the Lake Hotel tomorrow. I'd love company. If you're free."

"That sounds fantastic, I haven't been there in ages. I'll make the reservation for tomorrow. How about I pick you up at six?"

"It's a date." Winnie hardly believed she was going on a real date. "Here's my card with my cell phone number. Call me if anything comes up."

Jason called the number while Winnie was still in the car. When it rang, Jason hung up. "Now you've got my number, too, in case you need anything. I'm looking forward to tomorrow."

"Me too." Winnie got out. She waved goodbye to Jason as he pulled away, then turned and opened the door to her motor home. Patches came running forward, clearly happy to see her.

And so was her mother.

"Hello, dear." Her mom got up from the couch.

"Mom! What are you doing here?"

"Well, somebody has to keep you out of trouble. Besides, Martin was off at the last minute to some conference in Germany, and I thought it would be nice to see Yellowstone."

Sabrina Hackleshack stood and gave her daughter a long hug. "I missed you. I liked it better when you were living in Madison."

Winnie pulled out of the hug and took her mother's hands. "It's good to see you, too, Mom. But how did you get here? And why didn't you tell me when you called before?"

"I flew into Jackson Hole and took an Uber up here. And I wanted to surprise you. When I called, I was at the airport. I was hoping all those crazy announcements didn't tip you off."

Winnie was trying to make sense of it all. *A last-minute trip and then an Uber. Wait—did I hear that right?* "You took an Uber? You used to be afraid of busses because you didn't know the drivers, and now, you're getting in an Uber? What's gotten into you?"

"Nothing. But Martin swears by them, so I thought I'd give it a try."

Martin. Oh my. Someone's falling pretty hard. Winnie stared at her mother, unable to think of anything to say.

"I'm glad I remembered the spare key you gave me. Otherwise, I would have had to wait outside." Winnie must have had a strange expression because Sabrina frowned. "Aren't you glad I'm here, Winona? I could leave if I'm making you uncomfortable."

That snapped Winnie out of it. "Of course not, Mom. You have to understand this was a bit of a surprise, but I'm really glad you're here."

That brought a smile back to Sabrina.

"I need to take Patches for a walk. Would you like to come with us?"

"I took him for a walk about an hour ago. He certainly can tug on his leash."

Winnie looked over at Patches, who seemed relieved Winnie was back.

"Well, then, there's nothing left to do but to pour a couple of glasses of wine and relax. Want to sit outside? I can tell you about my day. And my date."

"Date? Why, Miss Winona Hackleshack, have you been holding out on me?"

Winnie chuckled as she opened the refrigerator. "I'll explain in a minute. But first, I need to think about what we're going to do for dinner."

"Don't be silly. We'll go out."

"I've been leaving Patches alone a lot lately. I was thinking of eating here. Let's get pizza. They make a good one at the Fishing Bridge General Store just down the road."

"Perfect. We can order in a few minutes. But first, tell me about this date."

"Wine first. Explain later."

After putting Patches on a leash and tying it to the RV, Winnie and her mom sat outside under the awning, enjoying the late afternoon. It was a sunny day, bright and cheerful. And it mirrored Winnie's mood.

Winnie took the first sip of the deep red elixir and closed her eyes, savoring the moment as the liquid warmed her throat. "There's really not much to tell about my date. I met another ranger today. His name is Jason. He seemed nice, and he offered to show me around, so we decided to go to dinner."

"When are you going?"

"Tomorrow." Winnie looked at her mom and frowned. "But you'll be here. I'll cancel. He'll understand."

"Nonsense. Patches and I will be fine. I picked up a couple of those mystery books you like to read before I left, so I'll have plenty to do. Tell me about Jason. I want details."

Winnie smiled. "He's tall, probably six-two. Rugged good looks. Tanned. And he has a great sense of humor. We talked on the way back from the mine, and I really felt comfortable with him."

Oops. Maybe she won't notice.

"What mine?"

Crap. "It's nothing. We were looking into Anita's death and the clues brought us to a couple of possible locations. The first one didn't pan out, but the second one looks like it might be the location Anita stumbled into that got her killed."

Her mother sighed. "I thought you were done with all of that, Winnie. Let the police handle it. I came all this way to be with you, not to get snarled in some murder investigation."

"But I am involved, Mom. Anita needed my help, and I tried to help her. I didn't know her for long, but that doesn't matter. I want to make sure her killer is caught."

Winnie told her mom the entire encounter, from taking Anita to dinner to finding the notebook in her car, Taggart, the mines, everything. When she was finished, her mom was silent for a long time.

"I understand, Winnie," Sabrina said finally. "I really do. Just promise me you'll be careful."

"Of course, Mom." Winnie gave her mom a big hug. "And it really is nice seeing you."

Patches was wagging his tail, and Winnie bent down to scratch between his ears. "It's nice to see you, too." She tossed him a treat.

Winnie smiled at the two of them. *My new normal, I guess. I'll take them. And Martin, too.*

"Time for pizza. I'm starved."

The three got into Winnie's Mini and took off for the short drive to the general store. Winnie and Sabrina took turns ordering while the other watched Patches. When Winnie came out, she was carrying two pizzas, a bottle of wine, and a bag full of dog treats.

"I've got some cheesecake in the refrigerator for dessert."

"Pizza, cheesecake, and wine," Sabrina said. "At least you've got the eating part of your vacation right."

Winnie's face burned. She *had* been overdoing it lately. And her pants might be a little tighter to prove it. "I'll make a salad, too. We can split a piece of cheesecake."

"I like that idea," Winnie's mother said.

When they reached the motor home, Winnie put out a table and the three enjoyed their meals outside. Plenty of people walked by, almost all of them waving or saying hello. She told her mom about Reggie and Cal and how they might meet up at some of the parks.

"That's great, Winnie. Traveling with friends would be much safer."

"So, Mom, I told you about Jason. Tell me about Martin."

Sabrina's eyes lit up at his name. "Martin and I are still getting to know each other. I like him—a lot—but we're so different. It's a bit like a swan dating a duck. Close but maybe not close enough. But for now, we're both having fun."

"I take it you're the swan?"

"Well, I'm certainly not the duck."

"Sorry," Winnie said. "I don't want to put you in a 'fowl' mood."

"Ha. Didn't you say something about cheesecake?"

Winnie was just about to get the cheesecake when a car pulled up. The windows were down and she heard Sally giving Jen a hard time.

Jen stepped out of the car. "Hi, Winnie. I'm sorry. I didn't know you had company. I guess we should have called first."

"Don't be silly. You're just in time for dessert. I'll be right back with cheesecake. This is my mom, Sabrina. Come and join us."

After introductions, Winnie got two more camp chairs and the four sat down. Sally brought a bag of dog treats and was now Patches's best friend.

After some small talk, Jen got to the real reason they came by. "So...Jason, huh? He's really nice."

Winnie smiled and bit her lower lip. "You heard about that already?"

"He called after he dropped you off, letting me know you were home safe. But he really called to tell me about your date. And ask for advice. He's nervous."

"Really?"

"Really. He likes you. And he hasn't been on a date in a while."

"What did you tell him?"

"I told him to be his usual charming self and the date would be over soon enough." Jen laughed. "Really, though, I just told him to be himself. He's one of the good ones. I told him you were a good one, too. So, both of you just go have fun."

"Thanks, Jen. What's happening with the mine?"

"All the mining equipment has been removed. They probably wore work gloves, so I doubt we'll get anything useable from it, but at least it's not there anymore. The body you found is on its way to the lab. The hands were pretty messed up, but hopefully forensics will be able to make an identification, determine the cause of death, and provide some clues as to why he was killed. Unfortunately, something like that usually takes a week or more."

"What about the mine?"

"It's been sealed, and a team from Cheyenne is coming up to work with our group. I doubt that there's much gold in the mine, but if there is, you'll have every prospector in the world trying to get rights to pan or dig."

"But it's a national park. They can't do that, can they?"

"If there's enough money involved, someone will find a way to get the permit. That's why I'm hoping there's not much there. Oh, we're trying to keep this quiet, so I'd appreciate it if neither of you would mention it to anyone. The less news the better, at least until we know what we're dealing with."

The rest of the evening was spent swapping stories, including some embarrassing ones about Winnie when she was younger. When it was time to say good night, Winnie walked Jen and Sally back to their car, while her mom stayed in the RV.

"Thanks for coming over. We really enjoyed it."

"I hope we didn't intrude. Your mom seems wonderful."

"She is. She drives me crazy sometimes, but I wouldn't have her any other way. She was there for me when my ex and I went through our mess. I guess she's always been there for me."

"She's a mom, and a good one." Jen gave Winnie a hug.

"Enjoy your date tomorrow. Hopefully I won't have to bother you with anything."

"You're no bother. Call anytime. Well, maybe not tomorrow night."

"Deal. But I'll call you the next day, and I'll want details. I'll bet he's a good kisser."

Winnie laughed and her cheeks warmed as she waved goodbye to Jen and Sally. "I feel like I'm in high school again," Winnie mused as she closed the door to her RV.

22

"Why did I agree to this date?" Winnie asked the mirror. She'd pulled a small chair into the bathroom and was trying different hair styles, frowning after each one. She still had twelve hours before Jason picked her up, but she didn't feel that was enough time. Not with her hair. "I look like Miss Frizzle after an electric shock."

"You look fine, dear." Sabrina walked past.

"Yeah, okay. I don't know what I'm doing going out on a date. Jason and I won't be seeing each other after I leave Yellowstone."

"It's a date, Winnie, not a life-long commitment. The only thing you need to do is have fun. Besides, what does it hurt to gain another friend?"

"You're right." *But it wouldn't hurt to have a little romance, either.*

"Of course I'm right. I'm your mother. Let's take Patches for a walk, have breakfast, and then I'll help you pick out an outfit to wear. Something that shows off your curves, and maybe a little cleavage."

"Mother!"

"If you've got it, dear, flaunt it. And you've still got it."

Winnie closed her eyes and counted to ten, letting out a deep breath. It was going to be a long day.

IT WAS a few minutes after six, and Sabrina had taken Patches for a long walk. Winnie was again standing in front of a mirror, frowning at the navy floral print dress she was wearing, turning to look at it from different angles. She might be showing off some curves, but there were a few bulges there, too. And not in the right places. Running her hands down her dress to smooth it out, Winnie heard a knock and froze.

Another quick glance in the mirror and she picked at her hair, sighing. "Why did I agree to do this?" But before her reflection could answer, another knock came, a little louder than the one before. Winnie tucked one last errant hair and went to the door.

Jason was standing there with a nervous smile. He was wearing a blue blazer, tan slacks, and loafers.

He cleans up pretty well for a monster-truck-driving cowboy. Winnie smiled as he handed her a bouquet of daisies. "Thanks. You look nice."

Jason chuckled. "I'm just a hick during the day. At night I'm a different man."

"I can see that. I like it. Not that I didn't like the look before, it's just that I, well I..." Winnie stopped her rambling and looked down. Her face heated, and she wanted nothing more than to turn and run back into her motor home, lock the door, and call it a night. Instead, she stood there, staring at her shoes. Then another pair of shoes came into view, and Winnie looked up to see Jason still smiling.

"Your dress is pretty. And so are you."

Winnie's face began to burn, but she was smiling broadly

when she looked up. "Thanks, and sorry. I'm just a little nervous."

"I don't blame you." Jason's eyes were wide open and playful. "I'm a scary guy."

Winnie bit her lip and smiled. "Let me put these in water."

She motioned for Jason to come in while she put the daisies in a vase.

He held out his hand. "Shall we go?"

Winnie took Jason's hand. It was warm and soft, and suddenly she felt safe. They walked to Jason's car, a Chevy Camaro, orange with white stripes.

"Nice ride," Winnie said as she slid her fingers along the side with her free hand. "Is this a sixty-nine?"

Jason looked over and nodded. "I'm impressed. It's the original paint colors, too. You know cars?"

"I know what I like." Winnie cocked her head and smiled.

Jason blushed and fumbled for his keys.

Hmm. Maybe I still do know how to flirt.

Winnie took a step and stumbled on a stone, catching herself before she hit the ground.

Okay. Maybe I'm a little rusty at this.

"It took me seven years to restore her. I found her in Yuma, Arizona. The low humidity kept the body in great shape, but I had to overhaul the engine and transmission. It's got a new paint job, new tires, and she runs like the day she left the factory.

"She? Does she have a name?"

"Maybe I'll call her Winnie." Jason smiled, tossing her the keys. "Want to drive?"

"Absolutely."

Winnie got into the driver's seat and looked at the floor. There were three pedals. She hadn't driven a manual transmission since her dad taught her when she was learning to drive. A long time ago. "Maybe you should drive. I haven't driven a stick in ages."

"That's OK. Give it a go. I'm sure you'll remember soon enough."

Winnie put the car in neutral and started the engine. She looked at the shift pattern on the knob, a standard H, with an extra leg for reverse. Pushing in the clutch, Winnie moved the shifter left and up, shifting into reverse. Or at least she tried to. Instead, the shifter shook as the gears ground. The sound was brief but horrific as Winnie put the lever back into neutral.

Jason looked over and smiled. "I did that a few times myself. Make sure the shifter is all the way over and up like this." Jason put his hand over Winnie's. "Push in the clutch and we'll try it again." Jason moved Winnie's hand over to reverse. "Okay, now let the clutch out nice and easy."

The car lurched and stalled. Something made a bumping sound in the trunk. Whatever it was shook the car a little as it settled.

"Sorry." Winnie pulled the keys out and handed them to Jason. "It's been a long time. I'll let you drive."

She started to get out of the car, but Jason took her hand.

"Nonsense. Unless you don't want to. But I think you should try it again."

"I'll try, but be warned, this could take a while. And what was that in the trunk? It sounded loud."

"Oh, it's nothing. Just an old duffel bag."

"Maybe we should check it to make sure nothing's damaged. I hope I didn't hurt your car." Winnie started to get out of the car, but Jason grabbed her hand.

"It's fine, Winnie. Really. Just some old stuff. I'll get it later."

Winnie noticed the strain in Jason's voice, but let it go. *First date jitters?*

She started the engine, put it into reverse, and let out the clutch. A little better this time because the car still lurched but didn't stall. After backing out, Winnie put the car into first gear and looked over at Jason. "Here goes."

The car stumbled its way forward but again didn't stall. Now came the challenge of shifting from first gear to second. She thought back to what her father taught her. She listened to the engine. Its roaring got louder the faster they went. When it sounded right, Winnie pushed in the clutch and pulled firmly on the shifter, making sure it was in position before releasing the clutch. The car shifted with a slight jerk, but much better, and Winnie breathed a sigh of relief.

"See? I knew you could do it."

Winnie looked over at Jason. His smile was warm and sincere, and Winnie smiled back. *Why couldn't I have met him twenty years ago?*

Winnie shifted into third, then fourth, her confidence in driving a manual transmission growing. Soon, they reached the Lake Hotel and parked. They approached the front door, and Jason opened it for Winnie as they stepped inside.

Winnie never expected any place in Yellowstone to look like this. The tables were covered with white linen tablecloths. Perfectly folded napkins were nestled next to gleaming silverware. Soft lighting and thick carpeting muted the conversations and the typical noises associated with a restaurant, and a view of the lake made the room look elegant. The chairs were simple but rich dark brown, which contrasted nicely with the white linen. Pleasant music was being played from a grand piano off to the side.

Much nicer than the pizza shack we ordered from yesterday.

They were taken to their table and Winnie could see Lake Yellowstone through the trees. "Wow. This place is even nicer than I expected. I love it."

Jason picked up the wine list. It was a couple of pages, and Jason thumbed through it before making his selection. "Can I order us some wine?"

"I'd like that."

When the server came, Jason ordered a bottle of Pinot Gris. After the server left, he explained the wine choice.

"Pinot Gris is a white wine with a grayish color. Gris means gray in French. This type of wine can be a little fruitier than other wines. Not overpowering, but you can definitely taste some pear and apple. I've had this wine before. I think you'll enjoy it."

"I'm impressed. All I know about wine is that I like it. Are you a wine critic on the side?"

"I do study wine, and I belong to a group called the Yellowstone Winos. When we get together, each of us brings a bottle of a new wine and we sample. It's fun. Sometimes we do it with beer instead, but we've run out of local breweries and most of us prefer wine anyway."

The server came back and poured a glass for Jason. Winnie watched as Jason swirled the wine, smelled it, and then took a taste. Nodding his approval, the server refilled Jason's glass and then poured a glass for Winnie. Winnie didn't know whether she should swirl it like Jason or just drink it. She was afraid she might swirl it right out of the glass, so she sat there for a minute, looking for a clue from him.

Jason looked over, smiled, and picked up his glass, stretching his arm. "To the start of a great night."

Winnie smiled and picked up her glass, lightly clanking it against Jason's.

The server came back to ask about appetizers. Jason didn't hesitate and ordered the duck and wild mushroom risotto. "I hope you don't mind me jumping in. The duck is fairly light, and, with the cream sauce, I thought it would be a good pair with the wine."

Winnie was used to ordering everything all at once, but the pace at this restaurant was much slower. She liked it. And she liked her companion. Winnie was already thinking about what might happen after dinner. It had been so long.

"So," Jason started, "are you retired, or do you work from your motor home?"

"I work as a freelance writer. I just got a new job, as a matter of fact. It's a corporate brochure. A little boring, but it pays the bills. It's not nearly as exciting as being a park ranger."

"It can be exciting. But it can be tedious at times. There's a lot of paperwork. It's not all riding around in a truck, but doing that makes up for the boredom."

The duck came and was delicious. It really did go well with the wine, and it was just enough to keep their appetite's ready for more. When it came time for entrees, Winnie ordered the steelhead trout, while Jason opted for the grilled quail. While they waited, they talked about their pasts and how they ended up in Yellowstone. Both steered clear of talking about Anita or the case. Winnie didn't want to tarnish the evening by bringing it up, and she suspected Jason didn't, either. The meals arrived and looked perfect. They ate and talked like old friends, and, before they realized it, the wine bottle was empty. The waiter offered to bring another, but they decided one bottle was enough. Winnie wanted a clear head for whatever might happen next.

The pacing of the meal meant neither one was rushed, and, by the time it came to dessert, they were both ready for more. More food, more conversation, and more flirting. They decided on coffees and split a fresh berry truffle. They lingered over dessert, and Winnie was listening to the piano in the background. The song selection seemed to be classic show tunes, and right now "As Time Goes By" from *Casablanca* was playing.

Absentmindedly, Winnie was humming the song and looked up to see Jason smiling at her.

"I love the old show tunes," Winnie said. "Why don't they make shows like that anymore?"

"I know what you mean. This music is great. It's a shame there's no dance floor."

Winnie laughed. "I haven't been dancing in ages. What with my two left feet and all."

"I doubt that. Maybe for our next date we should go into Gardiner. There are a few places with a dance floor. But be forewarned—it's country music."

"I'd like a next date." Winnie scooped up the last piece of truffle. "And I can do a basic line dance. All those fancy boot-slapping moves, though, I get lost in."

Now it was Jason's turn to laugh. "It's the spinning I can't do. I get dizzy."

The server arrived and placed the check in the center of the table. Jason grabbed it and put it next to him, setting a credit card on top. Winnie offered to split the bill, but Jason wouldn't hear of it.

"I'm old-fashioned." Jason smiled as the server took the credit card.

In a few minutes, Winnie and Jason were back in his Camaro. Jason was driving and Winnie leaned over the console, placing her arm around his. Jason gently placed his hand on Winnie's knee when he wasn't shifting, and a tingle zinged that she hadn't felt in ages. Her mind was galloping through all sorts of scenarios, the heat rising with each passing one, until Winnie realized that her mother was waiting for her back at the RV. That cooled her off quickly.

They both sat quietly, content to be together on the ride back. Winnie was hoping he would suggest a stop at his place and thought of suggesting it herself. It had been so long since she'd had a companion, and she found herself thinking about a long-term relationship. She hadn't expected to find someone during her adventure, but what if she did? She really liked Jason.

Winnie was jolted back to reality as Jason stopped suddenly.

Gripping Jason's arm tight, her eyes went wide when she spotted a bison standing in the road, staring at them. The bison's eyes reflected like a cat's, but the brown fur was difficult to spot in the darkness.

Jason pointed at the buffalo. "That's why you can't drive fast in Yellowstone. Especially at night."

He pulled over, put on his emergency flashers, and shut the engine off, leaving his headlights on. After a few minutes, the bison ambled off to the side and they were on their way.

"That was interesting," Winnie said as they got back up to speed.

"Happens all the time. Unfortunately, a lot of people don't follow the speed limits. A buffalo-car encounter usually doesn't bode well for either party."

"Where do you live?"

"I have a small apartment near Grant Village."

"That's convenient. Do you have a nice view?" *Like from your bedroom window, perhaps?*

"Mostly woods, but it's quiet, and I like it."

"Sounds nice." Winnie was a little deflated when she recognized the turnoff for the RV park. *A perfect gentleman. Too bad.*

Soon, too soon, Jason pulled up in front of Winnie's motor home.

"I had a wonderful time," Winnie said. "I'd like to see you again."

"I'd like that, too." Jason placed his hand on the small of her back, leaning in. Winnie leaned forward and the two shared a kiss. It was wonderful. Magical, even. She stayed close, hoping for a second one, but he pulled away.

"I've got some things I need to do." Jason opened his car door, moving around to open Winnie's. "Next time, we'll do some dancing. And more romancing. Promise."

Maybe it's just nerves. Winnie smiled and said good night.

She stood at the doorway as Jason got in his car, waved goodbye, and left.

I want romance. Now.

Winnie stood outside her front door, wondering what awaited her when she opened it. Would her mom be asleep? No, that would be too much to wish for. Winnie was hoping she wouldn't get hit with a barrage of questions as she pulled the latch. Instead, she found...nothing. Her mom didn't seem to be home.

"Mom?" Winnie called out.

Patches sauntered in, looking like he just woke up from a sound sleep.

"Some guard dog you are." Winnie scratched Patches's head.

After checking the bedroom, Winnie went outside, thinking her mom might be sitting with a group of campers. No luck.

"Maybe she went for a walk?" Winnie got back in the RV. She looked over and found a note on the table.

Winnie had to read the note several times to make sure it really said what she thought. Instead of a note from her mom, Winnie read this: Want to see your mom again? Bring us the gold you took and she'll be unharmed. If we don't get the gold, she'll be dead. AND DON'T EVEN THINK ABOUT CALLING THE POLICE. WE ARE WATCHING!

23

Winnie fell back into her chair. *Gold? They think I have the gold?* She called Jason's number, but it went to voice mail. After leaving a message, Winnie called Jennifer.

"Hi, Winnie," Jen said. "How was your—"

"My mom's been kidnapped."

"What? Kidnapped? Are you sure?"

Winnie sniffled, fighting back tears. "Yes, I'm sure. I'm reading the note they left. Whoever took her thinks I have their gold. They want the gold in exchange for my mom. The trouble is, I don't have it."

"Why on earth would they think you have their gold? Never mind. We can talk about it when I get there. I'll get a team assembled. I take it Jason's not there?"

"No. He dropped me off a little while ago. I tried to call him, but it went straight to voice mail."

"I'll try him, too, but reception is spotty, and his service doesn't work well at all at his apartment. Hang tight. I'll be there as soon as I can."

"Wait! They said no police."

"Trust me."

Winnie put the phone down and motioned for Patches to sit next to her. None of this made any sense. Why would someone think she had gold? She thought back to recent events. The notebook. Could there be something else in the notebook? Or could something still be missing?

Winnie put her head down on the couch, and Patches nestled up beside her. They both stayed there until Winnie heard a knock on the door.

"Winnie, it's Jennifer."

Winnie rushed to the door and found Jen with her arms extended. Two rangers she hadn't seen before were struggling to get out of a red Prius. Winnie fell into Jen's arms, and that was when the floodgates opened. She'd held back the tears as long as she could, but she was missing her mom.

"It's my fault," Winnie blurted between sobs. "If I hadn't left her alone, none of this would have happened."

Jen turned and told the two rangers to wait outside.

She patted Winnie's back. "It's not your fault. You know that. You're a good person trying to right a wrong. There's no fault in wanting to do that."

Winnie nodded and wiped her eyes.

Jen directed her to the couch and they both sat down. "Tell me everything you can think of."

Winnie cleared her throat. "You know my mom showed up yesterday unexpectedly. I was going to cancel my date with Jason, but she wanted me to go." Winnie sighed. "Why didn't I cancel my date? My mom would still be here."

"No, Winnie. My guess is both of you would be gone, which would have been worse. What else do you remember?"

"Nothing, really. My mom was out with Patches when I left for my date. When I came home, I couldn't find her. I looked around, checked outside, but nothing. When I came back inside, I saw the note. I called Jason, left a voice mail, and then I called you."

"Do you mind if we look around? We may find something that helps us locate your mom."

Winnie nodded absentmindedly, and Jen opened the door and brought the two other rangers in. They began searching the RV, causing Patches to bark at the intrusion.

Patches was at Winnie's feet and she reached down to pat him. He seemed to know when she needed him and stayed close. She couldn't blame him for what happened, but sometimes it would be nice if Patches was just a little more aggressive. *No, that's silly. He's great the way he is.*

Winnie got up to put some water in Patches's dish. He drank it up like he hadn't had water in days, and Winnie wondered if he'd been fed, so she filled up his bowl and Patches attacked it. Winnie mustered a smile and went back to the couch as Jen came over.

"I didn't find anything. I tried Jason again but got voice mail. Do you have a picture of your mother? We'll use it when we put out an alert."

Winnie went through her phone and found a picture of her mother and her together. They both looked so happy, and Winnie burst out into tears again. She pulled out a tissue, then reached for the box. It was going to be a long night. "This was taken right before I left Madison. I'll send it to your phone."

Jen received it a minute later. "Got it. Do you know if your mom left her phone here? We didn't see one. If she has it, we'll try to track her location. Maybe we'll get lucky. Can I have her number?"

Winnie wrote down the number and handed it to Jen. "I was about to call her after I came home and she wasn't here. When I found the note, I didn't think about it. I just called you."

Winnie called her mom's number, but it went straight to voice mail.

"We'll check outside for anything that might help us find your mom. My guess is that whoever took her isn't in the area, but we'll be discreet. Why don't you try to rest? We won't bother you unless we find something. Come on, guys."

"Wait," Winnie suddenly realized something. "What about the note? They think I took their gold. Why would they think that? They must have some reason, don't they?"

Jen was silent for a minute. "In the area that we found the mine, there were a few sets of tire and ATV tracks. I didn't think much of it at the time, but maybe someone else came out there and took gold the miners stashed. What I don't know is why they think you took it. You didn't go back out there, did you?"

"Me? Willingly go to a cave, which is next to an animal feeding ground? Of course not!"

"I didn't think so, but I know how curious you are, so I had to ask. I'll let you get some rest, but if you think of anything, please call—day or night. I'll have a ranger stationed outside, so if you look out and see someone, it's okay."

Winnie said goodbye to Jen and closed the door. Letting out a big sigh, she plopped down on the couch and looked at the picture of her mom on the phone.

"Where are you, Mom?" Tears dripped to Winnie's lap.

Patches sensed Winnie's pain and jumped up on the couch, resting his head on her leg. Winnie stroked his side and the two sat there quietly.

WINNIE HAD FINALLY DOZED off when the phone rang. She fell asleep on the couch with her head bent uncomfortably around the back. Her phone had fallen, and she felt a sharp pain in her neck from sleeping strangely as she bent down to get it.

"Mom?" Winnie asked. Her mouth was dry and had an acrid taste.

"Hi, Winnie," Jason said. "Sorry for calling so early. I just found out. I take it your mom hasn't shown up yet?"

"Jason? Hi. Um, no, my mom isn't here. At least I don't think so. Let me check."

She got up and looked around the RV, but there were no signs of her mom. "No, she's not here."

"Are you up for company? I'll bring coffee."

"That would be great. Thanks, Jason."

"Be right there. Keep your door locked."

Thirty minutes later, Winnie heard a knock on the door. She had taken time to change her clothes and try to pull a brush through her hair, but she still looked like a crumpled mess. She'd pulled her hair back into a ponytail and splashed some water on her face.

Winnie opened the door to find Jason looking like she felt. The sad eyes and fearful expression might have looked cute another time, but now they simply amplified what she was feeling. He held out two cups of coffee and a bag with something smelling wonderful. Winnie's stomach grumbled so loudly she was sure the campers next door could hear it. It upset her that she could even think of eating when her mom was out there, suffering God knows what. But a girl had to eat, didn't she? She forced a smile and motioned for Jason to come in.

"Thanks for coming over."

"Of course. And I'm really sorry about not answering my phone. Sometimes I can't get reception, and since I wasn't on call, I didn't have my radio on." Jason took Winnie's hand. "If I'd known what happened, I would have come right over."

Winnie clasped her other hand around his. "I know. And thank you."

"I haven't spoken to Jen this morning," Jason said. "Did she find anything?"

"Not last night. At least not that I'm aware of. She hasn't

called yet, so I don't think there's any news. I just don't understand why someone took her and what gold they think I have."

Jason opened the bag he brought. It had three breakfast sandwiches and three donuts. "I was hoping there would be three of us when I got here."

Winnie smiled. Patches, who hadn't shown much interest in the conversation until now, came over, sitting down beside Winnie. Winnie took the bacon out of the third sandwich and gave him one of the three strips. It was gone in an instant, and Patches licked Winnie's fingers clean, hoping for more.

"Slow down, buddy." Winnie took a bite of her sandwich.

Patches licked his lips, his eyes pleading, and Winnie tossed him another strip. Gone.

After finishing her sandwich, Winnie gave Patches the last strip of bacon, showing her hands and saying, "No more."

Patches held fast, holding a sliver of hope, but Winnie only scratched his head, and Patches went over to his food dish, nudging it before lapping up some water.

"I guess I should have brought more bacon," Jason said.

"He would eat it until he got sick, then eat some more. I love him but he can drive me crazy sometimes."

The conversation lulled, and neither had much to say. Winnie noticed Jason wringing his hands and wondered if something was bothering him, finally deciding he was just upset at the situation. But he looked more nervous than worried or upset. Was something else going on? Winnie shook the thought from her mind. She really didn't know Jason very well yet, and maybe she was simply misreading his expression. Tired of sitting there waiting, she decided to take Patches for a walk. She looked at Jason. "Would you mind waiting here in case my mom or Jen shows up?"

"Sure. Take your time. Maybe I'll sit outside and get some fresh air."

There's that nervous look again. And the hands. "Are you okay, Jason? You look like something's bothering you."

"I'm fine, just upset at what happened. The closest I've ever come to something like this were a couple of drunk and disorderly arrests. Nothing like kidnapping."

Winnie nodded, grabbed her phone, and took Patches out. Jason followed, unfolded a chair, and sat under the RV's awning. She turned back a couple of times to check on him, but he was still sitting there, head down, hands wringing.

As she let Patches drag her along, Winnie thought about Jason. He just seemed…off. Not confident, or even cocky. She didn't understand why, but something didn't seem right. Maybe it hit too close to home. She'd read about that. Even with short-term relationships, a sudden trauma can cause strange behavior. Winnie reminded herself to write all of this down when she got back.

A pull from Patches, who was interested in sniffing a nearby rock, distracted her. She forced herself to think of something else.

When Winnie got back to her motor home, the chair was empty and Jason was nowhere in sight. She started to call out, but he popped is head out of the door, donut in hand.

"I hope you don't mind. I got hungry, and I kept hearing the donut calling my name."

"*Mi casa es su casa.*" Winnie smiled. She thought it was a common expression, but Jason looked confused. "It's Spanish. My home is your home."

Jason attempted a smile, but it was forced. Something was definitely wrong. Winnie was sure of it. She just didn't know if it was about her mother or something else. Then a thought came over her. *Did I do something wrong on the date?*

"I had fun last night." Winnie suddenly felt guilty thinking about a date when her mom was missing.

Jason smiled. "Me, too. When your mom gets back, let's do it again. That is, if you want to."

"I'd like that." Winnie took his hand and pulled him close for a hug.

It was awkward at first, but Jason's arms wrapped tightly around Winnie. She was hoping for the warm comfort of a loving embrace. Instead, it seemed mechanical, like being hugged by a robot.

Cold. Winnie tried to hang on. She breathed a sigh of relief when Patches started to bark and pulled away to see what Patches was fussing about.

Patches had spotted a red squirrel and was pulling hard on the leash. Winnie's arm was being yanked as she took a few quick steps to catch up. The squirrel scampered away, and Patches stopped tugging.

"Thanks for saving me, buddy." Winnie scratched Patches's head as they came back to the RV. "Sorry, Jason. Patches never met a squirrel he didn't want to chase."

"That's okay. I need to get to the office, anyway. I'll call you later."

Winnie watched as Jason got into his car and left. He was still driving the Camaro, but all the fun Winnie had in it last night was gone.

Neither one waved goodbye.

"I think it's up to you and me to find my mom. What do you think? Are you up for it?"

A bark let Winnie know Patches was onboard. "Good boy. Ready to make some house calls?"

Winnie and Patches spent the next two hours canvasing the neighbors for anything they might have seen or heard. They walked past Reggie's site, but they had left and a new camper was parked. Most of the people at Fishing Bridge had talked to the rangers the night before and didn't know anything. Just as she thought it was hopeless, Winnie found someone with a campsite near the road who had been out when the rangers came by.

"Yeah, I remember her. Pretty lady. Walked a firecracker of a dog. Hey! There's the dog!"

The woman pointed at Patches. For his part, Patches wagged his tail, enjoying being the center of attention.

"I remember your momma because she was so proud of her daughter. Nothing but good things to say about you and your travels."

Mom is proud of me? A sudden burst of pride exploded in Winnie, followed by guilt at being annoyed with her sometimes.

"Anyway, not long after she walked off, a car pulled up with two big guys inside. Mean looking, like they forgot how to smile. I waved at them, but they ignored me. Couldn't see their eyes 'cause they had sunglasses on. And it was getting dark. I don't trust nobody that wears sunglasses in the dark. A short while later, the same car went barreling down the road, barely making the turn. One of the guys had moved to the back seat, and it looked like he was wrestling with someone. I couldn't see too good, but whoever it was looked small. Why would they take your mom?"

"They think I have something of theirs and they want it back. Unfortunately, I don't have it."

"My, my, here in Yellowstone? I can't believe it."

"Yes. Excitement is certainly following me on this trip." Winnie explained what had happened since she arrived. When she finished, the woman looked completely flustered.

"Gosh, girl, that's more trouble than a person should see in a lifetime."

Winnie smiled and thanked her for the help. "One of the park rangers will probably come by for a statement. If you wouldn't mind giving me your cell phone number, I'll pass it on to the ranger investigating the...incident."

My mom is an incident? That sounds better than kidnapped, I suppose.

Shaking the thought from her mind, she continued on. She still had more sites to check out. On her way, her phone rang.

"Reggie? Hi. Is everything all right?"

"No, it's not all right. Your momma is missing. Why didn't you call before?"

"How did you—"

"The rangers called us because they knew we stayed at Fishing Bridge. Even though we left before it happened, they wanted to talk to us to see if we had any information that could help them locate her. Now, tell me everything. You must be frantic with fright."

Winnie went over the story of her mom's arrival, the date, her mom's disappearance, and the note. "But I don't want to trouble you with this. You've got enough to deal with. How's Cal holding up?"

"He's fine. Everything was arranged, and he was able to reconnect with family members he hasn't seen in a long time. He has a lot of good memories of his aunt, and he was grateful for their time together. Back to you and your momma. What can I do to help? I know we just met and I don't want to seem pushy, but I know a good person when I meet them, and you're one of the good ones. And back in Sweetwater, we help each other."

"Thanks, Reggie. Just having someone to talk to is a blessing."

The two chatted for a while. The more they talked, the more Winnie realized they might have grown up differently, but the two were alike in many ways. It was like talking to a friend she'd known for years.

After both promising to get together soon, they hung up. Winnie felt better, and she felt hopeful for the first time since her mom's disappearance. She reached into her pocket for a tissue and pulled out the phone number for the woman who may have seen her mom being kidnapped. Winnie picked up the phone and called Jen.

"Ranger Malone."

"Hi Jen, it's Winnie."

"Winnie. I was just about to call you. I'm on my way over there now to see if I can find anything else that may help us. Have you heard anything?"

"I found someone who saw my mom being taken away. Well, she saw someone struggling in a car as it was speeding away, so it fits with my mom's disappearance. It's better than nothing, I guess."

"Any lead is a good lead, Winnie. I should be there in twenty minutes. And Sally's right behind me. She thought you might want some company."

"That's really nice of both of you."

"Oh, and we tracked down the kid on the ATV. The Cody police are picking him up as we speak. It will take a few hours for them to get here, so, when I'm done at Fishing Bridge, I'll go back and interview him."

"Really? That's great. He might hold the key that helps us find who's responsible for taking my mom. I'd like to sit in on the interview. I've been interviewing people for years, and I've developed a sense when someone is telling the truth."

"Thanks, Winnie, but we've got it covered."

"Jen, I'm not really asking. I'll be there."

24

Jen was ready when Winnie walked up to the ranger office.

"Really, Winnie," Jen said with a hand up. "I appreciate you coming out, but we've got this."

"Is he here?"

"The Cody police radioed they entered Yellowstone a while ago, and they should be here any minute. I was told his parents are following the police car, so this situation could get messy quick. To be honest, as much as I appreciate your concern, I don't need another distraction." Jen's face was hard as stone.

But Winnie wasn't giving up. "Jen, before I started this trip, I was a reporter. You may not have heard about this, but Governor Clark was forced out of office because of a piece I did on kickbacks he was receiving in exchange for highway contracts. I didn't luck into the story. I uncovered it, through lots of hard work. And a little skill. I may have been a pushover in my marriage, but not as a reporter. I can be a valuable asset for you, if you'll let me sit in."

"Winnie...I can't. It's not that I don't want to. It's simply against the rules, and I don't want anything to compromise the investigation."

Winnie smiled. "I think I have a solution that will satisfy both of us."

Fifteen minutes later, Jen got a call that the Cody police had arrived. She looked over at Winnie. "We'll do this your way. But any interference and you're gone. Agreed?"

"Agreed." Winnie got up, following Jen into the hall, where the Cody police were standing behind a clearly nervous kid. The two adults standing behind the police looked equally distraught.

The police took off the handcuffs, had Jen sign some paperwork and left. The two adults filled the void left by the officers.

Jen casually flipped through a notebook, occasionally glancing up. "Mark Connors?"

The kid nodded.

Jen looked past him. "You must be his parents."

More nodding.

"Please wait here while I bring Mark to an interview room."

Jen motioned for another ranger to follow her. She returned alone after a moment. Winnie had moved into the break room, where she could hear everything but not look like she was eavesdropping.

"Mr. and Mrs. Connors, I'm Jennifer Malone, the ranger investigating a murder which happened in Yellowstone recently. Your—"

"Murder?" Mark's mother wailed. "You're accusing my son of murder?"

"What? Heavens no. Nothing like that. Please, follow me into a conference room and I'll explain. Would either of you like a cup of coffee?"

Winnie could hear them walk down the hallway. She wanted to follow but couldn't think of a way to do it and not seem obvious. Instead, she gave Sally a quick call to check on

Patches. Just as she was hanging up, Jen stepped into the break room.

"Ready?"

"What did his parents have to say?"

"His mother lit into her husband for getting him the ATV, but they both agreed Mark needs to learn his lesson. They were more worried about how this might impact his ability to get into college. When I suggested keeping it off the record and having him perform community service and pay a fine, they were both relieved."

"Seems like they want him to learn his lesson. That sounds like a fair compromise."

"Shall we go? I think we've kept Mark waiting long enough." Jen grabbed two Cokes from the refrigerator, offering one to Winnie.

Jen led Winnie to a small room adjacent to the interview room where Mark Connors was sitting. The room was empty except for two chairs and a small ledge against a window. Jen pulled the curtain open to reveal one-way glass. She turned a knob near the window, instructing Winnie how to adjust the volume so she could hear the interview. Jen left and stepped next door, where she replaced the ranger sitting there. Winnie took out her iPad to take notes, although she knew from her own time in the interview room that the entire session was being recorded.

Winnie watched Jen walk over to the table, making a show of the thick folder she had, causing a loud thud as she plopped it down. Mark jumped.

"Good, Jen," Winnie said to the glass, watching as Jen pulled out the chair opposite Mark and sat down, gently placing the soda on the table.

"Mr. Connors, I'm Ranger Malone. I assume you know why you're here?"

Mark nodded. He kept his eyes on the floor, only darting occasionally between Jen and the Coke can.

"Mr. Connors, you broke federal law by your careless acts in Yellowstone. My job is to make sure whoever breaks the law within my park is brought to justice. Right now, you're looking at a five-thousand-dollar fine and up to eight years in a federal prison."

Mark looked up, startled. Tears were starting to work their way out.

"You go girl." Winnie again talked to the glass.

"We checked your record, and it doesn't look like you've been in trouble before. If you help me, I'd like to help you."

Mark wiped away the tears now starting to run down his cheeks. "Okay. How can I help?"

Jen slid the soda over the table. Mark glanced at it, then at Jen, who nodded.

He opened the can and guzzled about half of it down before coming up for air. "Thanks."

"You're welcome. Now, please tell me everything about your excursions into Yellowstone. Remember, you help me and I'll help you."

"I've only been there a few times. Outside of Cody, there are a bunch of trails. Once you're on a trail, you have no idea where you are. It's not like there's a sign telling you you've entered Yellowstone, you know?" Mark looked up from the table at Jen.

She nodded but stayed quiet.

"That's right, Jen." Winnie was taking notes. "Use the silence to get him talking."

It worked. Mark soon looked back down at the table. "So, anyways, like I said. I didn't really know where I was, but the trail was fun. Lots of bumps you could jump from and turns to lean into. And it was quiet. I rarely saw anyone else. One time, maybe my fourth time out that way, I went past the trail. I knew I shouldn't have done it, but it was fun and I didn't think I was hurting anything. I mean, it's just weeds and dirt out there, you know? I was having fun and lost track of time. Anyway, I got turned around, it was getting dark, and I was starting to run low on gas, so I stopped to check my phone. No signal. The GPS knew where I was, so I figured I could just point myself back and hopefully at least find a road. I was putting gas in from a spare can when I heard a noise. It sounded like a machine or something, and I thought that maybe they could help me find how to get back. So, I started that way, but then I thought I might get in trouble for being off a trail, so I went as quiet as I could, not that it mattered with all the noise they were making. I kept following the noise. That was when I saw them—three guys and a girl mining for something. We read about early mining for gold and silver in the area, so I guessed that's what they were doing. I watched them for a few minutes, wondering what to do. I mean, they seemed okay, but you never know. Then one of them spotted me. He grabbed another guy and pointed my way, and the two of them started running toward me. I got scared and took off as fast as I could."

"Probably a good idea," Jen said. "We think they killed someone else that stumbled across them."

"Killed? You mean, like, they're dead?" Mark swallowed hard.

"Why did you go back?"

"Shelly thinks she's a tough girl. Always rambling on about getting tattoos and piercings, even though she doesn't have any. We were talking at lunch, and I told her what happened. She kept saying how she wanted to go see it. I didn't want to, but, you know, it's hard to refuse her. She's so pretty and all."

Jen nodded. "Her accounts were a little different. She said you were the one that wanted to go."

"Maybe. I don't know. We both talked about it, trying to show how cool we were."

"Cool," Jen shook her head. "You risked your life to be cool.

And even after the first encounter, you decide to go back, this time with a date? I take it you're not up for a genius award. Or a common-sense certificate."

"I didn't plan to actually go there. I wanted to take her near it, but not actually there, thinking she wouldn't know the difference. She kept wanting to see the mine, so I got closer. That's when I saw you and took off."

"And just leaving her there—was that part of being cool, too?"

"No, wait. That was different. You guys looked different. You had uniforms and everything. Not like those guys. And I heard you shout that you were rangers. Besides, there was no sense in both of us getting caught. I mean, if you were bad people, we'd both be caught and probably killed or something. This way, I was free to call for help."

"And did you call for help?"

"Umm, no." Mark looked at the floor. "But I looked back and Shelly was already caught. I guess I figured you guys were rangers and that was that. Look, I panicked, okay? I'm a coward. What else can I say?"

"I think you summed it up nicely."

Winnie had never watched an interview from behind one-way glass before. It gave her a perspective she didn't think she could get from sitting in the room. It was kind of like being in a zoo. She watched as Jen leaned in, her face impassive, staring at Mark like a lion addressing her kill. Mark stared at the can of Coke, but his fidgeting hands told Winnie everything she needed to know.

"That's it. That's what happened. I screwed up." Mark looked at the table. "She'll probably never speak to me again."

"I know I wouldn't, but that's the least of your problems. You trespassed on government property, defaced a national park, and left a crime scene when ordered to stop. That's resisting arrest and whatever else I can find. Like I said before, you're looking at a lot of jail time."

Mark was sweating, and Winnie noticed tears starting to form again.

"And these are federal offenses, Mark," Jen added for emphasis. "No local jail for you. You'll be shipped off somewhere, maybe Colorado. And you're eighteen, so you'll be with the big boys."

"No, please. I didn't mean any—"

Jen held up a hand. "Save it, Mark." She leaned back, adopting a less aggressive stance. "Look, you screwed up, but I don't want to see you in prison. I'll talk to my boss and see what we can do. But he's going to want something in return."

"Anything. I'll do anything."

Mark sounds desperate. Perfect.

"Great. I need descriptions of the men you saw and any cars that were there. I'll also need your phone to see what we can get off of it."

"My phone?"

"Yes. Is that a problem?"

"It's just...it's private."

"I see." Jen stood and picked up her papers. "Well, that's your right, of course. But I thought you said you'd do anything to get out from under this. I'll let your parents know you won't be coming home today." She turned to leave.

"Wait."

Mark slid his phone across the table to where Jen had been sitting. She turned back and sat down.

"Thank you, Mark. I appreciate your cooperation."

"So, that's it then?" He stood up.

Jen laughed and motioned for him to sit down. "No, Mark, that's not it. I think a fine is in order. Something you can give to the Cody animal rescue. I think one thousand dollars is appropriate. I also think you need to do some volunteer time, so I'll have a talk with the rescue group. I see about eighty hours of service cleaning stalls. I've already spoken to your parents, and they readily agreed to make sure you comply. And they said you'll earn the money. They won't be bailing you out of this mess."

Mark put his head in his hands.

"If you do this, I'll drop all charges. If you don't, I'll have you arrested, and this time, you'll be talking to a judge, not me. And one other thing. If I ever, ever, catch you in my park on an ATV, I will make it my mission to see you behind bars for a long time. Understood?"

"Understood."

Winnie smiled. Jen was tough but fair.

Jen handed him a piece of paper and a pen. "I want you to write down everything we talked about. Where you were and when and where you started with the ATV and where you ended up. Describe the encounter you had and the equipment you saw. Basically, everything you can think of."

Winnie made a note to get a copy of what Mark wrote down.

When Mark was finished, Jen said, "Now your phone. Unlock it please and give me the passcode. We'll need it for a few days and then we can get it back to you."

Mark unlocked his phone and handed it to Jen. She wrote the passcode on a sticky note and attached it to the back. Winnie could see Jen swiping on the phone and occasionally caught a glimpse of what looked like a picture.

"What are you looking in there for?" Mark leaned over the table.

"There's a feature in Google Maps called Timeline. It shows where you went, and it can go back years."

"Years?" Mark looked worried.

"It will also tell me if you were lying in your statement. Care to change it before I look?"

Mark shook his head no.

Winnie couldn't see Mark's phone, but she took hers out. What did *her* phone show? Home, work, home, work. Boring. Until recently, when it had a new line pointing west. *Not boring.*

"I'm only interested in the days around our investigation. Unless, of course, you have other things to confess?"

Another shake no.

Winnie watched as Jen swiped through more screens.

"Here we are. My, my, you were busy with that thing." Jen pointed at Mark. "You stay here. I'll be right back."

Winnie heard her door open and turned to see Jen standing there.

"I need to get a computer," Jen said. "I don't think this will lead to much, but we need to follow through. Are you okay?"

"Yes." Winnie stood and opened her arms. "I'm sorry about before. I'm just so afraid for my mom."

"I know," Jen returned the hug. "I'm doing everything I can."

Jen pointed to the window. "Keep an eye on him. I don't think he'll go anywhere, but if he does, give a holler. I'll be down the hall. I need to download the contents of his phone. We've got a program I'll use to extract the data, and we'll send it to the FBI."

After twenty minutes, Jen escorted Mark out of the interview room. Winnie closed the curtain and stepped into the hallway just as Mark was being reunited with his parents.

"I'm sorry," Mark said to his parents. "I know I messed up. I want to make it right."

His mom smiled at her son's contrition, but not his dad.

If his face was any redder, he'd have smoke coming out of his ears. "Sometimes sorry ain't enough. You're finding out now you can make your own decisions, but you can't control the consequences of them. And believe me, there will be consequences." His dad pointed to Jen. "I believe there's someone else you need to apologize to before we leave."

Mark turned and looked at Jen. "I'm sorry for being reckless in Yellowstone. I won't do it again."

"That's what I want to hear. Do your community service, pay your fine, and everything will be okay. Show up here again, though, and it's big trouble."

Mark's parents shook Jen's hand, said goodbye, and left, promising Mark would follow through on his penance.

After the Connors left, Winnie and Jen sat down in the break room.

"Sorry that wasn't more useful in helping us find your mom. I looked over the notes, and they seem to match Anita's descriptions of the people, but I don't think we're much closer to finding them."

"Or my mom."

25

Winnie drove back, alternating between crying and resolve to find whoever took her mom. When she got back to her camper, she looked in the rearview mirror. Wild hair, puffy eyes, and a face as long as her RV. "You look wonderful."

She stepped into her camper. Sally was sitting there quietly reading, and Patches was by her side.

"You poor dear," Sally said as Winnie tried to wipe the tears still running down her cheeks. Sally went over and gave her a long hug, and Winnie hung on, not wanting to let go.

"It will be okay." Sally offered to stay the rest of the day, but Winnie insisted she go while she still had some sanity left.

Winnie sent her off with a batch of cookies she'd made earlier to keep herself occupied.

After cleaning the RV for the third time that day, Winnie looked out the window at the Mini. She tucked her cell phone in her pocket, then grabbed her vacuum and cleaning supplies, and headed off to the car. Once the outside was free of bugs and dirt, she moved to the interior. Winnie kept it fairly clean, but it could still use a once-over for good measure, and the floor hadn't been vacuumed in ages. She started at the front, took out the floor mats, emptied the trash, and wiped the dash and doors down.

Moving to the back, Winnie wiped the interior and reached to remove the back driver's-side floor mat. Shaking it out, she vacuumed it and put it back. Repeating the procedure for the passenger's side, Winnie vacuumed the interior. Almost finished, she heard the vacuum try to pull something and got stuck, creating a loud whine as the motor gasped for air. She reached down and pulled it off the nozzle, then stared at it. Blending in with the black carpet and black floor mats was a small black cell phone.

"What's this, Patchy? Have you been making calls without me knowing?"

Patches just wagged his tail.

Winnie turned it on, but it prompted her for a password. She asked Patches what it was, but he wouldn't give it up. She tried "1111," but that didn't work. Afraid it might lock her out completely, Winnie took the phone inside and plugged it in while she considered what to do.

"Where did this come from?" Winnie watched the phone charge. She'd found her mom's phone nestled in the couch cushions, so Winnie knew it wasn't hers. She couldn't think of anyone that would have left it in her car, until she had her "Ah ha" moment.

Anita. It has to be. Nothing else makes sense. That's why nobody could find the phone.

Winnie's mind came off her mom for a moment while she thought about Anita and how to unlock her phone. After considering it, Winnie placed a call to Martin Mellon.

"Professor Mellon? I mean Martin?"

"Yes, Winnie. It is I. I haven't heard from your mother in a few days. Is everything all right? I'll bet it was a surprise to see your mom in Yellowstone!"

With everything going on, Winnie hadn't remembered to call him. Or her sister, Lexi. Truthfully, she had remembered. She was hoping her mom would show up before she had to. Too late now.

"Oh. Umm, well. My mom is…missing."

"Missing? You mean lost?"

"No." Winnie's tears started to flow again. "She was kidnapped. The police and park rangers are looking for her now."

Winnie took a deep breath and waited for Martin to say something.

"Is this some sort of joke, Winnie?"

"Of course not. How could you even think I would joke about something so horrible?"

That did it. Winnie now had a river of tears flowing. Patches came over to comfort her. He always seemed to know what to do, and he curled up next to her, gently resting his head in her lap.

"I'm so sorry, Winnie. I didn't mean...what I meant was... how did this happen?"

"I went out to dinner with a friend and when I came back, Mom was gone. Vanished."

"But...but...why did they take her? What do they want with Brina? It just doesn't make sense."

Winnie's mind drifted for a moment. *Brina? He calls her Brina? And she lets him? When she gets back, she's got some explaining to do.*

"They took her because they think I have something of theirs, which I don't.

"What do they think you have?"

"I can't say, but I can tell you I'm working with the police and doing everything I can to find her."

"Did you try calling her?"

"Her phone was left here. It was on vibrate, and we never heard it when we called the number. Even if she did have it, I doubt the kidnappers would make it that easy to locate her." Winnie started to cry again but stopped herself after a few sniffles. "I just don't understand why they took her. I don't have any gold."

"They're after gold? And they think you took it?"

"Umm, yeah. I wasn't supposed to say that, though. The police don't want that to get out."

"Mums the word, Winnie. I'd never say anything that might endanger Brina."

Winnie suddenly remembered the reason she called Martin in the first place. "Martin, I was cleaning today. It helps me take my mind off of things. When I vacuumed the car, I nearly vacuumed up a cell phone. I didn't see it at first because it was all black, but the vacuum found it. I think it's Anita's. The problem is it prompted me for a passcode. I tried one one one one, but that didn't work, and I'm afraid if I keep trying, I might get locked out. I was wondering if you might be able to figure it out. Maybe something in her notebook will give us a clue. I mean, she left both of them in my car, she might have given us a way to unlock the phone."

"An excellent idea, Winnie. This might allow me to take my mind off of Brina for a while. I'll get on it right away, and I'll call you as soon as I know something."

"Wait. Aren't you supposed to be in Germany at a conference?"

"I was. I was at the airport when I got word the person I was going to see wasn't able to make the conference. I cancelled, but Brina was already on her way to visit you."

"Thanks, Martin. I'll let you know if I hear anything about Mom. I should hand this over to the police soon, so the quicker we can unlock it, the better. The phone was left in my car before Mom disappeared, but it might help us find her."

"Understood, Winnie. It's my top priority."

After talking to Martin, Winnie felt a little better. But she still had to call her sister. She thought about putting the phone down and calling later, but instead pressed the speed dial. Lexi's picture showed on the screen as the phone tried to connect. She heard it ring and hoped it would go to voice mail, but Lexi answered before she'd finished the thought.

"Winnie! I was wondering when you and mom were going to call. How is it going? Did she surprise you?"

"Hi Lexi. Yes, she certainly surprised me."

"You don't sound too happy about it. Is everything all right?"

"There's something I need to tell you. I went out the night after mom got here. I had a date and she wouldn't let me cancel it. Anyway, I—"

"You had a date? I want details."

"Not now. I don't know how to say this, but mom's been kidnapped."

"What? Come on. Is this a joke?"

Winnie started to cry. "I wish it was. Lexi, I was gone for just a couple of hours. When I came back, she was gone. Taken."

"By whom?"

"I'm not supposed to talk about this since it's linked to an ongoing investigation. But they think we stole gold, and they took Mom to force us to give it back."

"Gold? Are you drunk?"

"I wish I was. I know it's hard to believe, but it's true. The police are looking for her, but so far, nothing."

A silence followed that seemed to stretch for hours. "What do we do?"

"We're waiting for them to contact us. I'm doing everything I can, but it's not much."

"Why do they think you have gold?"

"It's a long story."

"I'm all ears."

Winnie told Lexi the story of meeting Anita and everything that happened since. There was another long silence after she finished, and Winnie thought the line might have disconnected. Finally, Lexi spoke.

"Are you okay? You've been through a lot."

"Patches and I are getting by."

"Should I come out there? I think I should be there with you. I'll come out there."

"Lex, there's nothing you can do. The last thing I want is to endanger another person. It's better if you stay home. I'll let you know when I have news. I promise."

The two talked for a while longer. When she hung up, Winnie felt better for telling her sister. She was also a lot more determined to be proactive and find her mother.

"Who else is going to do it, Patchy? I think it's up to me. Are you in?"

Patches let out a resounding bark.

"Thought so! Let's get to work."

The problem was, Winnie really didn't know what to do. The rangers had already talked to the only person in the RV park that saw anything that might be relevant, and so far, that had gone nowhere.

Winnie had moved from cleaning the car to the storage area under the RV when Martin called back. "Winnie, I've looked at the notebook you sent me, and I think I may have come across something. Is the phone you have a Samsung J1?"

"Let me see. Does the type of phone matter?"

"It might if I'm right about my findings."

"Okay, hang on."

Winnie went inside and grabbed the phone.

"Yes, it's a J1. How did you know that?"

"There were some references to a J1 in the notebook, but I couldn't understand them at the time, so I ignored them. When I took another look, I focused on cell phone models, and I concentrated on those frequently sold in Ukraine. Google really is your friend for questions like these. Fortunately, when I entered the most common phones into the search parameters of the notebook, only one match came back. The J1. So, I was hopeful it was her phone."

"Any idea why she even bothered to put the thing in code?"

"Good question. I also wondered about the code. Most kids her age would write in plain text, but the code intrigued me, so I did a little research on Anita. Did you know she studied computer programming at the university? I found a paper published about quantum computing, and she was one of the authors."

"Quantum what?"

"Computing. It's all quite technical, and I won't bore you with the details. Suffice it to say Anita was a bright young woman. She must have suspected something could happen to her and she decided to take precautions. Her notebook was written in code long before she met you, so she was probably doing that for fun. But once things started to happen, she probably added notes and other information. I believe Anita was planning on dropping these things with someone. She might not have known who at the time, but when you befriended her, she may have decided on you. She didn't want to tell you in case you objected, so she hid them in the back, hoping you'd find them. My guess is she didn't want to make it too easy to read what was there, so she gave us clues in her notebook."

"But how did she know we would be able to decipher it?"

"She didn't. Again, I'm guessing, but she must have thought highly of you because she entrusted you with everything. Her estimation of you was correct, of course."

"Me?"

"Don't be so modest. Anita saw in you what your mother always brags about. You're bright, resourceful, and determined. And, as your mom puts it, 'you don't take crap off nobody.'"

Winnie was both flattered and flustered at the comments. *My mom really said that? Time to change the subject before I start crying like a baby...again.*

"Thanks, Martin, that means a lot to me. But none of that will do us any good unless you figured out the unlock code. Did you?"

"I think so. The computer came up with five possibilities. If it's not one of those, then I'm afraid we're out of luck. Unfortunately, to complicate matters, the unlock code can be either four or five digits, and we don't know which."

"How confident are you in the results?"

"The computer indicates there's about seventy-two percent probability that one of these codes will unlock the phone. It's not the best odds, but that's what we've got."

"Okay. Let's give it a try."

They tried the first combination. No luck. The same with the second one, and the third. Winnie could feel her pulse quicken. She took a deep breath, then read the next sequence to make sure she had the numbers in the right order.

The fourth combination produced a warning that they had five tries left before the phone destroyed all information.

"Martin, we're down to five tries before we lose it forever. If this doesn't work, we'll have to stop."

"Fingers crossed, Winnie. Try this last one, four two four seven seven."

Winnie carefully typed in the numbers and pressed the OK button. The screen came to life, and she blew a sigh of relief. "Martin! You did it."

"That's such good news. Not only does it help you, but it means the computer program we're using is at least somewhat accurate. So, now that you have the phone open, what are you going to do?"

"First, I'm going to write down the passcode, so I don't forget it. Then, I'll go through the phone to see what I can find. I'll copy everything and send it to you. Then, I'll hand it over to the police."

"Very good, Winnie, but please do be careful. I don't want anything to happen to you or your mom."

"I'll be careful. I just want my mom back. And I figure I'm more motivated than anyone else."

"I'll let you get to it, then. Please let me know if you need anything—day or night."

"Thanks again, Martin." Winnie hung up and wrote the passcode down on a sticky note then taped it to the back of the phone. But then Winnie took a step back. She wasn't a forensic expert, and she really didn't know what to do. Pulling up her MacBook, she searched for a way to get information off of the phone. Most of the hits were about tracking down a cell phone number, and the only software available was either for law enforcement or too expensive. The only practical suggestion was to connect the phone up to Winnie's laptop and download as much as she could.

"I guess we'll give it a try. What do you think, Patchy?"

But Patches just stared.

"I know, I know, we should just hand the phone over to Jennifer. But I need to find Mom. If anything happens to her, I'll never forgive myself."

Patches seemed to understand. He wagged his tail and looked up, his big eyes staring at Winnie.

"I knew it. We're a team, buddy." Winnie scratched his ears.

She made a pot of coffee and plugged the phone into her computer. It didn't take long to download the photos, but there was no way Winnie could automatically capture the call or text activity, so she had to go through this manually, translating the text and copying down things that looked promising. After a couple of hours, Winnie's eyes started to hurt from staring at the screen for so long, and she needed a break. She had compiled the information but didn't take the time to really look at any of it. It was more important she get as much off of the phone as possible before she had to give it to Jen.

Standing up and stretching, Winnie yawned as she picked up her phone.

Jen answered after two rings. "Hi, Winnie. How are you holding up?"

"I'm stable, I guess. Thanks for asking. I just can't believe I got my mom involved in this. I can't believe I got *myself* involved with this."

"Winnie, this wasn't your fault. You know that, don't you? You've been a great help in getting to the bottom of it, but none of it is your fault."

"Yeah, I suppose. But it doesn't make it any easier."

"No, I imagine it doesn't. But it's true. Do you have any news? Sally said if you need someone to talk to, she'll come over anytime. I would, too, but I'm a little busy right now."

"That's so sweet of both of you. But, no, I don't need anything. Actually, I was cleaning my car to keep busy, and I might have found something useful. I think Anita left her phone when I gave her a ride. It's black and I couldn't see it on the floor before."

"Really? Do you think it's hers?"

"I'm sure of it. In fact...I sort of already looked at it."

"What do you mean, 'looked at it?'"

"Well, I didn't realize it was Anita's at first, but it couldn't be anyone else's. So, I turned it on and wanted to see if there was anything on it."

"Winnie, that's evidence. You shouldn't be messing with it. What if you got locked out? We couldn't get any information from it then."

"I know, and I'm sorry. But the good news is I got in. Well, not me specifically. I had some help from my friend in Wisconsin. You remember Professor Mellon? He's got some whiz-bang computer program and he figured out the passcode. I unlocked the phone and put the passcode on the back so anyone can get in."

"That's good news, Winnie. Your friend is amazing. I'm in the middle of a few things, so I'll send someone by to pick it up. Are you going to be there for a while?"

"We'll be here." She didn't mention she had already taken as much information as she could from the phone.

Winnie looked at Patches. "Jen's nice, but to her it's a job. To me it's personal. Very personal. Let's go for a walk before they show up. Then I want to go through the phone data."

A walk usually cleared Winnie's head and lifted her spirits. But not today. There were too many things bothering her to simply walk them away. Her usual stroll where she was led by Patches and meandered behind him was replaced by a march with Patches practically being dragged along.

"None of this makes any sense, Patches." Winnie tugged at the leash. "Why take Mom? What can she—or me—possibly have to offer? And what about the gold? Where is it and who has it?"

Winnie kicked a stone off the path as she tugged Patches along. She had a nagging feeling she just couldn't shake, one that had been with her for a while. Like most problems she was trying to solve, Winnie used Patches as her advisor. She was amazed at what Patches could say, just by the wag of his tail or the look he gave her.

"And where is Jason in all of this? He was acting kind of weird when he came by. Was he just nervous, or is something going on I don't know about? It was just one date, so I don't really know him, but he went from warm and caring to aloof and distant pretty quick. Maybe that's just how he is. If so, I've dated enough moody people for one lifetime."

Winnie stopped and covered her mouth.

"That's it, Patches. There's something going on the rangers don't want me to know about. That's why Jason was acting so strange. He couldn't tell me about it, and it was bothering him, I need to find out what it is. This has to be about Mom."

Winnie tugged at the leash even harder. "Come on, Patchy. I need to look over everything and there's no time to waste."

26

"Jen, I need to know what's going on," Winnie said. "Don't sugarcoat it. Is my mom dead?"

"What? Winnie, why did you ask that? Please believe me, we don't know anything other than what I told you. I would never hide anything from you about your mom's case. Did something happen?"

"It's just..." Winnie started crying again. She hated crying. After her divorce, she wanted to be as tough as nails. Or at least appear to be. *Show 'em you're tough and they'll respect you...or at least leave you alone.* But this was too much. She found herself breaking down a lot over the last two days.

"Winnie, I'm coming over. I'll be there as soon as I can, okay?"

"Okay," Winnie said through the sobs.

Jen made it to the Fishing Bridge RV Park in record time. Winnie was trying to fix her hair and noticed the bright red circles around her eyes. There was no denying it. She wasn't as strong as she wanted to be. Or needed to be. With a heavy sigh, she answered the door, finding Jen with open arms. Winnie fell into them.

"It's going to be all right, Winnie. We're doing everything we can to find your mom. And I promise we haven't held back any information."

Winnie pulled away and gave Jen a hard look. It had been a while since she trusted anyone, and she really wanted to trust Jen. Winnie nodded and tried to smile, holding the door so Jen could come in. She plopped herself on the couch and motioned for Jen to follow suit.

"Winnie, why did you think we were holding something back?"

"It's probably nothing. Just my emotions getting the better of me. When I saw Jason, he seemed really strange—distracted maybe—almost like he had something to say but couldn't."

"That might just be the ranger in him. We're trained to be passive about reporting news. It's important we stay calm when there are tragic events. I think that's what you probably felt."

"Maybe." Winnie wasn't convinced. "You're probably right. I guess I overreacted. I just want my mom back. I'm sorry I bothered you."

"You know you're no bother. I haven't seen Jason today, but I'm sure there's nothing to it. While I'm here, I'd like to pick up the phone you found. The sooner I get it off to the lab, the sooner we'll get results. The phone must have been in your car before your mother disappeared, so I don't know if this will be a help in finding your mom. We don't even know for sure Anita's death and your mom's disappearance are related."

"They have to be related. The mines, the demand for gold in exchange for Mom. Anita is the one who saw the people mining the gold. Nothing else makes sense."

"You might be right, but I try not to jump to conclusions. Let's get the phone analyzed and see where it leads us. I'll make sure it happens as quickly as possible."

Winnie nodded and handed the phone to Jen, not mentioning she had already downloaded everything she could.

"Winnie," Jen said softly. "Have you heard anything else from the kidnappers? We would have expected to see a follow-up letter, drop-off instructions, or something by now."

"No, nothing."

"Okay. There is one last thing. It's probably nothing, but I think you should know about it."

"What?"

"Well, I wasn't sure I should bring it up, but we haven't been able to find Jason. We started looking when he didn't report for his shift. He just disappeared. Vanished. We don't know where he is. I stopped by his apartment, his car's gone, and it doesn't look like he's been back to his apartment in a while. You don't have any idea where he is, do you?"

"Me? No, but I was wondering why he hasn't called. I tried his cell phone once, but it went straight to voice mail."

"Yeah, that's another thing. His phone was in his apartment. Turned off."

"Why would he do that?"

"We don't know. I only looked briefly, but there was no sign of a struggle. Right now, we're treating it as suspicious, and we've put out a BOLO."

"I've seen enough cop shows to know what that means. Jen, why didn't you tell me this before? I mean, we only had one date, but I like him. Now you're trying to hunt him down like a fugitive."

"Not a fugitive, but someone we need to talk to. I thought about telling you earlier, but you've got enough on your mind. Until we knew something more, I didn't see any reason to give you an additional concern. Plus...I wasn't sure if maybe you knew something about Jason and didn't want to tell me. You know, sometimes friends help out other friends."

Winnie took a moment to realize what Jen was saying. Then her eyes went wide and she raised her hand. "Now you wait just a minute." Winnie wagged her finger. "Don't you dare think I would do anything, ANYTHING, to hurt my mom, or hide someone. I—"

"Winnie, wait."

"No, you wait. I can take a lot. But I won't tolerate even the insinuation I would do anything like that. You have your phone. Please leave."

"Winnie, come on."

"Leave. Now." Winnie stood and pointed to the door. She could feel beads of sweat on her forehead, and her pulse raced as she stood like a statue.

Patches moved over to Winnie's side, staring at Jen. He must have sensed the tension because his tail wasn't wagging as he stood at alert.

Jen walked to the door. When she reached it, she turned and gave a last look at Winnie, but Winnie ignored her. Without another word, Jen turned and left. Winnie heard footsteps retreating, then the sound of a car door closing, followed by the crunch of gravel as Jen drove off.

Winnie dropped her arms and sighed, then flopped on the couch. Patches jumped up and sat beside her. "I know I overreacted. Again. But sometimes it's just too much, and I can't take it. I guess you've lived with me long enough to know how I am."

Patches nudged closer, wagging his tail against the cushion.

"Okay, you're right. I'll apologize later. Right now, we've got to go through the information we took off the phone and see if it helps us."

Winnie made a quick call to Reggie. She told her about the run-in with Jen and the disappearance of Jason.

"Jen seems like a trustworthy person. But I have to agree with you, Winnie, something about Jason doesn't add up. That behavior doesn't make sense. Do you think it's related to your mom's disappearance?"

Winnie hadn't considered that before. It couldn't be, could

it? "I don't see how. He just saw her right before we left for dinner, and she was gone when we got back."

But the coincidence was bothering Winnie, and, after she got off the phone, she couldn't shake a nagging feeling Reggie could be right. Trying to push the thought aside, Winnie made a pot of coffee and got to work, with Patches curling up next to her on the couch. Putting the photos aside for now, she examined the files. Two cups of coffee later, Winnie had finished the files and started on the pictures. There were a lot of them. Most were selfies and photos of people she assumed were her friends. But there were a few that looked like the area where the cave was. She flipped through them, ten in all. There were a couple of photos of people, but they were blurry. Winnie guessed Anita was moving too much to keep her phone steady. Unfortunately, she didn't see anything in the landscape pictures she didn't already know.

"I need a break. How about a walk?"

Hearing the magic word walk, Patches started to jump in excitement. Winnie got the leash and the two set off. The RV park was full, and Winnie had to dodge a number of campers loading or unloading. She started to pull Patches away from a duffel bag resting against a tree. "Patchy, let's not pee on people's stuff."

Patches looked disappointed but seemed to forget about it when he saw another tree to investigate. He started to tug his way over, but Winnie stood there, thinking. "Wait a minute, Patches. The duffel. Could that be it? Come on, let's get back."

Winnie tugged at the leash, but Patches still wanted to walk and pulled the other way. There were plenty of things left to sniff, and he hadn't done his business yet. Reluctantly, he followed Winnie back to the motor home, breaking into a run to try to keep up.

"Thought so." Winnie flipped through the pictures. "Right here."

Winnie pointed to a small duffel bag on the side of the cave entrance. "See it, Patchy?"

Patches nudged his bowl over, letting Winnie know what he was really interested in.

"Okay, buddy." Winnie got the dog food. "Eat up, because we've got something to do. I think we know where the gold went and the rat that took it."

As usual, it didn't take long for Patches to inhale his food, licking the bowl to get every morsel. Winnie didn't pay much attention as he pushed the bowl around with his nose, his tongue flapping wildly. Instead, she got out some paper and started making notes about the date she had the other night.

"You're an idiot, Winnie," she berated herself. "How could you be this stupid?"

She shook her head. "Getting old, I guess. Hopeful that someone could still find you attractive."

Winnie started pacing, stopping to write things down when she thought of them.

"The duffel was in the trunk. The clunk sound—that must have been the gold rolling around after I stalled the engine. And that's why he was so adamant about me not checking it out."

Winnie kept pacing. "I knew the bang was too loud to just leave. He knew if I saw the gold, I would know what happened. And my mom would still be here." She allowed herself a moment of panic before she formed a plan.

"Here's what we're going to do," Winnie said to Patches. "We're going to find Jason and bring him to the police. I know Jen is looking for him...but can we really trust her? After all, she is another ranger, and they could be in this together. I don't think so, at least I hope not, but right now we can't take that chance, can we?"

Winnie looked at Patches, but he only offered a wagging tail in response.

"I know, it's not likely, but right now we need to do this on our own. We need to find Jason and get him to confess. Any ideas?"

Patches kept wagging his tail.

"You're not a lot of help, sometimes, you know that?"

Winnie heard a car pull up and looked outside to see who it was. Sally was carrying a basket with her. Winnie debated whether to pretend she was away when she heard a knock.

Silence.

Knock, knock, knock.

Winnie wanted to be quiet for a moment and think about what to do, but Patches, ever the guard dog, started barking at the door. *How come he can only hear when I don't want him to?* Her cover blown, Winnie sighed and turned the handle, trying to smile as Sally stood there, smiling back. "Hi, Winnie. I hope you don't mind me stopping by unannounced, but, well, Jen told me what happened, and I thought maybe you could use a shoulder to lean on. Can I come in?"

Winnie nodded.

Sally stepped inside and put the basket down. An awkward silence hung for a moment, but Winnie relented and offered her a seat.

"I hope you know Jen and I care about you. Neither of us would ever think you did anything wrong We just want to help you."

Winnie nodded and motioned to the couch. They both sat.

"Jen was just being Jen, you know? Sometimes she just can't let the cop in her give it a rest. Besides, you think it drives *you* crazy? Sometimes it's like living in an interrogation room."

Winnie managed a laugh through her sniffles. "I know she means well. It's just...well, what if someone she knew did something wrong? Would she just ignore it?"

Sally pulled away and gave Winnie a hard look. "Did something happen? Jen would do everything she could to help you. But she is a ranger, and she took an oath to follow the law."

"It's not about me. It's about someone else. Someone she works with."

"It doesn't matter. She doesn't play favorites. If you know something, or even suspect something, you need to tell her. She will go after whoever or whatever it is. Trust me. And trust her. She's there to help you."

"I think Jason is somehow involved."

"Why? Has he said anything? Did he contact you?"

"No, we haven't spoken. Just call it a strong hunch for now. Based on the pictures I saw and something he said during our date, I have a feeling he's the one that took the gold."

"Oh, boy. That's what I was afraid of."

"What?"

"There's something you should know. Jen just found out Jason sent an email a while ago saying he was taking some time off to 'sort things out.' The BOLO she told you about before is now nationwide."

"Do you think something happened to him, or is he in it with whoever killed Anita?" She sighed. "And took my mom."

"I don't know, but we need to call Jen. Now."

Sally called Jen from her car, saying she and Winnie were on their way to Jen's office. Patches came along for the ride and was happily sticking his head out of the car window. When they arrived, Jen was standing outside, waiting for them.

"Winnie, I'm so sorry." Jen gave Winnie a big bear hug. "I can be a bit abrupt sometimes. Please forgive me."

"I'm sorry, too," Winnie said. "It wasn't your fault. I'm just so afraid for my mom."

"I know."

Patches barked to let everyone know he was there. It seemed to dispel any remaining tension, and the three started to laugh. After Patches finished sniffing everything on the front lawn, the three went inside.

Jen took out her notebook. "After Sally called, I looked through the pictures Anita took. I see the duffel bag you were talking about, but how do you know Jason has one with gold?"

"I don't. It's just a hunch based on what happened on our date." Winnie got out her notes and recounted the story of the loud bang in the trunk when she stalled the engine and how Jason acted strangely about it. Then at dinner when he mentioned things were looking up for him, Winnie put the pieces together. The final piece was all the hand wringing after her mom's disappearance.

"It makes sense." Jen said. "The problem is we don't have any proof."

"But he's on the run. That must mean something."

"We don't know if he's on the run or if something's happened to him. We don't know if the email was really from him. All we know is we can't find him. Until we do, we can't assume anything."

"Maybe you can't, but I can. I knew something was wrong when he stopped by the next morning, but I kept shaking it off, assuming it was just jitters. Then I thought it might be that he did know something—something bad."

"Boss," one of the rangers interrupted. "We got a hit on Jason. He was on a Delta flight at seven this morning, landing in Salt Lake City about eight thirty."

"What? Why are we just hearing about this now?"

"The airport didn't receive our alert until after eight."

"Wonderful. All this technology and it gets us nowhere. OK, where is he now?"

"Ummm, we don't really know. Not yet. We're working on it. It's not that easy to get the airlines to cooperate. In the meantime, we've asked the airports at Jackson Hole and Salt Lake for video, and we should have those sometime this afternoon. We do have the police and TSA on the lookout for him, so hopefully we'll find him soon."

"Check car rentals, taxi cabs, Uber, Lyft. See if he walked out of there. We need to find him. He just jumped up the list to a person of interest, wanted in the connection of a kidnapping."

Winnie looked at Jen. "And possibly murder."

27

While she waited for the video and reports from Jackson Hole and Salt Lake, Jen went back to do a more thorough search of Jason's apartment. The apartment was government property, and no search warrant was required. Winnie was invited to come along, and she sat quietly on the passenger's seat of Jen's car. Normally, she'd be happily belting out a Christmas tune, but not now. Jen was talking about Jason, hoping this was all a mistake. She'd known Jason for a few years, and he always seemed trustworthy and loyal. He was a ranger, after all, one of the best. But the facts were out there, and they didn't look good.

For Winnie's part, she seemed stunned the man she had a great time with the other night could be caught up in all of this, and was probably responsible for her mother's kidnapping. At least indirectly. Jason went from Winnie's nice to naughty list. It was a short list, but nobody wanted to be on it.

They arrived and were met by a couple of other rangers and the apartment building manager. Winnie stared at door 2F. She couldn't believe she would have willingly gone there after their date.

"I really shouldn't let you come inside, but as long as you don't touch anything, I think it will be all right. Here, put these gloves on just in case."

Winnie snapped the gloves on and stood behind Jen. Jen knocked out of protocol, but no one expected an answer. After a second unanswered knock, Jen motioned and the manager opened the door.

"Here we go," Jen said, and the group walked in.

Dust swirled up and sparkled through the sun coming in, and Winnie coughed as she entered.

"The last time I was here," Jen said, "I was only looking for Jason, not evidence."

This time was different, and Jen and her team went over everything. There wasn't much inside, but what they found was shocking. Aside from the usual TV, game console, and other electronic gadgets, Jen found stacks of betting markers tucked in the hallway closet. It would take a while to comb through them, but Jen found more on the dining room table. The betting amounts ranged from a few dollars to thousands, and they were mostly placed with the same group.

"He was a gambler?" Winnie looked over Jen's shoulder.

"Apparently, and not a very successful one, judging by these sheets. It's going to take some time to go through this, but my guess is he got in way over his head."

"That's why he took the gold." Winnie shook her head.

"It could be. We still don't know that he took it, but it's looking more likely that he did."

Winnie knew Jen wouldn't jump to any conclusions, but Winnie had no doubt Jason was involved. What Winnie didn't know was *how* involved he was. Was he responsible for Anita's death? Winnie couldn't believe Jason would stoop to murder, but desperation caused people to do things they wouldn't normally do.

Then she thought of Anita. She didn't deserve any of this.

Not the harassment from the fake ranger, not being chased after finding the illegal mining, and certainly not being killed for it. She was just a young, innocent woman. A kid, really, with her whole life ahead of her.

Winnie clenched her fists and was more determined than ever to get to the bottom of this. She understood addiction. She'd lived with an abusive alcoholic until she finally had the courage to escape. She'd hoped dealing with an addict was behind her. But Winnie didn't like turning her back on someone in need. If Jason wasn't involved with her mother's disappearance or Anita's murder, she would try to help. But if he had anything to do with either of those, Winnie would move heaven and earth to see he was held accountable. And that he got a swift kick in the you-know-where. Maybe two.

But first they had to find him, and, with every minute, that seemed less likely.

A ringing cell phone brought Winnie back. She didn't know who called, but she could hear Jen's side of the conversation. And it didn't sound pleasant.

"You're going to let a formality allow a suspect to get away?" Jen shouted into the phone. "I need your cooperation, not your stonewalling. All I want...yes...Okay, I'll wait to hear back."

"Bastard." Jen hung up, raising her eyebrows as she looked at Winnie. "Salt Lake isn't being cooperative about checking with cabbies. Lack of proper authorization, or so they claim. I think it's just a case of 'not my problem' syndrome. Unfortunately, even some cops aren't immune to it."

Winnie was crestfallen.

"We'll get him, Winnie. It just might take a while."

They went back to searching the apartment. Winnie stayed close to Jen, keeping her hands in her pockets so she didn't touch anything. They were combing over the kitchen, looking inside cabinets. It was a typical guy's kitchen—lots of junk food and big knives for cutting meat, but not a vegetable in sight.

The refrigerator had plenty of beer, wine, and a few containers of what looked like leftovers at one point. Now they were enemy combatants, battling each other for bacterial superiority. The smell let Winnie know the battle was raging, though no victor had won.

"Jen, come take a look at this," someone called from the bedroom.

Jen and Winnie hurried into the room to find the mattress propped up on the frame and people taking pictures of whatever was underneath. When the photographer stopped, a hand reached down and pulled out a beat-up green duffel bag, something that looked like it came from an army surplus store. It smelled like it, too, and Winnie wrinkled her nose at the musty smell. The duffel was well used, with a few small holes and the outside splotched with a generous amount of dirt. Dust billowed up as Jen grabbed the duffel and looked inside. She put a gloved hand in, scraping the inside.

"Yellow," Jen said. "I guess I shouldn't be surprised, but I am. Sorry, Winnie. I was hoping there'd be another explanation."

"So, the gold is gone. Where does that leave my mom? Without the gold, they might kill her. We've got to find Jason, get him to tell us what he did with the gold, and get her back."

"I agree, but we don't know who took your mom, or where she is. Jason has an alibi for when your mom went missing. He was with you. He may have been in on it, but we just don't know. Hopefully, finding Jason will help lead us to your mom. That's why we need to find him as soon as possible."

They finished up and were at the car when Jen's phone rang. Winnie couldn't hear much from the other end, but what she heard was shocking. And encouraging.

"Where? Are you sure?"

Winnie tugged at Jen's arm. "What's going on?"

Jen held up a finger and went back to her conversation. "Yeah, OK. I'll wait."

A moment later, Jen's phone trilled. Winnie started to say something, but Jen shook her head. She looked at her phone, then showed it to Winnie. A text message with a picture. Winnie squinted to see it, but when she recognized the picture, she let out a gasp.

The picture was a squad car. Jason sat in the back in cuffs. His hair was disheveled and the bags under his eyes showed a tiredness Winnie hadn't seen before. Was it remorse at what he'd done or frustration he'd been caught? The gray stubble of beard made him look old. Was this aging him as quickly as it was Winnie? Or maybe he was trying to change his appearance. He looked pathetic, but there was no doubt who he was.

"Where is he? Does he know where my mom is? Will he help us?"

Jen turned the phone back to her ear and motioned for Winnie to wait. Winnie called out to put the call on speakerphone, but Jen ignored her and took a step farther away. She was talking for quite a while, and when she finished, Jen turned around to face a clearly exasperated Winnie. She motioned for Winnie to get in the car.

Jen pulled out of the parking lot. "Sorry about that, but I still have to conduct this properly. I know it's personal for you and it's difficult to be on the sidelines. They found Jason at a rest area north of Salt Lake City on I-84. It was just lucky a Utah Highway Patrolman was there and noticed Jason getting out of his car. Once Jason spotted the patrolman, he got back in and took off, trying to avoid detection. They followed him onto the interstate while they ran the plates, and when it came back as a rental from Salt Lake airport, they pulled him over. For what it's worth, they say he's being cooperative. They think he's just glad it's over."

"It's not over until my mom's back safe."

"About that. He claims he doesn't know where your mom is. He did take the gold but didn't think they would take your mom as a hostage. And he doesn't want to say anything else until I speak to him directly."

"Well, we'll get the gold back and we can use it to get Mom."

Jen took a deep breath and didn't say anything.

Winnie's eyes got big as she looked at Jen. "He doesn't have it, does he?"

Jen shook her head. "They didn't find it on him. After your mom was kidnapped, he suspected somebody would figure out he took the gold, so he ran. After flying into Salt Lake City, he planned to take the rental car to Boise. From there he was going to try to get out of the country. They found his passport, but he only had about five thousand in cash with him. He said he has more information but will only talk to me about it."

"So, what do we do?"

"They're bringing him back here. I told them a life was on the line and they agreed the paperwork could wait. They'll be on the next flight from Salt Lake to Bozeman. I'll be waiting for him when he gets off the plane."

They pulled up to Winnie's RV.

"I'd like to be there, too," Winnie said.

Jen shook her head. "I can't let you do that, Winnie. Sorry. It might compromise things."

Winnie didn't say anything. She looked to her left when she heard a car pull up.

"Sally wanted to stay with you. I hope you understand."

Winnie nodded. She understood all right. Jen would understand soon, too.

28

After Jen left, Winnie said she needed to go for a walk, and asked Sally if she minded watching Patches for a while. Sally showed Winnie a basket full of treats she brought for him and was now Patches's best friend. Winnie grabbed her phone, said goodbye, and left. She unlocked her car using the key instead of the noisy clicker, slipped inside, started the engine, and took off before Sally could stop her. Winnie looked behind to see Sally at the door, phone in hand.

She was about three minutes behind Jen. At the speed Jen drove Winnie might never catch up. But she had to. She wanted to see Jason's face and judge his reaction. She put the pedal to the floor, hoping she didn't hit a person. Or a bison.

Winnie traveled about two miles when she saw a car in a pullout. A cop car. With no chance to slow down, Winnie sped past, and the car pulled out, lights blazing. *Crap.* Her Mini couldn't outrun a cop car. She pulled over and the car stopped behind her. Winnie shook her head when Jen got out and walked over.

"I thought we settled this."

"You said I couldn't come with you. I'm just out for a drive."

"To where?"

"I don't know. It's a nice day and I feel like exploring."

"I should give you a ticket."

Winnie said nothing. She tried to give Jen a "sad eyes" look.

Jen gave Winnie a long stare then sighed. "I guess I'm better off keeping an eye on you than letting you follow me. Maybe, just maybe, I can actually control you a little."

Winnie smiled. "There's always hope."

"You can't leave your car here. I'll follow you back."

"Thank you."

Jen smiled. "I would have done the same thing. Let's go."

Winnie offered a quick apology to Sally when they dropped the car off. Sally gave her a hug and smiled at Jen, who waited in the car. Winnie got in and Jen pulled out. She put her lights on. "We need to make up some time after our...delay."

After leaving the park, the two headed North on US-89 then West on I-90 to the Bozeman airport. Along the way, Jen was on her phone, coordinating the pickup of Jason with the Bozeman police. Winnie fidgeted the whole time, staring out the window and wondering what she'd say—or do—when she saw Jason.

They might need to put me in handcuffs.

As if reading her mind, Jen spoke up. "Winnie, I'm guessing your emotions are working overtime right now. I know mine would be. I can imagine a combination of anger, fear, uncertainty, disappointment, and loathing all fighting inside you. Maybe even a little excitement mixed in. But we can't let our emotions rule what happens. If we mess up, he might get to go free. His lawyer can argue some technicality about the arrest or treatment while in custody and he's gone. Poof."

"Got it. No poof. Hopefully, my foot won't act up again. Sometimes it does that and ends up in a very delicate place to anyone standing close enough. It would be a shame to see Jason doubled over in pain. Of course, it would be purely accidental."

"Winnie..."

"Okay, okay. No poof and no foot. Got it."

"Thank you. That's one less thing I need to worry about."

The Bozeman Yellowstone International Airport was located a few miles northwest of Bozeman in Belgrade, Montana. Winnie's pulse quickened as they got closer, the thought of seeing Jason racing around in her head. Winnie felt so embarrassed going out with him in the first place. What was she thinking? Winnie didn't think she was *that* unattractive, at least not for her age, anyway. But doubt crept in every chance it got.

"How could I have been so stupid to think he liked me?" Winnie blurted out.

"What? Winnie, that wasn't stupid. And you've got so much going for you. You're smart, pretty and you have a great heart. You make every life you touch better."

There was silence for a moment, then Jen went on. "And I think Jason went out with you with good intentions. He liked you. He probably still does like you. He just made a stupid, stupid mistake that will cost him. A lot. Park Ranger—gone. Friends—gone. Freedom—gone. But I don't think he was trying to use you or anything. I'm not excusing him, but I don't think he's a bad person. Jason's done a lot of good in the time I've known him. But he made a bad decision, and, unfortunately, in life there are no do-overs."

"Humph," was all Winnie could muster. Her face warmed, and the vein throbbed in her neck as they turned off the interstate.

Before long, they pulled up to the terminal, and Jen parked behind two police cars. Four officers got out of the squad cars and waved. Jen stuck her hand out of the window, returning the wave. Winnie was staring outside, her eyes tearing up and body slightly shaking.

"Are you going to be okay? Maybe I should have brought Sally and Patches with us."

Winnie looked over. "I'll be fine. I probably shouldn't have come. There's nothing I can do to help." She let out a long sigh. "I just want my mom back."

Jen nodded. "I know." She got out of the car. "You wait here. As soon as he gets off the plane, we're going to have to put him in cuffs, and it might not be pleasant. He's going to ride in one of the police cars, so you don't have to worry about talking to him."

"Can we find out what he knows about Mom before we go back? She's been gone a long time now, and I'm really worried."

"I'm going to talk with him in the airport before we go back. I'll make sure he knows it's in his best interest to cooperate."

After Jen and the Bozeman police officers entered the terminal, Winnie was alone in the car with little to occupy her time. She wished she would have brought a book, even though she wouldn't have been able to concentrate. She considered using the Kindle app on her phone just to have something to do. Instead, Winnie decided to check on Patches.

"Sally, it's Winnie. We're at the airport. Jen went inside to get you-know-who while I wait in the car. I just called to see how Patches is doing."

"I know it must be rough to go through all of this. Patches and I decided to go for another walk, and he's pretty busy sniffing on one thing and peeing on the next. He seems to have a pretty good system down for it, too. Tug-sniff-pee, tug-sniff-pee. He never gets tired of it. But he's also a lot of fun, and we played catch for a while before the walk. I was thinking of asking Santa for a dog for Christmas. I don't know, though. Jen's not really into pets anymore, and we have such a crazy life sometimes."

"Pets are a lot of fun, but they're a lot of work, too. I love Patches, but he's like a kid that never grows up. Sometimes that can drive you crazy." Winnie was happy for the distraction while she waited. She wondered if Sally was doing that on purpose. It would be just like Sally. In the short time she'd known her, Sally struck Winnie as a person that went out of her way to make someone feel better. Maybe that was why she was a teacher. She was such a great person, and it bothered Winnie that some people made a fuss over her and Jen being a couple.

I'd rather be with this happy couple than the SOB I was married to, any day.

"Winnie!" Sally whispered, interrupting her daydream. "We're just getting back from our walk, and I think there's someone in your RV."

"What? Get out of there, now!"

"Oh. My. God." Sally said, and then the line went quiet.

"Sally? Sally!" Winnie started to get out of the car to find Jen. She didn't want to disconnect her call with Sally in case she got back on the line.

"Winnie, your mom's here!"

"What? Really? When? How?" Winnie had already gotten out of the car and was pacing around it.

"I'm Sally, Winnie's friend," Winnie heard Sally say.

"Where's Winnie?"

"She's on the phone with me now. Here."

"Winnie?" a familiar voice said.

"Mom! Thank goodness. Are you all right?"

"Well, that's a relative term, I suppose. I could use a glass of wine and a nice hot bath, maybe something to eat. But other than that, I'm fine."

Yep, it's my mom all right. At least she got her priorities straight —wine then bath then maybe some food.

"What happened? Did they just let you go?"

"I guess. I was either locked in a room or blindfolded most of the time. When they put the blindfold on this morning, they pulled me outside. I thought they might kill me.

Instead, they dropped me off about a mile or so from your RV."

Her mom started crying, and Sally took the phone back. "She's just a little shook up, Winnie. She doesn't look hurt."

"Thank God. Can you stay there with my mom? We probably won't be back for a couple of hours."

"Absolutely. As soon as you see Jen, tell her, and I'm sure she'll have a couple of rangers stop by to take her statement. Do you think I should take her to the hospital to have her checked out?"

"As long as she looks okay, I would just leave her there. She'll likely fall asleep as soon as she calms down." Winnie looked over to see Jen coming out of the terminal, four police officers surrounding someone Winnie suspected was Jason.

"Jen!" Winnie shouted. "My mom's back."

Jen looked over then said something to one of the Bozeman police officers and dashed over to Winnie. "Really? When?"

"Just a few minutes ago. Sally was out walking Patches when I called. When she got back to the RV, my mom came out and said whoever kidnapped her just dropped her off."

"That's fantastic news. I can't wait to see her again. I had a talk with Jason, and he said he didn't know your mom was going to be kidnapped, but once she went missing, he was able to make a deal with someone. He exchanged the gold for your mom then left town before his bookie could find him. They were supposed to drop your mom off sometime today. We're lucky they kept their word and didn't just, well, you know."

Jen looked back at the squad car as Jason was being stuffed into the back seat. Jason looked over at Winnie, who was standing there staring.

"Winnie," he blurted out. "I'm sorry. I never meant for this to happen." That was all he could get out before the door was slammed. Jen rushed over to the cars before they could take off. She came back a moment later.

"He's going to be held at the local Bozeman jail. For now, anyway. Federal prosecutors are coming to take this over, and since we don't need him to find your mom, I'd rather not have to deal with it. I asked the guys to hold up a minute. If you want to go over and talk to him, they'll wait."

Winnie folded her arms, bit her lower lip, and tapped her right foot. Letting out a sigh, she marched over to the car holding Jason. As she approached, the window went down.

"Win—Win—Winnie," Jason stammered. His eyes were puffy and red.

Winnie held up her right hand and Jason stopped.

"Were you a part of my mom's kidnapping? Tell me the truth."

Jason shook his head. "No, of course not. I had no idea that was going to happen. Look, I took the gold. I was in debt way over my head. I was desperate."

"So, you didn't make the killers think I took the gold and then ask me out just so they could get to my mom? Because that's exactly what it seems." Winnie clenched her jaw as she glared at Jason. She'd been fooled once, and she wasn't going to be fooled again. Not if she could help it, anyway.

"That's not what happened. Please, believe me."

Winnie stared at Jason, her gaze boring a hole through his eyes, trying to read his mind.

"Winnie," Jen called out, looking over at her.

Time to go.

"Bye, Jason. I hope it works out for you."

The window went up and the cars drove away, leaving Winnie standing there, staring.

Jen walked over to where Winnie was standing. "Let's go see your mom."

That snapped Winnie out of her fog. She smiled at Jen and they got in the car. As they pulled onto the interstate, Winnie called Lexi, who was relieved to know Mom was safe. Then she made a quick call to Reggie, who had been texting her to find out about her mom. When she hung up, Winnie told Jen how she and Reggie met and how Reggie was fast becoming a good friend. Then she called her mom back and they talked until Winnie's cell phone ran out of battery. Jen spent her time coordinating with federal authorities for the transfer of Jason into their custody. Winnie started humming "I'll Be Home for Christmas," already making plans to be back in Wisconsin for the holidays.

After Jen got off the phone, Winnie looked over. "What's going to happen to Jason now?"

"He'll sit in a federal prison. I don't think they'll give him any sort of bail, especially since he's already proven to be a flight risk." She took Winnie's hand. "We can't worry about him anymore, okay? He's just one bad apple, but there's a whole orchard out there."

Winnie started to chuckle, then found herself laughing so hard tears were rolling down her cheeks. She knew Jen was just trying to cheer her up, and she was so happy to go through this with a couple like Jen and Sally. The world needed more of them.

"Wait," Winnie said. "If Jason traded the gold for my mom, he must know who has the gold now. Wouldn't they be the ones that killed Anita?"

"Oh, I never finished telling you about my conversation with him at the airport. I asked Jason about that. He said he was out there the day before to bring an animal over and noticed the lock was off. He found what looked like recent activity heading toward the mine, so he went to investigate. Whoever it was left in a hurry and didn't take the duffel with gold. When Jason realized he could sell it and get out of debt, he took it."

"But why would they leave the gold? They risked a lot to mine it. I would think it would be a priority to take it."

"Nobody knows, but I'm guessing there was more than one

bag. Maybe it was from the guy that got killed. They probably got spooked and thought they would leave it and come back later for it. Those bags are heavy, and it takes time to load it."

"That still doesn't explain why they thought I had it. Why not someone else?"

"I have a theory about that, too. My guess is someone was watching the area when we approached. They knew the bag was missing when we left. You and your mom were easy targets, so they started there. Maybe they saw me leave and knew I didn't take it, then they followed you and Jason back to your RV. Unfortunately, we may never know all the answers."

"But how did Jason know who to exchange the gold for my mom with?"

"You really do think like a detective, Winnie. Jason claims he knew someone that knew someone, and he arranged a drop-off of the gold. He never saw any faces. I'm not buying it, but now it's the fed's problem. Thank goodness he crossed state lines."

"Yeah, I guess." Winnie wasn't feeling entirely convinced. "Why didn't he drop off the duffel bag, too? As soon as we found it, we knew he took the gold. Seems kind of stupid."

"I don't know, but I'm guessing he didn't think it through. Maybe he already had the gold out and didn't put it back. Maybe he panicked. I'm sure we'll find out eventually. For now, it's just good your mom is back."

Before Winnie knew it, they were turning into the RV park. Winnie sat up straight, both nervous and excited to see her mom, hoping she was going to be all right.

Two ranger cars were parked next to Winnie's Winnie. A group of people were standing outside, and when they heard a car approach, they all turned to see who was there. Winnie could see her mom through the crowd, and she opened the door and jumped out before Jen came to a full stop. Winnie ran to her mom, and they both were locked in a tight embrace.

"Oh, Mom." Tears streamed down Winnie's face. "I was so worried."

"Me, too, dear. But I'm fine, so let's not dwell on it."

Winnie pulled away and stared at her mom. It was so un-mom-like to just shrug something like this off.

Sabrina seemed to read Winnie's mind and must have seen the confused look on her daughter's face. "Winona, dear, I know I'm acting a little different. But ever since I started seeing Martin, I've decided to be more zen."

Zen? My mom's a monk now? What's next, incense and chanting?

"It's both Martin and you, dear. You both showed me I need to live my life a little more fully. Take risks. I guess after this you can say I jumped in with both feet!"

"Yeah, Mom, and look where it got you. Kidnapped. I was so worried for you. Maybe we should both just go back to Madison. I think I could use a little normalcy."

"I don't think that's you, Winnie."

"Mom, I caused this. None of it would have happened if I hadn't left. You'd still be safe in your house."

"And, I wouldn't have met Martin. Even more importantly, I wouldn't have realized how little I've been living these past few years. That wouldn't have happened if it weren't for you. Besides, you didn't cause this. You didn't kill Anita. You befriended Anita and probably made her last night much better than it would have been."

Sabrina took Winnie by the hand and led her away from the crowd. "Winnie, you were bored stiff in Madison. Out here, you're alive. I heard it in your voice when you called. I like you better this way. In fact, both Martin and I have talked about following in your footsteps. Well, at least to some extent. We talked about getting a small camper for weekend outings."

Winnie still wasn't sure if her mom was suffering from

shock or if she was changing. "I don't know. Maybe. Let's just get through this and see where it takes us."

Winnie's mom wrapped her in a bear hug and planted a kiss on her cheek. "I know I don't act like it, but I'm so very proud of you. You're a terrific person."

Winnie returned the kiss. She whispered, "I love you, Mom," in Sabrina's ear, and was rewarded with a tighter hug, which threatened to force the wind out of her. But it felt good, and neither one broke away for a long time.

29

By the time the police finished, it was getting dark. They retreated outside, and it didn't take long before the adrenaline rush left Sabrina and she crashed. Hard. Winnie got her comfortable in the bed in the RV, and Sabrina was out quickly. Patches seemed to know what to do, and he stayed by Sabrina's side, keeping watch. Winnie stepped back outside.

The rangers didn't think Sabrina or Winnie were in immediate danger, so they left, promising to make frequent patrols. Winnie thanked each of them for their help. Sally and Jen stayed behind.

"You're a true friend," Winnie said to Sally as she and Jen got ready to leave. "Both of you are. My life is so much better because you two are in it. I can never thank you enough."

Sally rushed over and gave Winnie a hug. Jen, back to her professional, reserved self, just smiled and nodded.

"We're throwing you a party!" Sally blurted out.

Jen looked over with a confused expression on her face.

"I just thought of it." Sally looked at Jen.

Jen smiled and nodded.

"Tomorrow night. Bring your mom and Patches. We need to celebrate. Love and friendship. What could be better?"

Winnie looked over at Jen, and Jen smiled. "Sally can be spontaneous, but I couldn't agree more. Tomorrow. Come over about five."

"Thank you," Winnie said. "We'll be there."

After everyone was gone, Winnie was left standing there. "Whew." She plopped down on a lawn chair. She didn't have a chance to put her feet up before she heard the phone ringing inside the RV. She left it there charging, not thinking anyone would call her, and now she was scrambling to answer it before it woke up her mom.

"Hello?" Winnie panted into the phone.

"Winnie. It's Martin."

Martin. Ouch. Kinda forgot about him. "Martin!"

"Hello, Winona." That time his voice dropped an octave.

Whoa, now Martin's calling me Winona? Geez, they're going to start ganging up on me. And he sounds mad, too. "Martin. I was going to call—"

"Winnie, I know it's late, but I believe you owe me an update on Brina. I must insist you provide me one now. I've waited far too long."

"I agree, Martin, and I'm sorry. Things got a little crazy, and I didn't follow up with you like I should have. But I've got good news. Mom's back."

"She is? When? Is she all right? Put her on the phone."

"Easy now, fella," Winnie laughed. It felt good to say something silly like that. "Mom's sleeping. She just got back a short while ago, and as you can imagine, she's been inundated with police and medical personnel checking her out and asking her questions. After they left, she about collapsed. I know she'll want to talk to you as soon as she gets up, but right now I need to let her sleep."

"I see. But she's all right? No harm came to her?"

"I'm sure it was rough, emotionally, anyway. Physically, she doesn't look harmed. The medics checked her out and said she was fine. They offered to take her to the hospital, but she refused. Instead, she had the best medicine around—a big glass of wine and a chocolate chip cookie. Nothing could be better."

"I believe that's a case of 'like mother, like daughter.' Wouldn't you agree?"

"Yes, Martin." Winnie laughed. "I'll have Mom call you when she gets up, but I don't think that will be before morning. I'm sure you understand."

"Very good, Winnie. Until then."

Too stressed to sleep, Winnie put on a sweater and sat outside, enjoying the light breeze. The campground was too bright to see many stars, so Winnie closed her eyes and let her other senses take over. She could smell a campfire burning somewhere, and the sounds of crackling wood mingled with muffled voices. She took deep breaths. Each time Winnie exhaled, she tried to push her anxiety out. She finished with a prayer of thanks for her mom's safe return.

Feeling better, Winnie went back inside and sat on her couch. She picked up her Kindle and started a new fudge shop mystery series, which took place in Door County, Wisconsin, a place Winnie's family visited many times when she was growing up. After an hour of reading, Winnie drifted off to sleep. But sleep wasn't peaceful, and Winnie found herself jumping at the slightest noise.

~

THE NEXT MORNING, her mom was still sleeping soundly, but even without a good night's sleep, Winnie was a bundle of energy. Pent-up energy, because she was afraid to stray too far from the RV. She took her yoga mat outside and went through her poses. Winnie missed Patches jumping on her while she changed positions, even though she grumbled about it when he did. Without Patches to scurry around her, Winnie finished her yoga in record time and went in to check on her mom. Faint snoring wafted in from the bedroom. *Good. Right where I left her.*

As she went to make coffee, Winnie glanced at her phone, which was flashing. "Two missed calls and a voice mail." Winnie remembered she put the phone on silent so as not to disturb her mom. But with her mom safe, nothing was more important than her morning caffeine, so she put the phone on the counter while she mixed some fruit, yogurt, and granola in a bowl. She poured her coffee and was just about to take a sip when she heard scratching. Soft but constant, like someone sending a message. Someone named Patches.

"Really?" Winnie quietly opened the door. Patches sauntered out, circling Winnie's legs and wagging his tail. "You need to go out now. Of course you do."

The leash came out, and Patches did his happy dance. She tried to keep him from making too much noise, but there were still a few yips and yelps. Winnie locked the door on the way out, double-checking it was secure. She made sure all the windows were shut, and only then was she comfortable leaving. Even so, instead of their usual long sniff and pee on everything walk, Winnie kept Patches on a very short radius, not wanting to stray too far from her mother. She kept her RV in sight at all times, frequently turning to make sure she could see the door, then whipping her head around to check the road for any signs of trouble.

True to their word, a ranger's car came up slowly, asking if everything was all right. Winnie said yes and thanked the ranger, who said she'd be back soon to check again. That made Winnie much more comfortable, and she allowed herself to relax a little as she directed Patches back to the RV.

Back inside, the bedroom door was still closed, and the

snoring continued. Winnie's now-cold coffee sat on the table, right next to her phone and the bowl of yogurt.

The phone! I knew I forgot something.

Winnie picked up the phone. It now showed three missed calls, a text message, and a voice mail, so whoever it was wanted to talk. The text was from Reggie, checking on Winnie's mom. She included a smiling face emoji that made Winnie smile. Then she checked the missed calls—all from Martin. She knew the voice mail must be from him, too. "He's going to be a Nervous Nellie until Mom's back in Madison." Winnie took a spoonful of yogurt and decided to answer the text message first, calling Reggie instead of replying.

"I'm so glad you called," Reggie said. "I prefer talking over an impersonal text, but I didn't want to disturb you two. How's your mom?"

Winnie kept her voice low while her mother slept. "She's still sleeping, but fine. She seems to be taking it really well, which isn't mom-like at all. Oh, and remember Sally and Jen, the two I told you about? They're throwing us a party tonight. You're not coming back today, are you? I'm sure they'd love to meet you."

"Unfortunately, we're going to be a few extra days. The funeral was today and we thought we were leaving tomorrow, but the lawyer has asked us to stay for the reading of the will, which isn't for two days. We'll come back the day after that."

"That's too bad. I know you would have gotten along really well. I've been thinking about my itinerary. The Grand Tetons will still be there, so I'm planning to go to Glacier instead. Maybe we can spend some more time together, if that's okay. I can use some hiking partners."

"Okay? That's fantastic. It sounds like we might get there a day or so later than you, but we'll do our best to catch up. Have you made reservations yet?"

"Not yet. As soon as I get my schedule arranged, I'll let you know. Oh, I signed up for Drove There, Did That. I got my first newsletter already."

"Great! You'll meet lots of new people that way. Cal's pointing at his watch, so I better run. I'm glad we'll be catching up at Glacier. Hope your momma feels better."

After Winnie hung up, she noticed the voice mail indicator and entered her password to listen.

"Winnie, it's Martin. You're not answering, so I hope everything's all right. I took another look at Anita's notebook. Something was bothering me about it, and I wanted to give it another go. And I'm glad I did. Call me when you get this and we'll go over what I found."

After calling Martin back, Winnie eyes went wide as she took notes as fast as she could.

"Martin, are you sure?"

"Very sure."

"Wow. Okay. Thanks."

Then she made a call of her own. To Jennifer, who picked up on the first ring.

"Jen, do you have a pen and paper? You're not going to believe this."

30

"You mean Anita listed names?" Jen asked over the phone after Winnie told her the news.

"Well, sort of. She read two of the names on their name tags, and she translated them into Ukrainian. It was just a first initial followed by the last name. Then she reversed the name, putting the initial last. So, when Martin fed the information into the computer, it came back as gibberish. The third person didn't have a tag, which is why she used 'Mr. X,' although it was spelled 'X-M-i-c-t-e-p.' And Anita went over it a number of times, which distorted the letters. The Ukrainian alphabet has some different characters, too. All of that meant it was easy to dismiss and easy to confuse Martin and his computer."

"But all the pictures were from a distance," Jen said. "How could she read them?"

"I don't know if she says. Maybe when she looked out from her position in the shrubs, she noticed them. Anita wore a name tag when she was working, so maybe she knew where to look. I'll ask Martin if there's more information the next time I talk to him."

"Speaking of Martin, how did Martin figure it out? And why now? I mean, he's had Anita's notebook for a while."

"At first, he didn't pay much attention to it. He assumed it was just some sort of doodle. Or words he couldn't translate. But as the messages became clearer, he decided to give the things he couldn't originally translate another look. According to Martin, it was the placement and the tracing that caught his attention. Martin thought that Anita kept tracing over it because it was important and she was mulling it over. Or maybe she tried to draw our attention to it. It was actually the scribbling of 'Mr. X' that clued him in. He said he noticed the 'mister' and wondered about it. Then he did it for the other names. Then it all came together. I think it's the best lead we've gotten so far."

"Absolutely. It might be the break in the case we've been looking for. I've got personnel looking for a 'K. Jeffers' and 'R. Wilson.' Unfortunately, the request is going through headquarters, so it might take a while. They don't move quickly for anybody. How's your mom doing?"

"She's okay, I guess. She's been sleeping since last night. I almost wonder if I should go in and check on her."

"I would give her some time. She's been through quite an ordeal, although luckily, she wasn't harmed. At least not physically. Let her sleep, just as long as she's not late for the party. Sally's been busy all day, and I think you know her enough to know how she is when she makes up her mind."

"We won't miss the party. I don't want the wrath of Sally. I was thinking that tomorrow I'd spend the day with Mom doing something she'd like. Maybe we'll go shopping or something."

"Sally and I thought about that. Why don't you let us keep Patches tonight. You and your mom can check into a hotel in Gardiner after the party and spend Sunday wandering around. Maybe go to a spa. I bet she'd love that."

"That sounds right up Mom's alley. Thanks."

"My pleasure. Oh, before I forget, I wanted to let you know we spoke to the people running the RV park. You can stay there as long as you like, and the bill is already taken care of. It's our way of thanking you for all of the help."

"Wow. I don't know what to say. Thanks! I appreciate it. I can't wait to see you tonight."

"Sally just handed me a note that The Laughing Bison Resort is a spa just outside of Gardiner. I should have remembered that because she's been trying to get me to go. I'm not much for being pampered, but maybe I'll check it out someday."

"Maybe tomorrow?" Winnie said. "We could have a girls' day."

"I heard that," Sally called from a distance. "That's a great idea. We could all use a relaxing day. I know the manager, so I'll call her as soon as I'm finished getting the food in the oven."

"I guess I'm going to be pampered after all," Jen chuckled. "But none of that seaweed wrap, cucumber eyelid nonsense," she said loud enough that Sally could hear. "So, leave it to Sally. I'm sure by the time you get here, she'll have the whole thing planned out. Yay, me."

"It won't be *that* bad, will it?"

"Not really. But if I don't make a fuss and complain, she'll wonder why. It's just one of those silly dances couples do."

Sally said something but Winnie couldn't make out what it was.

"Duty calls, Winnie. I guess my fun time is done and I've got to get back to work. I swear, she's a tougher taskmaster than my boss. I have to go to the office sometimes just to relax."

Winnie laughed when "I heard that, too" came through the telephone. Offering quick goodbyes, Winnie hung up just as her bedroom door opened and her mom came out, rubbing her eyes and yawning.

"Did you sleep okay? I hope I didn't wake you."

"I'm fine, dear. Just not used to sleeping this long, I suppose, and I feel a little disoriented. I woke up a little while ago, thinking about Martin. I should give him a call."

"He's been thinking about you, too." Winnie smiled. "But I'm sure it can wait until you've had some coffee and wake up a little more. You still look a bit groggy. Are you hungry?"

"Starving." Sabrina grabbed a cookie from a tin on the counter.

"Cookies for breakfast, Mom?"

Sabrina shrugged. "I know, but I think I'm entitled this one time. How about some coffee to go with it?"

Winnie poured another cup of coffee and refilled her own. "Martin called while you were sleeping. He was able to decipher more of the notebook, and he found a few names. They're tracking them down now, but I wouldn't be too surprised if they're fake. Everything else seems to keep us running around in circles. But it's something more to look into, and hopefully, it will pan out."

"I really should call Lexi and Martin. I'm sure they're both worried."

"We'll call Lexi after we eat, and I told Martin you were sleeping and would call later. He understood, Brina."

"Oh." Sabrina's cheeks turned rosy. "Martin likes to call me that. It's silly."

"It's cute. So, are you and Martin getting serious?"

"I don't know, dear. I like him, and that's enough for now."

"Well, I like him too, in case you want to know."

"Thanks. It's important that you like him. Even if we don't get serious, he'll always be a friend. How about we change the subject? I'm not ready to discuss my love life with my daughter just yet."

"We've got a party to get to tonight, and I have a special treat in store for tomorrow. We're going to have a girl's day out at the spa."

"Really? There's a spa in Yellowstone?"

"Just outside in a small town. Sally's making the arrangements, and we'll finalize them at the party."

After they ate, Winnie checked her pantry. She had just enough ingredients for oatmeal-raisin cookies, and decided to make a batch to bring. While she baked, Sabrina spoke to Lexi on FaceTime. When they finished, Winnie called Martin and pressed the speaker button so her mom could hear, too."

"Hello, Brina! It's so good to hear your voice."

"Yours, too, Martin."

"Are you all right?"

"I'm still recovering, but I think I'll be fine. Guess what? We're going to a party tonight and a spa tomorrow. I am so looking forward to a nice massage."

"You deserve it, my dear. I'm sure it will bring your spirits up. When are you coming home?"

"The day after tomorrow. I'll be home before you know it. And Winnie is getting out of here right after that." Sabrina looked over at Winnie. "I think we've both had enough excitement for a while, haven't we?"

WINNIE, Sabrina, and Patches arrived shortly after five. Winnie had brushed Patches, and his coat had a nice shimmer to it, at least until he found the nearest dirt patch to roll around in. On their way, they picked up a bottle of *Rendezvous Red* from Jackson Hole Winery.

Sally opened the door before they could knock. "Winnie! Sabrina! Welcome." She looked down. "And you, too, Patches. I'm so glad you made it."

Sally led the group inside. The family room was set up with serving stations, each one offering a different small plate. Next to each serving station were beverage choices that paired well with the food, and Winnie placed the wine next to another red. Sally took the cookies and put them with the other desserts. Winnie could see Jen and six other people milling about.

Jen came over, and she and Sally took Winnie and Sabrina around, introducing them to the other guests, while Patches was free to roam. Everyone there knew the abridged version of what happened, and all of them were curious. Winnie and Sabrina were the center of attention for a while, but the conversations naturally drifted to other adult topics, and soon half the group was discussing book club fiction while the other current events.

The evening was fun, but when the clock turned nine, both Winnie and Sabrina were stifling yawns every few minutes. The rest of the guests filtered out, wishing Winnie and Sabrina well. With everyone gone, Winnie turned to Sally. "Thanks so much for doing this. I can't remember the last time I had this much fun."

"My pleasure. I know you're both tired, but I have the details about tonight and tomorrow I'd like to go over with you." Sally went to the counter and came back with a slip of paper. "Here's the hotel I reserved for you tonight. It's called the Gardiner Old West. I know the manager and got a great deal on a room. Breakfast is included, so fill up before we pick you up for the spa."

She turned the page. "Jen and I will pick you up at ten. The Silvermans, the couple you met tonight, will be taking care of Patches for the day. They love dogs and will take good care of him. Here are the contact numbers for the Silvermans, the hotel, and the spa, just in case. The hotel is tucked away from the main road, so Jen and I will show you where it is."

After saying goodbye to Patches, Winnie and Sabrina followed Jen and Sally the few miles to the hotel. Sally went in to make sure everything was ready and wished them a good night.

Winnie and Sabrina were tired, but neither wanted to sleep. They hadn't had a chance to spend much time together and decided now was probably their best opportunity. Sally, who seemed to think of everything, had a bottle of wine, two glasses, a corkscrew, and strawberries on the table. The note in front of the glasses read "Enjoy! Sally and Jen."

Winnie made quick work of the cork, pouring two glasses, and stepped out onto a patio overlooking the mountains. The sun had long-ago set, and Winnie slipped on a sweater before sitting in one of the lounge chairs. She could still see the outlines of the mountains and heard the rush of water as the Yellowstone River flowed past.

Sabrina took her glass and joined her.

"To new friends," Sabrina said, the two clanking glasses.

"And to each other," Winnie added.

Her new adventure was turning out all right after all.

31

Winnie was sitting on the patio when the sun came up, highlighting the mountains in a beautiful red, orange, and yellow glow. She could still hear the river, but the tranquil flow was joined with boaters launching rafts for a day of fun on the water. Waiting until the sun rose and washed out the colors, Winnie left a note for her mom and went down for breakfast.

Winnie's thoughts turned to her mom while she took in the buffet, wondering if her mom would ever get back to normal. *She's been through so much over the past few days. It may take a while for her to feel comfortable and trusting again.* Winnie thought about ways she could help, but, for now, all Winnie could do was be supportive and a good listener. Skipping over the fruit, Winnie's eyes were drawn to the huckleberry pancakes. She took four of the plate-sized cakes, smothering them with whipped butter and maple syrup. She found a table overlooking the hills, where she could enjoy the view. The smell of the huckleberries and maple syrup made her mouth water in anticipation. The pancakes seemed to melt in her mouth, and, without Patches begging for scraps, she ate in peace, savoring the gooey creation. Well, relative peace. A few kids made a fuss about something, but Winnie tried to block all of the noise out. Until she couldn't.

"Don't eat too much for breakfast, dear, especially that." Sabrina ambled into the dining room. "We've got a busy day today, and all those pancakes will do nothing to flatter your figure."

"Hello to you, too, Mom." Winnie wiped a bit of syrup running down her chin. *Yep, she's back to normal. I shouldn't have worried.*

"You left your phone upstairs. Sally sent you a text. She finished walking Patches and fed him leftover steak. She said the Silverman's dog, Bitsy, and Patches got along during the walk, so she'll drop him off on their way to pick us up."

"I knew I left Patches in good hands."

"Yes, dear, you did. Now, about your breakfast choices—"

"Mom! Back off, okay? I normally don't eat like this, but they looked so good I couldn't resist. I'm going to indulge and not worry about it today. It's one of the few days I do that, so don't spoil it for me."

"Sorry. I just can't help myself. Anyway, it's going to be a great day for the spa. Sally said she signed us up for the 'queen for a day' package."

Winnie and Sabrina were waiting outside of their hotel when they saw Sally's red Prius come into view. Winnie looked over at her mom, who was practically jumping up and down in anticipation. She rolled her eyes at her mother's giddy demeanor, but she had to admit a day of pampering was going to feel good. Sally was sitting in the passenger's seat with a goofy grin that matched Winnie's mother's, and Winnie couldn't help but laugh when she saw her.

"What is it, dear?" Sabrina asked.

"I guess I'm just happy we're all together."

But Winnie looked over at Jen, who had a death grip on the steering wheel. *I guess not everyone's happy*.

Sally put down her window. "Let's go, girls! We don't want to be late."

The Laughing Bison Resort was located right outside of Gardiner, hidden off of a gravel road that wound its way into the hills. The only indication it existed was a small sign next to the highway of a smiling bison holding an arrow pointing to the turnoff. Jen was driving and missed it the first time, making a U-turn like Sally's Prius was a cop car.

"Easy does it," Sally snapped, patting the dash in an attempt to soothe the car's spirit.

Jen just smiled as she hit the accelerator, taking the turnoff with the tires squealing, making all three passengers grab onto something as they were flung sideways. But once they hit the gravel road, Jen slowed down considerably, and everyone was able to relax again. Sally gave Jen a look but then took her hand.

"Thanks for doing this," Sally said. "I know it isn't high on your list of things to do."

"I'm with friends, so it's all good. Besides, we haven't spent enough time together lately, so this will be a nice break." Jen squeezed Sally's hand.

After another turn, the resort came into view. It looked fairly new, but it still had an Old West feel to it, with a log cabin exterior and wide front porch, complete with wooden rocking chairs. To the right of the main building, there was a horse stable, the heads of a few horses peering out from their stalls. To the left was a gigantic hot tub, the steam rising from the water like a thermal from Yellowstone. Solar panels and a wind turbine could be seen behind the main building, and a trail wound along the hill behind the solar panels, where a couple of hikers were walking.

"I love it already," Sabrina said as they walked toward the entrance.

A wooden sign posted above the door read "Relax, Unwind, Rejuvenate." It was surrounded by red and yellow roses carved into the wood, with green stems providing a border. While the outside made them feel like they were in the west, opening the door changed Winnie's perception immediately. Stepping in, she felt like she was transported to another place. The lighting was subdued, with a blueish tinge. Soft music drifted from hidden speakers, and a waterfall off to the side added to the calming effect. The floor was a thick deep blue pile carpet Winnie was sure she could get lost in.

As they entered, a woman came over with glasses of champagne and a bowl of strawberries and chocolate sauce. "Welcome to The Laughing Bison. My name is Audrey, and I'll be getting you all set up. You're the Claire party, right?"

"That's us." Sally took a flute of champagne and a strawberry, dipping it in the chocolate sauce. "I'm Sally Claire."

"Great. If you can come with me for a moment, I'll get you signed in and we'll get started."

The other three each took a flute of champagne and dug into the strawberries.

"This is going to be wonderful." Sabrina looked excited.

Jen smiled at Sabrina, and Sally followed the receptionist, taking care of the registration. She came back, carrying a set of instructions, and handed one to everyone.

"We're going to start with hydrotherapy." Sally sounded thrilled. "A sauna first for a little dry heat then off to a steam room. Then it's time for a cool dip in the pool and then we jump into a water massager. After that, it's time for more champagne and the outdoor hot tub. Then a nice, relaxing massage.

Finally, we'll unwind by the pool. We'll have our own table and all the wine, cheese, and fruit we want."

"I may not want to leave," Sabrina said. "This is fantastic. Thanks for setting this up, Sally."

Before they got started, Jen's phone rang. She answered it quickly, but Audrey rushed over. "I'm sorry, but, for everyone's enjoyment, I must ask that you turn your phones off. We want all of our guests to enjoy a peaceful day with no interruptions."

Jen nodded and stepped outside.

"Jen is a park ranger at Yellowstone," Sally said. "Sometimes she has to take a call. Occupational hazard, I'm afraid."

"I see," the receptionist said. "Well, please have her keep the phone on vibrate to minimize any disruptions. Right over there we have a couple of cell phone rooms, if she needs to take a call." She pointed to the two doors just past the waterfall.

"Thanks. I'll make sure she puts her phone on vibrate. And if it gets to be too much, I'll take her phone and 'accidentally' drop it into the hot tub. It's happened before."

They all laughed as Jen approached. "Did I miss something?"

"We were just warned about cell phone use while we're here," Sally said. "There are a couple of booths for using a phone if you have to, and you need to switch it to vibrate. I told her if I have to, I'll take care of it like the last time we were on vacation."

Jen clutched her phone. "No you don't. I'm still paying for this one." She put it on vibrate and tucked it in her pocket. "But I'm glad I took the call. That was Greg from human resources. They tracked down the names for us."

"Really? Do they know where they are?" Winnie looked over at her mom, who was staring at Jen with wide eyes.

Sabrina looked a shade of pale Winnie didn't think possible, like she was reliving her captivity just hearing about them.

Sabrina barely breathed out, "It's okay, go on."

Jen looked at Winnie for approval, who nodded and took her mother's hand.

"K. Jeffers is Kelli Jeffers and R. Wilson is Ronald Wilson. Luckily for us, both were fired recently from the Park Service for stealing. HR had their records flagged, so that made it easier to narrow down the list. They're alerting all the state and local police forces, and the FBI has been informed. Maybe I should get back to the station and help out."

Jen put her champagne flute down and was turning to leave when Sally grabbed her arm, pulling her away from the others. "You're not going anywhere."

"Sally, I'm more useful there than here."

"No, you're not. Look at Sabrina. Does that look like a woman who feels relaxed? You need to stay here and be with us. If for no other reason than to help her."

"Sally, I can't guard her twenty-four/seven."

"No, but you can do what you can. And that means being here for her. Today."

Jen looked at Sally and nodded. "You're right."

Sally gave Jen a quick kiss on the cheek and pulled her back into the group.

"On second thought," Jen said, "I think I'll stay here. A day with my friends is just what I need."

Winnie looked over to see some color return to Sabrina, and she mouthed a thank you to Jen, who smiled in return.

"Ready, ladies?" The receptionist motioned for them to follow her. She led them to a locker room, if you could call it that. It didn't smell like any locker room Winnie had ever been in before. It smelled more like a flower shop combined with a juice bar. Another floor-to-ceiling waterfall added a peaceful sound. Inside the locker room were individual compartments for them to change in, each with their name on it. Winnie found the one with "Winnie H." and opened the door, taken aback by what she saw. Inside her compartment were towels, slippers, and a robe. All of them were on heating racks. There was a drawer to put her clothes in, and two spa outfits, neatly folded and labeled First and Second. A note explaining the outfit labeled First was to be put on now, and if there were fitting problems to press the red help button. Once changed, she was instructed to put the robe and slippers on, take a towel, and step outside where a therapist would escort her to her first treatment.

Winnie slipped out of her shoes and the warmth from the heated floor seeped into her. "Wow, they thought of everything." She changed into her spa clothes. Slipping on a warm robe and slippers, she grabbed a towel and stepped out of her compartment, finding Jen already there, followed quickly by Sally and finally Sabrina. They were all excited when the therapist came up and led them to the sauna. When the door opened, a waft of heat rushed at them. It was mixed with the soothing smell of eucalyptus.

"Okay, ladies, time to relax. Hang your robes on the hooks, and I'll come back and get you when it's time for the next treatment."

"When will that be?" Jen asked.

"We don't want our guests to worry about the clock while they're here. I'll get you when it's time." She smiled and held the door open as the four got in.

Instead of typical wood bench seats, this sauna had individual chairs that reclined slightly, with footrests that popped up to relax your entire body. Soft music was playing, but not loud enough to keep them from relaxing. As soon as they got settled, the music stopped and a quiet, soothing, woman's voice came on, encouraging them to close their eyes, breathe deeply, and enjoy the therapeutic benefits of the heat and the eucalyptus. The music started again, and the lights dimmed. Winnie snuggled against the chair and wondered if heaven was like this.

Winnie was very relaxed as she became aware that the lights were getting brighter and the music a little louder.

Too soon, the door opened and a quiet voice said, "Hello, ladies. I hope you found that a relaxing beginning. It's time to start our next treatment. Ready?"

Three of the women started to get up, but not Jen. She was sound asleep. Sally nudged her and told her it was time to go. "And you didn't want to come, huh?"

Even in the sauna, Winnie saw Jen blush.

The attendant laughed. "That's why we check on you during your treatments. We don't want you to relax in here for too long. Follow me."

Winnie didn't want to leave her comfy chair, but she was enjoying her time and wanted to experience all of the treatments, excited for the next one. The steam room they moved to was invigorating, and Winnie's sinuses opened. The layout was different, and tropical music played while they enjoyed the steamy heat. About halfway through, an attendant brought them each a fruity drink.

The first two stops were a wonderful combination, but Winnie was a little shocked at the contrast from the dip in the pool that came next, putting her foot in and hastily pulling it out. The therapist recommended they get in quickly, so Winnie went for it, jumping in and making a mini cannonball as she entered the water. She splashed the others, and her mother chastised her, but the rest just laughed.

As much as Winnie enjoyed the water treatments, she was really looking forward to the massage, and when the time came, she couldn't wait. The massage rooms were individual cabanas, with more soft music and warm lighting, a heated massage table, and that same eucalyptus smell permeating the area.

Winnie wore a towel and slippers as she walked down the aisle, looking for her name. She found her mom's, Jen's, and

Sally's, and continued past a few other names. Susan K on the left and Kelli J on the right before finally seeing her name and stepping in. A therapist came in shortly afterward. After introductions, Winnie found herself face down on a massage table, with warm hands working the kinks out of her back. Winnie's body gently swayed as pressure was applied to different areas, creating the perfect atmosphere to relax and drift off.

Winnie was just about to completely zone out when she popped her head up and opened her eyes.

"Is everything all right?" the therapist asked.

Winnie jumped off the table, clutching her towel and sliding into her slippers. "Sorry. I'll be right back."

Before the therapist could say anything, Winnie was out the door. She looked across the hallway and spotted the name "Kelli J."

Kelli J. This can't be K. Jeffers, can it? She'd be long gone by now, wouldn't she? Maybe not. Not if she didn't think she was going to get caught.

As she put her hand on the doorknob, Winnie didn't really expect to find a cold-blooded killer on the other side of the door. Instead, she expected to find a middle-aged woman startled at the intrusion, with Winnie making profuse apologies. But she had to find out, so she knocked, quickly turned the handle, and stepped in.

The only middle-aged woman in there was Winnie.

Startled by the intrusion, the therapist turned toward Winnie and said something, but Winnie blocked out all noise, her eyes locked on the massage table and the person lying on top of it.

Mid-twenties, long blonde hair, skinny as a rail. I hate her already.

Their gazes met, and something told Winnie it was her. The woman's eyes were cold and alert but not afraid. Her body language showed tension, and Winnie could see subtle changes in the woman's posture. She was preparing for a fight.

The woman on the table continued to stare at Winnie. She must have sensed this intrusion wasn't a mistake, her gaze never leaving her intruder. Winnie knew she was being sized up.

"Are you Kelli Jeffers?" Winnie took a step forward.

The woman on the table was silent.

Suddenly, she jumped up, pushed Winnie to the floor, and took off, grabbing her robe off the hook on her way out.

"What's going on?" the therapist asked, helping Winnie off the floor.

"No time to explain." Winnie secured the towel around her and headed off to catch her prey. "Find Jen and tell her I'm chasing Jeffers. It's important."

"Who's Jen?" the therapist asked. "And who are you?" But Winnie was already out the door.

Jeffers only had about a thirty-second head start on Winnie, but she was younger, faster, and highly motivated to get away. Winnie assumed Jeffers would be heading to the parking lot, and she tried to make her way there, getting lost a few times in the maze of rooms. When she burst out into the open, Winnie squinted in the bright sun, covering her eyes and scanning for her target.

Jeffers was nowhere to be seen.

Looking behind the spa, Winnie spotted a white blob making its way along the trail that headed up into the hills. The blob stopped and turned. It was her.

"The trail. Really?" Winnie moaned as she ran around to the back and started trudging up the gravel path. It didn't take long before Winnie was winded, huffing and puffing. Winnie's "run" was best described as a trot, and with each step, Jeffers was slipping farther ahead. She wished she'd taken her mother's advice about breakfast. Those pancakes settled hard in her stomach, and it made trying to keep up with Kelli that much harder.

Too much syrup, not enough kale.

Winnie was barely able to keep the towel covering her as she continued up the trail, wrapping her right arm around her body as the back of the towel blew with the wind. Modesty had taken a back seat to catching Anita's killer and mom's kidnapper, and Winnie was bound and determined not to let Jeffers slip away. No matter how much her stomach, legs, and lungs protested.

Or how much her backside flapped in the breeze.

"We know who you are," Winnie shouted between pants. "The police are right behind me. Make it easier on yourself and stop."

Jeffers stopped and looked. Winnie could see her scanning the area.

"I only see you," Jeffers shouted back. "And there's no way you can catch me. See ya."

Jeffers turned to run. Winnie knew she couldn't keep up. She looked back at the spa and could see someone pouring out. Jen.

"Up here!" Winnie shouted.

Jen looked up, and Winnie alternated between waving her hands and pointing at Jeffers, who was quickly getting away. But instead of running, Jen got on her phone.

"What is she doing?" Winnie was exasperated Jen didn't join the chase.

Winnie turned back to see Jeffers farther ahead, reaching a turn. Jeffers looked back at Winnie and smirked as she started to disappear behind the hill. But Jeffers wasn't looking where she was going and collided with a hiker coming down. The hiker managed to lean into the hill for support, but Jeffers didn't fare so well. She fell hard backward against the trail, landing on her shoulder as her leg smashed against a rock.

Winnie trotted up the hill, watching Jeffers writhe in pain. She was gaining on her target when Jeffers hobbled to her feet and started staggering back up the trail. But she was no longer faster than Winnie, and the gap narrowed until Winnie was in arm's length.

"Give it up, Jeffers." Winnie reached for the back of Jeffers' robe.

Winnie missed the robe but managed to grab a handful of hair, and Jeffers howled in pain as her body was jerked backward. Jeffers fell back onto the trail, and Winnie pounced.

Pounced was a little generous. Winnie's slipper got caught on a small stone and she fell directly onto Jeffers, making an "oof" sound as the wind was knocked out of her. Thankfully, Jeffers seemed content to stay on the ground.

As Winnie rolled off Jeffers and stood, she looked back down the trail. Jen was fast approaching, looking like she did this every day—which she probably did—and not slowing down as the path got steeper. Jen had managed to put pants and a shirt on but appeared unarmed. Not that it mattered. Jeffers was still rolling in pain when Jen pulled her to her feet.

"You're under arrest." Jen grabbed her by the arm.

"I'll be out before you know it. You don't have nothin'."

"A double negative? Well, we at least have you on poor grammar. Maybe the book the judge throws at you will be a dictionary. You're mistaken, though. We do have evidence. A lot of evidence. By Anita herself, including a notebook and cell phone records. But before you say anything else, let me read you your rights."

Jen recited the phrase heard a million times in cop shows, but Winnie had never heard it applied to a real person, and it felt surreal.

When Jen was finished, she looked over at Winnie. "Good work. You should be a detective. Oh, and you might want to tighten up that towel a little."

Winnie looked down, her face burning at what she saw, quickly bunching the towel around her. She looked at the parking lot. Her mother and Sally were standing there, both fully dressed. Sabrina was holding a robe. Winnie walked as fast as she could without risking the towel billowing up again, making her way to her mom and quickly spilling into the robe. Jen was still talking to Jeffers on the trail, and the confidence Jeffers initially had seemed to be gone, replaced with what appeared to be pleading.

By the time Jen got to the parking lot, three police cruisers had arrived, and one took a very distraught Jeffers away. Jen walked over to Winnie and the rest of the group.

"You throw a heck of a party, Sal," Jen teased. "I'll bet you had this whole thing planned out from the beginning."

Sally smiled and gave her a hug. "I think the last part was more Winnie than me."

"You mean our newest ranger? Of course it was. By the way, tough girl up there folded like a map after it sunk in she was caught. She gave up her partner's location. We're picking up Wilson now. It turns out they were getting ready to leave town later today, but she needed a spa day to help soothe her back." Jen looked at Sabrina. "She said you had quite a kick."

"Mother! You kicked her?"

"I tried to get away by any means possible."

"My mom the ninja." Then Winnie turned to Jen, her brow crinkled. "Wait a minute. What about Mr. X?"

"Jeffers gave me a name I've never heard of before. Ted Walkins. Said he was a local in Gardiner. He's the one who knew about the mine and the gold. He needed partners to help with the mining, so when he found two park employees willing to help, he and another guy—the one Walkins killed—started up the mine. Walkins was especially happy Wilson worked in the maintenance department because he had access to tools. According to Jeffers, Walkins was also the one that wanted to kill Anita. Jeffers and Wilson wanted to take what they had and run, but Walkins wanted to make a big score. It doesn't really matter. They're all going down for murder."

The group stood there in silence for a moment. Nobody knew what to say.

Finally, Jen gave Sally a hug and took a step away. "I hate to break things up, but I have to go. I want to be a part of taking down the other two. You three stay and relax, and I'll catch a ride with one of the officers over there. Besides, I've had all the pampering I need for a while." She raised her eyebrows at Sally, who started to laugh, and soon the four were cracking up.

"Can you believe Jen said Jeffers folded like a map?" Sally said after Jen left, laughing so hard tears were rolling down her cheeks. "She's been watching way too many cop show reruns."

Sabrina started humming the *Law and Order* theme song, and soon all three were doubled over with laughter.

When she could speak again, Sally said, "I'm glad we ended on a high note. Everyone's safe, so I'll call it a successful day, even though it wasn't totally relaxing. How about an early dinner at my house? Jen will be forever with the case, but that doesn't mean we can't celebrate. I'm sure Patches will be happy to see us. Are you ready to go?"

Winnie and Sabrina nodded. Everyone had had enough of The Laughing Bison for one day. And from the looks of the faces on the employees, they were happy the three were leaving, too.

"It's too bad we couldn't have finished our spa day before you spotted Jeffers," Sabrina said. "I was thoroughly enjoying my day of being pampered."

"I'll find you a new spa, Mom. Preferably one that doesn't have a murderer client."

"I know just the place," Sally said.

The rest of the day was spent enjoying each other's

company. Patches was excited to welcome them home, and the three had lively conversations over takeout pizza.

Jen came in just as Winnie and Sabrina were leaving. “We got Wilson, but Walkins is still out there. We have his description, and everyone around is looking for him. Chances are, he’s long gone.” Jen showed his mugshot from a prior conviction.

He had a big gash on his cheek, and his nose looked flattened from too many punches. Tattoos of teardrops adorned both eyes. He wasn’t smiling, which wasn’t a surprise, but Winnie imagined a couple of teeth missing, too.

“I was blindfolded most of the time, and I never saw his face, thank goodness.” Sabrina said. “He looks frightful,”

“He is, but I wouldn’t worry about it. He’s got to be on the run by now. He’d have to be a complete idiot not to know we’re looking for him.”

They said their goodbyes, and Jen promised to keep Winnie apprised of any new developments.

32

It was still early when Winnie and Sabrina left, so Winnie suggested they walk around Gardiner, looking at shops. Sabrina was yawning, but Winnie seemed energized by everything that happened, so Winnie proposed they spend an hour browsing the shops then call it a night, and Sabrina agreed.

Winnie had Patches on a leash, so she stayed outside and window shopped while Sabrina went into stores that interested her. A light mist hung in the air, and Winnie slipped on a cap to keep her head dry. But it felt good to be out, and Patches didn't seem to mind, either. Craft and souvenir shops were interspersed with bars and restaurants, and they enjoyed wandering around, peering through the windows at the different displays. Winnie was walking toward Sabrina, who had just come out of one of the shops, when a heavyset man stumbled out from the bar next door, barely catching himself against a post before he hit the sidewalk.

"What'r yer lookin at?" he snapped as Winnie took a step back. The man looked up and his eyes were cold and mean.

Soulless. Then she noticed the other features. Next to each eye were three teardrops.

And a scar ran down his left cheek.

The man pushed off of the post. He wobbled and his eyes narrowed as he stared at Winnie. "Missy, I ain't afraid to hit a woman. Best you leave me alone."

Patches started barking and growling, tugging at his leash to protect his master.

The man looked past Winnie and saw Sabrina, who was still looking at a window display, unaware of the commotion. He blinked a few times, then his eyes went wide as he seemed to recognize Sabrina's face. He took a step toward them, but more people came out of the bar, so the man turned and stumbled down the sidewalk.

Before he got five steps, Winnie yelled, "Hey, Walkins."

The man turned and Winnie snapped a picture of him with her camera, the flash causing him to recoil. He started after her, but, in his condition, Winnie easily outran him. She caught up to Sabrina, who had moved to a different window down the street.

"Mom, that's Walkins." Winnie took her mom's arm, leading her to the Mini.

"What?" Sabrina turned to see, but Walkins had disappeared.

Winnie searched through her recent calls and pressed the number for Jen. It went to voice mail. Winnie left a message that they'd spotted Walkins and where he was as she hurried Sabrina and Patches to the Mini. Patches jumped inside the back, and Winnie and Sabrina were just about to get in when they heard a screech. Winnie looked back and saw a blue SUV veer around a corner.

Walkins was driving.

And he wasn't out for a Sunday drive.

Winnie jumped in and shut the door just as the SUV

reached the car, occupying the space Winnie had been in moments before. "Stay here! I'll be back" Winnie yelled to her mom.

"No way," her mom scrambled in.

Winnie took off, squealing tires as she sped away.

"What are you doing?" her mom tried to get her seat belt on while being tossed around. "I thought you were going to the police station."

"We can't let him get away."

"Winnie, he'll kill us. Let the police handle it."

Winnie tossed her phone over to her mom. "Try Jen again. If you can't reach her, call nine-one-one. Call anybody and tell them we're chasing a killer."

The SUV ran a stop sign and kept going. But Winnie's Mini was faster and more agile, and she was able to keep up with the lumbering car ahead of her. Walkins must have figured out he couldn't outrun the little Mini, because his window came down and a hand came out.

With a gun.

"Gun!" Sabrina screamed. They heard the explosion but didn't see the bullet.

"He missed!"

"He's firing with his left hand," Winnie said, "and I'll bet he's right-handed. Plus, he can't really make that hand turn backward very well. Hopefully, his shots will stay wild."

"Uh oh," Winnie said when she saw Walkins' right hand swing over. Winnie watched as the rear window of the SUV shattered, followed by a much-better-placed round, which hit the parked car they just passed.

"Get down!" Winnie screamed to Sabrina. She looked over to see her mom as close to the floor as she could. Winnie ducked down, peering out over the steering wheel.

Sabrina's hands were shaking when she dialed Jen. This time, Jen answered. Sabrina put it on speaker.

"Winnie, where are you?"

"It's Sabrina, and we're chasing Walkins like a couple of deranged maniacs."

"I've notified the Gardiner police, but they've only got one patrol car operating tonight, and it's on another call. I'm on my way, but please don't do anything rash. Keep way back. Where are you now?"

"We just turned onto Highway 89 toward Bozeman. After we were shot at, Winnie slowed down a little, so we're about a quarter mile behind. We're far enough back that he stopped firing on us."

"I'll alert the Montana Highway Patrol. I'm in my car now and will get there as soon as I can. I'll call you back when I know more."

Both cars were moving at the same speed. When Walkins sped up, Winnie matched it. For now, it was a stalemate, and Winnie hoped it would stay that way. At least until the police or Jen arrived.

The phone rang, and both Winnie and Sabrina jumped at the noise.

"It's Jen." Sabrina put it on speaker.

"Are you still on eighty-nine?"

"Yeah, we're still following him."

"Great. I just got on the highway, and I've got highway patrol coming the other way. If he makes a turn, let me know. Otherwise, stay as far back as you can. Has he fired again?"

"Not recently," Winnie said. "I wonder if he's conserving his ammunition. He probably figures we're not much cause for concern."

"Maybe. I let the patrol know he's armed. But don't kid yourself. He's already killed two people and taken shots at you. I don't think he'll hesitate to take more if he's threatened."

"We'll be careful."

"Once I overtake you, fall back. When it's safe, turn around and go to my house. I'll meet you there."

But they never got the chance.

"Crap!" was all Winnie said.

Winnie's Mini screeched to a halt on the side of the road.

"Winnie? Sabrina?"

Winnie could hear Jen's voice, but the phone was nowhere to be found.

"I'm coming, Winnie. Hang on."

Winnie rubbed her head where she'd banged it against the door, then looked over at her mom, who was clutching her seat belt and staring straight ahead. Seeing no obvious signs of injury, she checked the back seat, breathing a sigh of relief when Patches looked okay. In Winnie's haste, she forgot to harness him in, and she never wanted to put Patches in harm's way.

"What happened?" Sabrina finally spoke.

"Are you hurt?"

"No, but—"

"No time to talk now, Mom. We can't let him get away." Winnie opened her door and got out, with Patches right behind.

Sabrina opened her door, too, wobbling a little as she stood.

"Mom, wait here."

"I'm right behind you, dear."

"Mom!"

"Please don't argue with your mother. You go on, and I'll catch up."

About one hundred yards away in the middle of the road, a blue SUV sat on its passenger side, smoke slowly rising from the undercarriage. The driver's door was open, and fluids dripped from the engine. The hiss from the mist hitting the hot engine was loud enough Winnie couldn't hear anything else as she scanned the area.

But apparently Patches could.

Patches pulled Winnie to the other side of the road. After she cleared the smoke from the SUV, Winnie saw the outline of a man limping.

"Good boy, Patches." Winnie gave Patches a quick hug then looked over to see her mom coming up. She was walking a little better.

"Where is he?"

"He's walking along the side of the road. He looks hurt."

Just then, Patches barked. Walkins turned and took a step in their direction but then turned back and kept walking.

"He doesn't have his gun," Winnie said, "or he would have taken a shot at us."

Winnie heard sirens in the distance, but they seemed far away. Walkins must have heard them, too, because he turned to look. As he did, his bad leg collapsed, and Walkins went into the drainage ditch on the side of the road.

"Let's finish this, Patches."

Patches barked and trotted next to Winnie, and they followed Walkins into the drainage ditch.

WINNIE TOOK a step back to admire her handiwork when she heard Jen call her name. "Down here."

Jen scrambled down the embankment, weapon drawn. Walkins tried to move, but Jen shouted to stay still. When Jen got next to Winnie, she looked over at Walkins and started to laugh. He was tied up using Patches's leash. Not only was he tied up, he was hog tied, with his hands and feet bound together behind him.

"How did you manage that?"

"Once his car flipped over, we pulled over and got out. When we got past his SUV, we saw him stumble away. He didn't have his gun, so we kept an eye on him. He saw us and tried to get away, but he was hurt, and I think his leg gave out because he fell down the ditch. That's when I followed him down, with Patches barking all the way. I chased after him with the leash, and when I got down there, Walkins was holding onto his ankle and Patches was barking like mad. I think Walkins might have hurt his foot when he went over the side. I used the opportunity to tie him up."

"That's amazing, Winnie. Where did you learn to tie knots like that?"

"I knew that when I went off on my own in an RV, I'd have to be resourceful, so I taught myself a bunch of things, including tying knots."

Jen bent down and put handcuffs on Walkins, untying the knots around his wrists but leaving his legs immobile. Winnie heard police cars in the distance, and Jen called in her status and location. Once the police arrived, Jen untied the knots around Walkins's legs. A few minutes later, an ambulance arrived and took Walkins away on a gurney, a police escort following the ambulance to the hospital.

"What made him flip over?" Jen asked after the highway patrol left.

Sabrina piped up, sounding peeved but looking like a proud mom. "Mario Andretti here got the brilliant idea to switch off her lights and sneak up on him. We were almost on his tail when a bull elk moved into the road. When Walkins swerved to miss the elk, Winnie kissed the bumper on the way by. The combination put the SUV into a spin, and then it flipped over."

Jen looked at Winnie. "That was very brave. A little foolish, but brave. And thank you."

"You can thank the elk. You should deputize him. He might come in handy more often."

"Did the elk get hurt? If it was a male. it probably weighed seven hundred pounds, but a run-in with an SUV could still cause serious damage."

"The elk ran away as soon as he saw the SUV. I had no idea something that big could run that fast."

"Now you know one of the reasons we don't allow dogs in a lot of places within the park. Patches may think he's ferocious and fast, but he's no match for the animals out here."

"Well, Winnie," Sabrina said. "I can't remember a spa day quite like this. Wait until I tell my friends back home. My daughter, the hero. I'll be the talk of the book club."

33

Winnie took her yoga mat outside and went through her morning ritual. She was a little sore from the action yesterday, and some of the poses were difficult to get into. But she felt good. When she finished, she went inside to pour a cup of coffee, glancing at her phone. It was after nine and there were no missed calls and no messages. Winnie never thought she'd be happy about a lack of calls, but she was. Very happy.

Her mom was leaving today, and she would miss her. Winnie started this journey to find herself, and so far, all she'd found was trouble. Soon, it would just be her and Patches again, and that was fine. Then she remembered Reggie and Cal. Winnie couldn't wait to tell them her adventure, and she was looking forward to spending time with them at Glacier.

"We're better than fine, right, Patchy?" Patches seemed more interested in his morning walk than thinking about the future. Unless the future meant food. Now.

After the walk, Winnie found Sabrina up and packing. The smell of coffee permeated the little space, and Patches's bowl was filled with food. Someone was in a good mood.

"I talked to Martin this morning. He's picking me up at the airport. And...he said he's got something special planned for tonight." Sabrina was grinning so much Winnie thought it might hurt. But seeing her mom so happy made Winnie smile, too.

"Are you sure you're going to be all right, dear?" Sabrina continued packing. "I can stay longer if you want me to. I want to make sure you'll be safe. I think we've both had enough excitement to last us a while." Forcing the suitcase closed, she struggled to drag it out of the RV until Winnie came to help.

"We'll be fine, Mom." Winnie plopped the suitcase to the ground. "We're leaving tomorrow, and we'll put this behind us. Well, except for our friends. Jen and Sally are keepers. We're going to stay in touch. And I told you about my new friends. They'll be meeting me at Glacier, so I have some people to travel with."

"That's great. I hope I can meet them sometime, too."

"I know you'd love them. And if you ever do get a camper, we should meet somewhere."

Sabrina smiled. "I'd like that."

Winnie tugged at the suitcase, groaning as she lifted it into the trunk. She got in and shut the door, her little Mini Cooper stuffed with luggage, people, and one hyper dog.

The windows were up, and, even with the fan on, it got stuffy quickly. Winnie crinkled her nose and looked to see if her mom noticed. She did.

"Somebody needs a bath." Winnie looked at Patches while she put the window down to get some fresh air.

Patches sniffed but seemed to shrug it off with a look of "Who, me?"

Winnie's mom, who was usually fussier about these things than Winnie, shrugged and took her travel pillow out, wedging it between her seat and the window and closing her eyes. By the time they got out of the RV park, Sabrina was fast asleep and Winnie settled in for the two-hour ride to the Jackson Hole airport.

So far, the day was pleasantly uneventful, and Winnie was grateful for it. She was glad her Mini Cooper saved her from crashing yesterday, and Winnie patted the dash, happy the car was still in one piece, even if the bumper had a slight reminder of yesterday's chase.

The ride to the airport followed US-20 around Yellowstone Lake, meeting up with US-191, where she turned south on the Rockefeller Memorial Parkway toward Grand Teton National Park. The southern part of Yellowstone was pleasant, but nothing as spectacular as the boiling mud pots, pluming geysers, and steaming rivers she had seen in other areas of the park. Winnie was beginning to wonder if Grand Teton would be a nice but boring park, something she could see almost anywhere.

She was wrong.

Once inside the Grand Teton Park, Winnie was amazed at the transformation of the scenery. She couldn't believe how the park could be connected to Yellowstone yet still be so vastly different. The jagged mountaintops extended above the tree line and seemed to go on forever, each more spectacular than the other. Winnie pulled into a small parking lot and got out to take a look around, quietly closing the door so her mom could rest. Patches was staring out of the back window. He seemed to know they were someplace new and exciting.

"It's on our list, Patches," Winnie said quietly. "But I think we need to get a little farther away from Yellowstone. At least for a while. And we've got new friends."

When they arrived at the Jackson Hole airport, Winnie had to nudge her mom awake. She helped her get checked in and walked her to security. Both had tears in their eyes.

"Goodbye, dear," Sabrina said as they embraced in a big hug. "Please don't do anything dangerous."

"I'll be fine, Mom. I love you."

"I love you, too." Sabrina kissed Winnie's cheek and turned to go through security.

Winnie stood and waited until her mom disappeared toward the gates, wiped the tears from her eyes, tugged on Patches's leash, and started the journey back to her RV.

Winnie spent the rest of the day getting ready to leave. Jen and Sally stopped by to see how she was doing. They brought a pizza, and the three sat and talked. Sally got her last playful moments in with Patches. Sadly, it was soon time for them to leave.

Winnie opened her arms. "What an adventure I had in Yellowstone! The best part was meeting you two. You are both true friends, and I'll miss you."

"You're a remarkable woman, Winnie," Jen said as they hugged goodbye. "I know you're on a mission to discover yourself, but from an outsider looking in, I think you'll discover what we see already. A bright, caring, compassionate person. You're the real deal, girl. You just need to find it out for yourself."

THE NEXT MORNING, as Winnie pulled out of the RV park, she thought about what Jen had said the night before.

"Maybe Jen's right, Patches." Winnie glanced over at her companion. "Maybe I just need to believe in myself. Time will tell. But for now, we've got more places to explore. Are you ready?"

A bark and a wagging tail said it all.

ABOUT THE AUTHOR

M. S. Peke loves writing mysteries about interesting places involving quirky characters. His passion for travel and adventure influence his writing. When he's not at the computer, you can find him reading or enjoying a cup of coffee.

Visit his website, https://mspeke.com, to find out more and get a free ebook.

ALSO BY M. S. PEKE

The Happy Camper Mystery Series:

And So It Begins (Prequel)

Frozen In Death (Book 2)

Merlot and Murder (Book 3)

Grand Prairie Mystery Series:

Critiqued to Death

FROZEN IN DEATH

Enjoy this excerpt from book 2 in the Happy Camper Mystery series, *Frozen in Death*.

1

Winnie Hackleshack's bright blue motor home sputtered its way north along US-89 in Montana. It took a full day's drive to go from Yellowstone's Fishing Bridge RV Park to Glacier National Park, but the drive was pleasant and uneventful. Which is just what she needed after her harrowing experience at Yellowstone.

When she stopped for gas, the people at the pumps next to hers stared at her thirty-five-foot Winnebago. A caricature of Winnie emblazoned each side, with a curly mop of red hair and wearing a yellow sundress. A warm smile and a few freckles dotted her face. Along with the drawing were the words "Winnie's Winnie." Behind the RV was a Mini Cooper, the same electric blue color and caricature, with the words "Winnie's Mini" on each side. Winnie smiled at the gawkers. She was used to all the attention she got from the unique artwork, and she used it as a billboard for her freelance writing business, with the words "Creative, Professional Writing . . . Explore New Possibilities" on each side, along with her email address and website. Since Yellowstone, Winnie noticed an uptick in web traffic to https://winniehackleshack.com. Business was booming so much she had to turn customers away.

It was the end of June, but Winnie was listening to her usual Christmas music. "Feliz Navidad" blared through the speakers, and Winnie was singing just as loud. But she was hopelessly off-key, and she didn't know Spanish, so she made up the words or hummed as she went along. Her faithful companion, a rat terrier/Jack Russell rescue dog named Patches, sat strapped in just behind her. He stared out of the partially opened window. Most dogs would howl at the noise, but Patches was partially deaf and seemed immune to it, although he tugged at his harness when Winnie screeched a high note. The harness kept him safe but restrained, so Winnie stopped every hour to let him stretch, eat, and play.

Before leaving Yellowstone, Winnie made reservations at the KOA in St. Mary, Montana, a small town near Glacier. The KOA offered amenities not found in national parks, and Winnie wanted a little pampering. Just a few days before, she was thrust into a murder mystery which nearly cost her and her mother's lives. But that was behind her, and now she could focus on her mission ahead—to explore, rejuvenate, and revitalize both her body and her spirit, her mission since leaving Madison, Wisconsin.

Patches was restless and tugged on his harness when Winnie pulled into the KOA. After she parked, Winnie slipped his leash on, and the two went into the registration office. The person behind the counter smiled as they approached. She looked about the same age as Winnie, maybe a little shorter, with salt-and-pepper hair that seemed to have a mind of its own, shooting off in different directions. Winnie could commiserate with hair that couldn't be tamed. Her own mane provided similar battles. The woman wore yellow-framed glasses with a yellow strap dangling from each side. A yellow KOA polo shirt and khaki pants. Winnie took an instant liking to her and smiled back. Her name tag said, "Welcome to KOA. I'm your host Barney."

"Good afternoon. Checking in?"

"Yes, I'm Winnie Hackleshack. Are you Barney?"

"What? Heavens no. Barney's my husband."

"Oh." Winnie pointed to the tag. "It's just that your name tag says Barney."

The woman pulled her shirt out and looked down. When she looked up, she was red in the face. "We must have gotten our tags mixed up this morning. I'm Betty. Betty Bains. My husband and I own this KOA."

"Barney and Betty Bains." Winnie smiled. "I like it."

"Yes, Barney and Betty Bains baked beans beside big beaches." Betty chuckled. "We have fun with our names. I like the name Winnie, too. It's uncommon, but it suits you. And the hair! I love the color, and it's frizzy like mine." She looked at Patches. "And who's this bundle of energy?"

Patches was busy sniffing the ground in his constant search for food.

"This is Patches. He's my Barney."

Betty pointed to a bowl of dog biscuits, and Winnie took one. She tossed it to Patches, who caught it before it hit the ground. He looked up for more, gave a smirk when another didn't come, then went back to sniffing.

"I've never seen a motor home that color before," Betty said as she glanced out the window. "It's beautiful. And the caricature is wonderful. A true likeness."

"Thanks. My friend painted it before I left Wisconsin. The picture might flatter me more than reality does, but I like it. Before I forget, I wondered if someone else has already checked in. The Millers, Cal and Reggie. I was hoping we could have sites next to each other."

While in Yellowstone, Winnie met Cal and Reggie Miller, traveling vagabonds like herself. They all belonged to an association called Drove There, Did That, an online group that connected travelers. Winnie and Reggie became instant friends, and they planned to camp together while they were in Glacier. They were the only other Drove There members scheduled to be at Glacier at the same time as Winnie.

Betty typed on her keyboard, frowned, and typed some more. Another frown, more typing. "Hmmm. They did have a reservation, but it looks like it was canceled."

"Yes, Cal's aunt died, and they had to go to Texas for a while. But I thought they rebooked."

Another "hmmm" and more typing. "I don't see it. Would they have used another name?"

"I don't know. Maybe, I guess. Can I book a site for them? They should be here in two days."

This time, the typing was followed by head shaking. "I'm afraid not. We're booked solid for the next three weeks. That might be why they couldn't rebook. When they get close, have them call me and I'll see if there's something I can do."

Betty took a few pamphlets from under the counter. "Here are some other places for them to try. We've checked each of these out, and they're all good places." She chuckled. "Not as good as ours, of course."

Winnie took the pamphlets and moved toward the door, offering a thanks as she left.

"Shoot, Patchy," Winnie said when she got back into her RV. "We're not going to be next to the Millers. I'd better give them a call."

Reggie picked up on the first ring. "Hi, Winnie. Cal and I just got into Jackson. We thought about getting on the road tonight to try to get there a day earlier, but it's too late and we're tired, so we'll set out in the morning. We'll be there in two days like we originally planned. Sorry you have to go it alone for a while, but keep some sites saved for us. Did you make it to the KOA yet?"

"I just got checked in. I asked about getting our campsites together, but they don't have a reservation for you. They see where you canceled the original one, but they don't have a new one. Unfortunately, they're booked for weeks, but the owner gave me information on other sites and told me to have you call them when you got close, and she'd see what she could do."

"They don't have our new reservation? Hang on."

Winnie could hear Reggie talking to Cal, but she couldn't understand the conversation.

"Cal's not sure if he made a new one after he canceled the old one. I can't find it in our emails, so we probably didn't. We were making flight reservations, trying to find a place to store our RV, and dealing with the trauma of his aunt's death. It may have gotten lost in the shuffle. Let me make some calls and I'll call you back. Can you send me the information on the other campgrounds?"

Winnie took a picture of each brochure and texted it to Reggie, then drove to her campsite. It was big enough for her RV, but she had to disconnect her Mini and pull it alongside. She had an end site, but there was a smaller RV next to her on the other side. She leveled her motor home using the automatic levelers to keep the coach balanced while it was parked. After the RV was level, she engaged the slides—mechanisms that expanded the living space and bedroom, which added several feet of room. Finally, she connected the hookups for water, sewer, and power, allowing her to take longer showers and not to worry about running out of electricity. It also eliminated a trip to the dump site to empty the waste tanks, a definite plus in Winnie's eyes. With that messy job out of the way, Winnie took Patches for a nice long walk.

On the way back to her campsite, Winnie checked at the reception desk on the status of Glacier's roads. Even though it was the end of June, the main road through the park could still be covered in snow and impassible. It frequently didn't open all the way until about this time, and Winnie hoped she could drive its entire length.

"You're in luck," Betty said. "The Going-to-the-Sun Road just opened completely two days ago. They're still plowing some of the pull-outs and parking areas, so be careful while you're on it. Also, they don't allow RVs on the road, so you have to drive a car. I don't remember if you towed one when you checked in. If you don't have one, we can arrange a tour."

Winnie smiled and held up her keys. "Thanks, but I have a car. I think we'll try the road in a couple of days, after my friends get here."

"Sounds like a plan. Speaking of your friends, I checked with the other campgrounds around here. Unfortunately, it doesn't look like there's any availability on this side of Glacier Park. Your friends may have to stay on the other side. They usually have a few spots on the western campgrounds. I know it's not ideal, but I don't think there's any way around it."

"Thanks for checking. I'll let them know. While I'm here, do you have any suggestions for dinner?"

"There are a few choices around here, but if you want to start experiencing Glacier right away, I suggest you drive to the Many Glacier Hotel. It's inside the park, has spectacular views, and great food. It's on the bank of Swiftcurrent Lake, and moose often frequent the area, especially in the evenings, so you may get dinner and a show."

"Thanks. Sounds like a perfect place to eat."

"It really is. They have a nice dining room and a pub, so you've got choices. It's about twenty miles from here and will take about forty minutes. I would get there a little earlier than you want to eat and have a drink in the pub while you put your name down on the waiting list."

Winnie wrote the directions and said goodbye. She was already thinking about a hearty meal. And a hearty dessert afterward.

As they approached their campsite, Winnie noticed a tall, slender man exit the motor home next to her spot. "Howdy, neighbor," he said, a broad smile across his tanned face. "Just get in?"

Slender and handsome. Tall. And a smile that would melt any heart. "And those jeans fill out nicely." *Wait, did I just say that out loud?*

Winnie mumbled a quick "hi" and looked away. She pulled her hair to cover as much of her face as she could. Then she let Patches, who was busy sniffing and peeing on every rock he could find, tug her away. For once, she was grateful that Patches pulled her along. She looked back to steal a glance. The man was staring with a confused expression on his face. She shrugged and waved, then turned back as she continued to follow Patches.

Fifteen minutes later, Winnie returned to her campsite. Thankfully, she didn't see any signs of her new neighbor, so Winnie and Patches hurried inside their RV. *No sense facing that again.*

After Patches was settled for the night, Winnie took off in her Mini. As soon as she entered the Many Glacier entrance of the park, her phone beeped to let her know that she no longer had service. She hoped for at least some connection in case Reggie called, but without a cell phone booster like she had in the RV, she was out of luck. Shortly after they met, Reggie had to leave to attend a funeral, but the two kept in close contact. Late-night phone calls that went on for hours, the two became more like sisters. She was closer to Reggie than her own sister, Lexi. That was something Winnie vowed to change.

Just like she did at Yellowstone, Winnie jumped out at the entrance sign for the park and snapped a few selfies. Off in the distance, Winnie could see mountains with peaks of snow and took a few pictures before moving on. When she made the turn for the Many Glacier Hotel, she couldn't believe it. Plopped in northern Montana, it looked like a scene from the Swiss Alps, complete with a chalet-style hotel. Winnie giggled when she approached and saw the front bell staff unload cars all dressed in traditional alpine lederhosen, with white shirts and brown leather shorts held up with suspenders.

She bypassed the bell stand and drove around to the parking lot. It was crowded, but more with people than cars. The people gathered at the far end, and after she found a spot for her Mini, she went over to see what was going on. As she got closer, Winnie could see people taking photos. They traveled like a beehive as they moved further down. Winnie caught up to the crowd and saw a bighorn sheep casually stroll through the parking lot. The sheep's casual meandering through the lot made it look like it had just dropped its car off and was ready for dinner. She took out her phone and snapped a few pictures as she watched the sheep meander out of the parking lot and down the road. A ranger stood off to the side to make sure everyone kept a healthy distance.

The throng of people dispersed, and Winnie followed the crowd into the hotel. It was just as alpine-looking on the inside, with an open foyer that exposed wood beams to the ceiling, a wooden railing surrounded the foyer on the second floor, and a beautiful copper fireplace open from all sides. Sofas surrounded the fireplace, and people gathered around, talking or playing games. Winnie climbed the wide wooden staircase. The treads creaked like an old house welcoming its guest. Each room had a Swiss flag adorned with the room number, and the door looked like an entrance to a ski hut. Winnie thought she may need her passport to go to dinner.

As she stood on the second floor and overlooked the fireplace, her phone rang. *Reggie*. No data service, but she had two bars for voice.

"There you are. I wondered when you'd call back."

"It took me a while to find any place with vacancy, but we

got lucky. Inside the park at the Apgar campground, we found a vacancy that would fit our motor home."

"That's great."

"Yeah, that's the good news. The bad news is that it's on the other side of the park from you."

"Oh, maybe I can move over there."

"I thought of that, but we took the last vacancy. Unless you want to sleep in a tent."

Winnie's idea of roughing it didn't include tent camping.

"Or, I could take your spot and you could take the tent. That sounds like a better arrangement."

Reggie laughed. "I guess we'll have to commute to each other. We're hoping to make it from Jackson to Bozeman tomorrow, so we'll see you on Wednesday. S'mores and wine?"

S'mores was a treat they both enjoyed. A little too much on Winnie's part and she could feel her pants complain about it. But they tasted wonderful. Winnie imagined biting into the gooey concoction of roasted marshmallow, graham crackers, and chocolate, and her stomach grumbled.

"Of course, s'mores and wine on Wednesday. My place or yours?"

"We'll figure that out Wednesday. I'll call you when we get close. And Winnie, try not to get into trouble before we get there."

"No trouble. I'm at this beautiful hotel overlooking the glaciers. It looks like a Swiss chalet. I keep expecting yodelers to wander through. Just like Yellowstone, this place has magic to it. We'll have to plan some things around here."

"Sounds good. I'll try to call tomorrow and let you know where we are, but if I can't reach you, I'll see you on Wednesday."

After they disconnected, Winnie went back downstairs to put her name on the waiting list for dinner. Along the way, she stopped at an activities board, where a thumb-tacked paper caught her eye. Red print announced an additional ranger-led hike to Grinnell Glacier.

Just added, a ranger-led hike to the beautiful Grinnell Lake and glacier. Come join us for a challenging but rewarding eight-mile hike. Meet at the Swiftcurrent trailhead at 8:45 a.m. sharp. Wear sturdy, comfortable shoes and bring water and a snack. Bear spray required.

Eight miles? Bear spray? I don't know if I'm ready for this. But as she continued down the hall, she thought it would be good to challenge herself. *It's part of the journey. But so is an ice cream sundae. And wine.*

Winnie encountered bear warning signs at Yellowstone and even spotted a few bears from a distance, but she read about bears in Glacier, how active they were and how sightings were much more common. She asked someone looking at the board about bear spray and was told that the gift shop sold it. *I'm running out of excuses,* she thought as she walked to the restaurant.

The Ptarmigan Dining Room, located at the end of a long corridor, continued the charm of the Swiss Alps, with high wood ceilings and a stone fireplace on the far side. Winnie peeked in and smiled with anticipation before putting her name on the list. Told it would be about a thirty-minute wait, she retreated to the Swiss Lounge, a brightly lit, cozy pub with wood paneling and bench seats. Winnie found an open stool at the bar and sat down. She smiled when the bartender came over. The bartender was dressed in a traditional Swiss off-white dress with brown trim and a lace-up top. The lacing pushed up and showed off her cleavage. It looked cute, but Winnie wondered how impractical the getup must be. About the only part of the outfit that looked comfortable was her shoes.

"Welcome to the lounge. What can I get for you?"

Winnie looked at the board behind the bar. "I think I'll have the Moose Drool Brown Ale." While she typically preferred wine, there was something about being in moose country that drew her to the selection. After taking a sip, she knew she made the right choice. Not strong or bitter, and smooth. Winnie nodded her approval as she paid for her drink.

"Well, hello again," Winnie heard next to her.

She turned to see the man with the campsite next to hers. He smiled and made a flicking motion on his upper lip. Winnie reached up and felt beer foam, grabbed a napkin, and wiped it away. She tried to smile but could feel her face contorting into a goofy smile-smirk combination. She hung her head and turned to sulk over the bar.

Is my table ready yet?

"I noticed you're from Wisconsin. I'm originally from Chicago, but I moved out to LA a few years ago. I'm Pete."

Winnie looked and saw Pete's hand extended. She took his hand and wondered what stupid thing she was going to do next. Pete smiled and held on until Winnie became uncomfortable and pulled her hand away. "Winnie." She turned back to her beer.

Seemingly undeterred, Pete kept going. "I assumed so by your RV. I love the color, and the name 'Winnie's Winnie' is fantastic. Did you do the artwork?"

"No, my friend did it for me. She painted it to match my car."

"Let me guess . . . Winnie's Ford?"

Winnie chuckled. *Okay, besides the stupid hand thing, he is kinda cute.* "Nope. It's a Mini Cooper. I love the car, and the name fits, too."

Pete thought about it for a moment, then laughed. "Winnie's Mini. I love it. I spend so much time staring at numbers on a computer screen. I don't think I have a creative bone in my body."

Pete's smile was warm and broad, like he didn't have a care in the world. He was still wearing those jeans but changed from a t-shirt into a nice, blue-striped button down. His deep tan showed his love of the sun. A pair of loafers completed the look. She noticed what looked like an expensive watch on his left hand.

Winnie smiled and felt her face warm from the attention. The hostess from the dining room came over and told Winnie her table was ready. Winnie nodded and grabbed her beer. As she slid off the barstool, she made an impulsive decision.

"Would you care to join me for dinner?"

Pete had the expression of a dismissed schoolboy. He looked over in surprise. "I'd love to."

There's that smile again.

The server brought them to a table by the window. Winnie got her first good view of Swiftcurrent Lake and the mountains behind it. "Wow, it's beautiful."

Pete nodded. "Everyone feels that way at first. It'll wear off after four or five thousand times."

Swiftcurrent Lake was a pristine, mirror-like surface that reflected the mountains. Winnie could see some of the remaining glaciers between the jagged peaks, and she could see why they gave the hotel an alpine theme.

She turned back to her dinner companion. "You seem to know the area. Do you come here often?"

"I try to come up a few times during the summer. In fact, I just bought some land on the west side of the park, and as soon as I have the electric run and septic system dug, I'll move my camper over there. At some point, I'll build a small cabin."

Winnie could see motion out of the corner of her eye and turned her head. She jumped when she noticed a man bounding over to the table. He looked like a ball of fire, and he closed the distance quickly.

"We need to talk. Now." The man fixed his eyes on Pete and clenched his jaw as he pulled back Pete's chair.

Made in the USA
Monee, IL
21 September 2024